PYROPHOBIA

Titles by Jack Lance published by Severn House

PYROPHOBIA

PYROPHOBIA

Jack Lance

This first world edition published 2015
in Great Britain and the USA by
SEVERN HOUSE PUBLISHERS LTD of
19 Cedar Road, Sutton, Surrey, England, SM2 5DA.
Trade paperback edition first published
in Great Britain and the USA 2015 by
SEVERN HOUSE PUBLISHERS LTD.

Originally published in the Netherlands as *Vuurgeest*,
by Suspense Publishing in 2014.

This English edition translated from the Dutch by Lia Belt,
with additional editorial input from Bill Hammond.

British Library Cataloguing in Publication Data

Lance, Jack, author.
Pyrophobia.
1. Suspense fiction.
I. Title
839.3'137-dc23

ISBN-13: 978-0-7278-8490-9 (cased)
ISBN-13: 978-1-84751-597-1 (trade paper)
ISBN-13: 978-1-78010-648-9 (e-book)

Typeset by Palimpsest Book Production Ltd.,
Falkirk, Stirlingshire, Scotland.
Printed digitally in the USA.

The fire that seems extinguished, often slumbers beneath the cinders

Pierre Corneille

Never light a fire you cannot douse

Chinese proverb

PROLOG

A s soon as he opened the door the man in black pounced on him like a mad demon. Broad-shouldered, he had a muscular, impressive frame. His eyes were squeezed nearly shut and held a vicious sparkle as he clenched his fists and snorted like a wild animal.

His victim, older than he, could never hope to stand up to him. Before he knew it, he was shoved face down on to the floor, his cheek hard against the white floor tiles. The intruder placed the heel of his shoe squarely on the back of his head, increasing the pressure until the older man felt his nose break. Warm blood filled his facial cavities and flowed freely from his nostrils. Never had he experienced such excruciating pain. The scream he uttered emanated from his very soul.

The nightmare had started one hour and fifty-eight minutes earlier, even though for the older man the minutes had seemed more like hours.

The orange-red glow of the last sunset he would ever see had long since yielded to starlight. It had been almost ten thirty when the man had decided, a bit earlier than usual, to retire. He had hoisted himself from his hanging chair on the porch and had slid open the door to his living room.

As he did so, he was surprised to hear the doorbell chime.

He had decided not to answer the door immediately, but had instead crossed over to the window on the opposite side of the living room. His off-white bungalow featured a brick stoop that protruded a few feet from the front of the building. If he took a sideways glance through that window, he might be able to see who was calling at this hour.

The feeble glow from his sitting room and from the street lights beyond his small, colorful flower garden failed to shed much light on the figure who was standing by the front door. All the older man could make out in the dim light was that the man, whoever he was, was dressed entirely in black.

The older man was suspicious. He'd had a sudden premonition that this man's intentions were as dark as the clothes he wore.

But if that were true, he mused, why would he have rung the doorbell? If his intentions were sinister, he could simply have burglarized the house during the night.

Maybe a friend had had a seizure, he thought, or a heart attack. At this late hour, when a stranger came to call, the news could only be bad.

That was when the older man decided to go ahead and open the door.

Almost two hours later, he lay on the blood-smeared floor beneath the foot of the man in black.

'Right,' a lisping, quiet voice snarled above him. 'This is revenge.'

The older man, unable to answer, could barely breathe.

The bulky assailant pulled him up by the collar of his green-and-white checkered shirt and rammed a knee into his back, causing a new wave of flaming agony to course through his entire body and another tortured scream to explode from him. Then he flung him back down like a sack of potatoes. The older man squeezed his eyes shut, struggling to breathe, and pressed the ball of his right hand against the bloody pulp that used to be his nose.

The horror ended quickly. He was dragged upstairs into his attic where the man in black put a rope around his neck and tugged something tight beneath his chin. It felt like a necktie, but no, it was something else. With great ease he was lifted up, to where he stood wobbling on a wooden chair from which the paint had long since flaked off. The intruder gave another yank on the rope that was cutting into the skin of the older man's neck, forcing him to fight for balance on his toes.

He suffered through it all, offering no further resistance. He had no strength left, no resolve. He could not think. His skull was throbbing unbearably where the attacker had put his full weight on it, almost crushing it.

He was physically and mentally broken, a shadow of his former self.

Only then did he notice that the rope around his neck had been looped up and over a massive wooden support beam located directly above his head and was tied securely to it.

He stared into the face of his murderer. The man stank of sweat, and fire glowed in his eyes like the dying embers of a once raging blaze.

The man in black kicked the chair, hard, and it fell away and over.

Jason, was the older man's final thought as he dangled in agony. *Oh God, Jason!*

ONE
Polaroid

Jason Evans was worried. Usually he had scant cause for concern or complaint. But on the day the trouble began, something nagged at him.

On that Monday, July thirteenth, he was making slow progress on a promotion campaign he needed to complete. Was it his client, or was he just having a bad day? Probably both. He had to come up with something original for Tommy Jones's car dealership – or more specifically, for the used-car emporium of the 'Automobile King', a label repugnant to Jason. Tommy Jones had proclaimed himself the king of automobiles and was damn proud of the crown he had placed on his head.

'Genius, ain't it,' Jones this morning had crowed to Jason and his colleagues. 'I should go into advertising myself!'

What new ideas could Jason possibly present to a man for whom, during the past thirty years, every advertising concept imaginable had been cooked up and warmed over, and whose product he detested? Jason's mind wandered back to the days when, as a naive eighteen-year-old, he had bought one of Tommy's second-hand rust buckets. The ageing red Plymouth Road Runner had given up the ghost after only two months. That had been the first and last time he had purchased a car from the Automobile King. And now this auto entrepreneur was his customer, a client with Tanner & Preston, the prestigious Los Angeles advertising agency where Jason worked as an art director.

Of all people, the agency's CEO Brian Anderson had selected Jason to head the team assigned to seal the deal with their newest client who had jumped ship from Foote, Grey & Hardy, a hard-nosed competitor of Tanner & Preston.

Jason brushed strands of unruly black hair from his eyes and stared up at the ceiling, searching in vain for inspiration. But more reveries haunted him instead.

Since forever, or so it seemed, Tommy Jones's dazzling toothpaste-ad-smile had beamed down at him from posters and billboards scattered around town. Today was the first time he had looked the man in the eye and shaken his hand. Tommy, at age sixty-two, had looked a lot different from his public persona. He appeared older, balder and grayer in real life, without Photoshop's false promise of eternal youth. Only his famous grin and plump face – and his indomitable energy – remained the same. He was a short, sturdy little man who stood chin-high to Jason.

'I want something new, something exciting,' Jones had grandly exclaimed during the morning meeting, when he had graced everyone at Tanner & Preston with his presence. 'Make my cars stand out from the competition. Make them more attractive, better looking. Christ, Brian, make them *sexy*.'

Fuck you, Jason had thought as he sat there, listening, the memory of the rundown piece of crap the Automobile King had sold him assaulting his mind.

Of course, he hadn't said anything derogatory out loud. Tommy Jones carried around a fat wallet and besides, times had changed for Jason. He was far better off financially these days, and the silver metallic Buick LaCrosse CX he was currently driving could not be found on any of Tommy Jones's sales lots. It was too expensive and had too much class, *even* as a used car.

But since he had assembled his Tommy Jones team, Jason hadn't sketched as much as an outline for a campaign aimed at making the Automobile King's emporium appear sexy – or even viable. His loyal and dependable copywriter, Anthony Wilson, hadn't come up with much usable copy either.

Jason's gaze wandered around and he took note of the desk clock in the shape of two hearts, a birthday gift from his wife Kayla. It was after six o'clock. The other members of the team – Carol, Donald and Anthony – had gone home for the night. He was the last one still at work, and thus had the twenty-fourth floor of the Roosevelt Tower to himself. He stared out the window into the heat and haze of a Los Angeles summer evening. Just four more weeks, he thought, as if with a prayer. Just four more weeks and he and Kayla could finally leave the smog and chaos of this city behind them and immerse themselves in the glorious majesty and intimacy of the Rocky Mountains.

But first he had Tommy Jones to deal with. He sighed with frustration, knowing he wasn't going to pull off a miracle tonight. He stood up and was about to leave his office when George, Tanner & Preston's mail delivery man, entered waving a manila envelope in the air.

'Late delivery,' George said, as he handed Jason the envelope. Without another word, he wheeled around and walked out of the office.

Jason stared at George's broad back as he strode down the long hallway. When he saw the delivery man disappear around a corner, he glanced down at the envelope bearing his name and company's address written in a bold angular script, but with no sender's logo or return address indicated. Frowning, he fished his silver letter opener from the pen stand on his desk and slid open the envelope. Inside he found a Polaroid photograph of a tall, rusty iron gate set between two wide-trunked oak trees. Behind the gate stood rows of gravestones jutting crookedly out of the earth. At first blush it appeared similar to an old graveyard he had once visited in downtown Boston. But on closer inspection this graveyard seemed more unkempt than the one on Tremont Street.

Jason peered into the envelope but saw nothing else inside. His first thought was that Shaun Reilly had sent the photo. It would not have been the first time that Shaun had neglected to add a note. When Jason turned the photograph over, he noticed words on the back written by the same hand.

You are DEAD

He stared at the words, dumbfounded. Then he flipped the photograph back over and studied the gravestones once more.

'What's this?' he mumbled to himself. He flipped to the back again.

The same three words stared back at him.

He was stumped. Struggling to make sense of it, he turned the Polaroid over and over. As he studied the photograph intently, he became convinced of one thing: he had never seen this cemetery. The grass between the headstones was tall; the field surrounding it gave the impression of going to seed; in the background, beyond the graveyard, was a distinct line of small, gnarled trees.

Had Shaun sent him this? No, Jason reasoned; it was not his hand-writing. And he would never do anything this morbid. So who had sent it? And why?

He inspected the envelope, but it offered nothing beyond a stamp, his name and his work address. Nor could he make out the postmark, although clearly the letter had been delivered by the U.S. Postal Service.

Jason didn't know what to think. And George was long gone.

He wondered how this letter could have only just arrived. There were no mail deliveries at this hour, were there? As far as he knew, office mail was dropped off early in the morning and again around one thirty in the afternoon. But never at the close of business.

Had George gone home yet? If not, maybe he could shed some light on this mystery. Jason found the extension for the mail room, punched in the three numbers, and let the phone ring a dozen times. No answer. Perhaps, Jason's thoughts whirled, George was still on his way back to the mail room, or maybe on his way out of the building. Acting on that hunch, Jason hurried toward the elevator. It seemed to take forever to reach his floor.

The door hummed open. He stepped inside and pressed the button for the ground floor. The elevator door closed, but only after what seemed like needless delays. It was as if someone was trying to prevent the door from closing by inserting a hand or foot into the opening.

Then, with a barely perceptible jolt, the elevator started its descent. When it reached the ground floor, Jason ran out of it toward the mail room.

'George!' he yelled as he entered the small office, its walls hidden behind stacked-up brown parcels and boxes of paper and stationery. It appeared empty. On a whim, Jason scanned through the neat piles of envelopes and memos on the desk, hoping against hope to find there the solution – or at least a clue – to the mysterious Polaroid. But his search proved fruitless.

God *damn* it, Jason silently cursed, where was George? Roosevelt Tower had forty-two floors. Going in search of the man seemed a hopeless exercise. His thoughts wandered back to the photograph. Who would do such a thing? Who in heaven's name would go to the trouble of sending him this photo with its bizarre message? It was a sick prank; it made no sense; why then, Jason asked himself, was he so worried?

At that moment George entered the room, surprised to find Jason there.

'Good evening, Mr Evans,' he said, formal as always.

'George, listen,' Jason blurted out, 'I have a question for you. That envelope you handed me in my office. Where did it come from? Who delivered it? The mail truck doesn't usually swing by at this hour, does it?'

'Well,' George said, scratching behind his ear, 'it was in my in-tray. I must have overlooked it earlier.' His bushy brows arched down as he pinched his lips together. 'I could've sworn . . .' He shook his head and cast Jason a worried look. 'Was it important? Were you . . .' He hesitated. 'Are you all right?'

'What do you mean?' Jason snapped.

'Well, excuse me,' George fumbled. 'But if you don't mind me saying so, you look a mite pale.'

Jason fought to calm himself. George was an endearing sort of guy, a bear of a man who would never hurt anyone. Jason felt guilty for making George apologize to him.

'You only just found it in your in-tray?' he asked in a calmer tone.

George nodded. 'That's right, Mr Evans.'

'And you don't know who put it there?'

'I'm sorry, I don't,' he said contritely. 'I'm always extra careful when I'm sorting mail. Everyone will tell you that. But sometimes something goes wrong and that . . .'

He paused and shook his head again.

'I don't understand it, Mr Evans. I could've sworn I had emptied out my in-tray. And then, when I glanced at it a half hour ago, just out of habit, I saw your envelope in it.'

Jason gently gripped the man's shoulder.

'Think carefully, George. Letters don't just appear out of thin air. Someone must have put it there.'

In reply, George hung his head.

'Were you here the whole time?' Jason pressed.

George looked up. 'Not the whole time, Mr Evans. I went out for coffee with Lori. And Mr Albright from Accounting called. I went to his office, as well. He had some questions about our postage expenditures. As you know, he insists on everything tallying up to the last cent. And then—'

'So you were away from your desk a few times,' Jason concluded.

'That's right,' George confirmed.

'And then, suddenly, this letter appeared in your in-tray.'

George nodded. 'That's God's truth, Mr Evans.'

'I believe you, George,' Jason said, releasing his grip. 'Thanks for your help. See you tomorrow.'

Jason returned to his office to see a list of rejected concepts for Tommy Jones's advertising campaign glowing on his computer screen. He ignored them. The king and his clunkers were now in full retreat from the front lines of his consciousness.

He picked up the Polaroid photograph and scrutinized the gate, the headstones and the handwriting. He then slid the photo back into the envelope, tucked it into the inside pocket of his jacket, and grabbed his briefcase. After turning off the computer, he left his office.

You are dead.

Macabre mail. Was this some moron's idea of a joke? Perhaps, but a voice deep within him warned that it wasn't. He felt his face flush. A drop of sweat trickled down his brow. Angrily, he swiped it away.

TWO

Kayla

He was awakened by the feel of her hand sliding across his bare chest. Blearily he opened his eyes and found himself looking up into Kayla's sea blue eyes. Her long black hair was mussed and hung down appealingly. Her smile turned the moment soft and endearing.

'Good morning,' she said in that husky, sexy voice of hers. It was her voice that had first drawn him irresistibly toward her.

He pushed himself up on his elbows. 'I see your smile at the crack of dawn, and suddenly I forget to yawn,' he quipped. 'What more could a man want?'

Indeed it was the crack of dawn. The alarm clock on his bedside table registered 6:02.

'Or a woman,' she quipped back.

'You're in a good mood.'

'Of course.' Her smile widened. 'Your deep brown gaze puts me in a daze, and it's your body I craze.'

'The word is "crave", not "craze", and it doesn't rhyme with "daze".'

'It does in my book,' she said, and her hand slid lower.

'Oh good Lord,' he breathed. As his head slumped back against the pillows, she came to him, her long, lithe body hard against him, her mouth open and her tongue searching. Deftly she moved the tips of her fingers to his inner thigh, teasing him, playing with him.

'Your fingers chase away the sleep that lingers,' he whispered in her ear.

'Hmm, not very inspired,' she murmured as her hand found its mark. 'Now *this*, my dear, is what I call rock-hard inspiration.'

He moaned with pleasure as she squeezed gently.

'Late breakfast today?' Kayla whispered.

'Screw breakfast,' he breathed. 'I'd rather screw you.'

'Then *do* it, Romeo!'

After showering together, they hurried through the evolutions of getting ready for work.

Kayla served as a management secretary for Demas Electrical, a manufacturer of engine parts. Her boss, Patrick Voight, had told her many times that he would be lost without her – and upset with her when she was late for work.

While she was applying make-up in the bathroom, Jason scrambled a few eggs, heated water for coffee, and popped two slices of wheat bread into the toaster. Their bedroom romps had made him hungry, and he was sure it was the same for her. As he was setting out jam and butter on the table, she came up behind him and hugged him. He turned around. Her hair was still damp, and her cheeks fresh and rosy.

She brushed her lips against his. 'God, how I love you,' she said, from the heart. She gestured at the kitchen table. 'Not only are you a woman's dream in bed, you're a gentleman in the kitchen.'

'I wish I was more like that boss of yours,' Jason allowed. 'You know, I envy him sometimes. You do whatever he tells you to do.'

'Not everything, Jason Evans,' she said, stepping away from his embrace and wagging a finger at him. 'Not by a long shot, and you know it. Some things are just for you. This, for example.' She ran a hand from her ample breasts down to the curve of her thighs.

He reached for her but she spun away.

'No more of that,' she admonished. 'I'm in a hurry. So how's that toast coming? And where's the cutlery? Either give me what I require, or tonight you shall not have what you so desire.'

'Nor shall you, my love, in that case.'

'Oh, yes. That's right. I forgot.'

She smiled at him and sat down.

Jason sat down beside her. 'See what I mean?' he sighed. 'I try my damnedest to organize things around here, to make you happy, and still you give me grief. Isn't it you women who are always complaining that men think you're good for only one thing? That, and cooking and cleaning.'

'Oh, but you're doing such a great job,' she laughed. 'It must be your line of work. You advertising types sure know how to appeal to your target audience.'

'Ah, my sexy target audience,' he said.

'Yeah, but who's complaining? Your product's deft manipulations have once again ensured maximum customer satisfaction. I'm sold on whatever you have to offer.'

'Glad to be of service,' he said in a mock grumble. 'Always good to have a happy customer.' He poured out two cups of coffee. 'Well, if you need cutlery, you know where to find it.'

She arose and started rummaging through the kitchen drawer.

'Another disappointing line,' she teased. 'Your marketing skills need some more work. You're not perfect yet.'

'A man always needs room for improvement.'

Jason plucked two slices of slightly burned bread from the toaster and added, 'By the way, I'm stopping by my father's house after work.'

'Want me to come?'

He shrugged.

'Dad probably has everything sorted out for his party, and that means I won't have to do much of anything beyond sitting with him for a while. So unless you're up for a social call, you might as well come straight home. We'll be going there tomorrow anyway, and I won't be long. Just an hour or so.'

*　　*　　*

They finished their breakfast, cleared the dishes, and then drove in separate cars away from Fernhill, a town nestled in the lush Santa Monica Mountains between Malibu and Santa Monica. Jason had grown up in a town called Cornell, seventeen miles away. Kayla had been born and raised in Palm Springs.

Five years had passed since Jason had bought the house at 160 Cherokee Drive. Truth be told, his father had bought it for him. He knew Jason wanted the house, and so he had purchased it. At the time, Jason had just started working for Tanner & Preston, and the local bank hadn't judged him sufficiently creditworthy to buy the property on his own.

It hadn't cost all that much, perhaps because it needed quite a lot of work. Jason and his father had completed the basic home improvements in under a year, calling in professionals only when the complexity of a project exceeded their combined skills and experience. The result was a distinctive, whitewashed, wooden country house reminiscent of the neo-colonial style of the Go West era. The facade of the house stretched five feet across a lawn surrounded by flower beds containing Kayla's cherished white and purple lupins and some sizeable hydrangeas.

But their favorite place to be outside was on their back porch, where commanding views of the canyons around Fernhill took one's breath away. Canyon View, they called their home. It wasn't a big place: living room, kitchen, one and a half bathrooms and two bedrooms, one of which Jason had converted to a study. But that was all they needed.

As Jason followed Kayla along Tuna Canyon Road toward the Pacific Coast Highway, he recalled the day when he had literally bumped into her. It had been about ten months after his break-up with Carla Rosenblatt, one of three women in his life with whom he had been seriously involved.

As he approached the exit for Pacific Coast Highway, he waved goodbye to Kayla, who kept driving straight toward Interstate 405.

Not until he joined the traffic jams on Interstate 10 near the LaBrea exit did his thoughts drift back to the Tommy Jones campaign. With those thoughts came a headache and the death of his good spirits. Come what may, he had to get a draft on paper by the end of the day. He then thought about his father who would

turn sixty-six tomorrow and mentally checked off the list of things
he had promised to do for him.

The strange mail he had received the day before never entered
his mind.

THREE

Fuss

Jason's resolve to get serious about the advertising campaign came
to naught. He had just started reading through his new emails
when Barbara Baker stepped into his office. Barbara was an
essential girl Friday: she answered the phones, performed clerical
jobs, and was a junior designer. She worked closely with senior
designer Donald Nelson and art director Carol Martinez. But Barbara
and Carol did not get along, and Barbara had recently been hinting
that Carol was cutting corners.

'I'm a junior associate, but I do most of the work around here,'
she griped to Jason. 'My work is not appreciated. The least management could do is strip the *junior* off my title, right?'

Jason was in no mood to explain, once more, that Carol had been
working for the company six years longer than Barbara, and that
she had brought a lot of dollars into the firm during those years.
He certainly didn't want to explain that she was having problems
at home. Carol's marriage was steering toward the rocks. Jason
knew it, Donald Nelson knew it, but few others among the office
staff were aware of how tenuous the situation had become. Carol
Martinez was, in a word, preoccupied – in one of the worst ways
possible. Although Jason felt sympathy for her, there was little that
he or others in senior management could do for her despite their
admiration of her as an employee. They had to wait it out, and try
to keep the lid on a boiling pot.

'You're doing a great job for us, Babs,' he said, calling her by
her popular nickname. 'I can see you making progress every week.
Your ideas and solutions are solid. Be patient. Your time will come,
I promise you.'

He cast a meaningful glance at her tight jeans and tight top that exposed her navel. Earlier, Jason had mentioned Barbara's provocative way of dressing to Kayla, who had warned him not to take undue notice. It was a warning that Jason had found unjustified. In his mind he was unavailable, no matter how young and attractive Barbara or any other woman might be.

Today, Barbara had more to complain about. If he thought she was doing such a great job, she asked him sternly, why wasn't she being assigned to more design work?

'I'm tired of answering phones and playing secretary,' she groused. 'And I'm sick to death of bookkeeping. What I want is DTP work.' She was referring to artistic work as a desktop publisher.

Jason again appealed to her patience, in vain. Finally she slouched off to her work desk without a glance back at him. He gazed after her with concern. Barbara had talent and ambition, no one could deny that. The agency should cherish and protect such an employee. If nothing happened soon, she would find a job at another advertising agency, and that he didn't want to happen. He made a mental note to discuss the matter with Brian, but it would have to wait. Tommy Jones came first.

But it soon became apparent that today was not the day for the Automobile King either. Brian entered his office under the guise of a work meeting, although it wasn't long before his real purpose became clear. Brian started complaining about his wife Louise, who had suddenly lost interest in their long-planned trip to Las Vegas. This sorry state of affairs, Jason immediately suspected, was related to Brian's love of gambling that bordered on addiction. Louise had told Jason more than once that whenever Brian traveled to Vegas, he gambled away whatever cash he happened to have on hand, often several thousand dollars. He imagined she was getting tired and resentful of his passion. But how could he make Brian see the folly of his ways? He couldn't ever seem to find the right words. Luckily, on this morning, Brian received an important phone call and had to excuse himself.

Next up at his desk was Carol. Last night, she told him, things had come to a head with her husband. After what had apparently been a ferocious fight, Carol had packed a bag and driven to her mother's house. She hadn't had much sleep, despite several stiff nightcaps. And now she couldn't control her tears.

'It's over,' she sobbed. 'Twelve years of marriage down the drain.'

Jason was starting to feel more like a social worker and marriage counselor than an advertising executive. Nevertheless, he put his arm around her shoulder. 'Take the rest of the day off,' he urged.

She gave him a grateful look. 'I was hoping you'd say that,' she sniffled. 'I thought I might go shopping with my mother, to take my mind off things. Thanks. I'll be in tomorrow.'

She swiped at tears that had reduced her mascara to a blur of gray and left his office. Jason was watching her walk down the hallway when Donald suddenly materialized from a side office and wrapped his arm around her waist. Jesus, Jason mused, here was another office problem that had nothing to do with business. The truth was, Donald was in love with Carol. Jason had often wondered how much Donald was to blame for Carol's marital crisis. Their affair had by now become an open secret. Even Barbara knew about it, and it was probably another reason for her to hate Carol. If the relationship between Carol and Donald grew any closer, there would never be room for Barbara to improve her position in the company, she probably figured.

Jason sighed with frustration as the last member of the Tommy Jones team, Anthony Wilson, appeared in the open doorway glancing back over his shoulder at Donald and Carol. When his eyes met Jason's, he arched his thick, dark eyebrows and his mouth broke into a broad grin.

'Not good?' Tony asked, pointing down the hallway. His voice was as non-committal as his expression was unflappable. In the often troubling waters of office politics and office affairs, Tony Wilson, unmarried and uncomplicated, was the one safe harbor Jason could always depend on. He also happened to be one of the most gifted copywriters of his acquaintance.

Jason shook his head. 'No. Not good.'

'Well then,' Tony commented, 'I guess you and I will have to man the fort today.'

'We'll man the fort, Tony,' Jason conceded, unavoidably smiling at Tony's choice of words.

He glanced at the clock. Almost eleven thirty.

'Time for the Automobile King,' he said.

FOUR
Edward

At first blush Edward Evans appeared to be a healthy fifty-year-old man. His hair was military gray and well-trimmed, he had hardly an ounce of fat on him, and his arms were lean and muscular. Plus, he sported the rich brown tan of an outdoorsman. But in fact he was almost sixty-six and a good four inches shorter than his son. As Jason walked inside the house, his father gave him a pensive once-over.

'You look tired, son. Are you OK?'

'I *am* tired, Dad,' Jason allowed. 'It's been one of those days when nothing turns out right.'

'Busy at the office,' his father assumed.

'If only that were all.' Jason sighed.

Edward's eyebrows arched up in question. Jason considered spilling the beans – about Carol, Barbara, Donald, his boss, all of it – but he kept his emotions in check. Priding himself on not being a worrywart, he had long ago resolved never to bring work home with him.

'Let's talk about your birthday, Dad,' he said, changing the subject. 'Is everything set for the big party tomorrow?'

Edward Evans frowned. 'You act as if I can't handle this,' he said. 'But you know better than that, I hope.'

'Of course I do. I just mean that if anything needs to be done, Kayla and I could run some errands for you. Or whatever.'

'You just said you were busy.'

'I'm never too busy to help out my family.'

Their conversation had settled into its usual pendulum-like, back-and-forth pattern. Jason would offer help, and his father would decline that help, kindly but resolutely.

'You don't have to worry about your old man,' Edward avowed. 'I've already done all the shopping. Tomorrow I'll move the furniture around a bit, and after that, I'll just be sitting around waiting for the guests to arrive. All *you* have to do is show up with that lovely bride of yours and leave the rest to me.'

His father was right, of course. He didn't need Jason's help. Jason understood his father's strength because he felt that same strength inside of himself. 'Never show weakness' was the unspoken mantra of them both. Anything you can do yourself, you do yourself.

The only time Edward had reached out for his son's support was when his forty-seven-year-old wife had been diagnosed with incurable lung cancer. And then again in the months after she died.

Edward had loved Donna dearly. But she had passed away nine years ago, and if time cannot heal the pain of a grievous loss, it can at least numb it. So he had moved on as best as he could. Things are what they are, was his motto. A simple one, perhaps, but to his mind a compelling one.

Jason had inherited his father's pragmatism. Life could be *made* complicated, perhaps, but normally it wasn't. Crying or feeling sorry for oneself accomplished nothing. Worse, such emotions revealed weakness in a man. His beliefs bothered Kayla sometimes. She believed that men who cried now and then were expressing their true selves. They were not wimps or softies; often just the opposite. But Jason rarely cried. The few hard times he'd had, he had resolved the matter on his own, without having or wanting to lean on anyone.

Jason conceded that he'd had a happy childhood. Even though his dad was by no means rich, he had always put aside as much as he could for his only son. Jason had gone to the college of his choice and had picked his own major. As a result of receiving such assistance, Jason wanted to 'repay' his parents in his own way.

While his father made coffee, Jason gazed out the window, where a rich tapestry of canyons and forests shimmered beneath a clear azure sky. He and his father shared a love of nature. They were country people, not cut out for city life. The magnificent view that Jason enjoyed from his front porch in Fernhill was one his father had known for most of his life. It was also the view his father hoped to see on his last day on earth. He would never move, not even when he was old and decrepit and no longer able to care for himself. Jason well understood that when that time came, he would have to address his father's stubbornness, which after all was part of his own genetic make-up. But he would cross that bridge when he came to it. In the meantime, Edward Evans was a strong man capable of tending to his every need – and then some.

Jason turned away from the window and accepted the steaming mug of coffee his father held out to him. For a moment, their eyes met. No smiles, no frowns, just a simple, knowing expression.

'Your first party without Uncle Chris,' Jason commented softly.

'Yeah,' his father said.

Jason decided not to push the subject of Chris, who had hung himself because of his incurable cancer, unable to endure the pain any longer. After several moments of quiet reminiscing, Jason drained his coffee mug and put it down.

'Well, Dad,' he said, 'if there's nothing I can do here, I guess I'll mosey on home to Kayla. See you tomorrow.'

'See you tomorrow, son.'

Jason arrived home at Canyon View half an hour later. Breathing in the pleasing aroma of freshly cut flowers, he searched for Kayla and found her in the bathtub, her head and neck visible above a thick layer of suds.

'Hey, my hubby's home,' she said cheerfully.

He knelt down beside the tub and kissed her. 'I am,' he said. 'And I'm glad to see you taking some quality time for yourself.'

'Uh-huh. It's heavenly. How were things at your dad's?'

'Just fine. He's all set. How was your day?'

She blew bubbles at him from the palm of her hand. 'Nothing special. We had to step it up for a while to get the holiday mailing out. Patrick insisted on it. I felt it could wait until tomorrow, but what the boss wants, the boss gets. How about you? Any progress with the Automobile King?'

'A little, thanks to Tony. He had a flash of inspiration this afternoon, and after a few hours we had turned blank paper into a pretty decent outline. I have until the beginning of next week to finish the draft. We need to finish production for the campaign before you and I leave for vacation.'

'That's wonderful,' she said, straightening up. 'Care to hop in? There's plenty of room. It's a big tub.'

He smiled. 'Thanks for the offer, but I think I'll go read the paper.'

She gave him an arch look. 'You don't want to scrub my back? And other body parts?'

When he didn't answer right away, she dismissed him with a wave of her hand. 'OK then, off with you. You're no use to me.'

As usual, today's mail was piled beside the phone on his home office desk in what he and Kayla dubbed the postal basket. Casually he flipped through the stack of bills and brochures until he came upon a manila envelope with no return address. Only his name was printed on the front. Jason tore it open.

The temperature in his home office seemed to soar as he fished out the contents. It was another Polaroid photograph. His heart pounding, he noted a cluster of gravestones depicted on it, but different from those in the previous photo. He turned the photograph over and instantly recognized the angular handwriting.

You think you're alive, but you don't exist

Jason stood stock still. He shook his head, as if in denial of what his eyes beheld, trying to understand. The words seemed to jump out at him and slap him across the face. He flipped the glossy paper over again.

In this photo there was no gate between the trees and other elements were different from the previous photo. The photographer had trained the camera lens on a pyramid-shaped structure seemingly made of dark marble. The pyramid looked to be a tomb and was positioned in the center of the photograph. Behind it, more headstones.

As if he were handling some kind of explosive, he gently placed the photograph and its envelope on his desk. With sweat breaking out on his brow, he looked around the room without a clue of what he was searching for. Hesitantly, he picked up the envelope and examined it. On its upper right-hand corner was a regular stamp – just as the first one had had – indicating it too had been delivered by the U.S. Postal Service.

Nothing unusual about that.

What *was* unusual was the photograph with its macabre message. As his thoughts focused on the words, he shook his head in utter bewilderment. As far as he could tell, he was still very much alive.

Could the sender be planning to murder him? Was that what those words foretold? Was this a death threat? If so, *why*? And *who* was behind it? Mentally he listed the few people in his life with whom he'd had a serious disagreement, but no one of consequence came to mind. He had no real enemies – certainly none who might want to kill him.

He stood where he was, staring at nothing, his mind blank, until he felt something touch his shoulder.

FIVE

Doubts

Jason whirled around and found himself eye to eye with Kayla, wrapped in a skimpy bath towel.

'Oops. Did I scare you?' she apologized.

'No,' Jason quickly assured her. 'My mind went somewhere else for a moment.'

He slipped the photograph into his pocket. 'By the way,' he asked as casually as he could manage, 'did you happen to be here when the mail was delivered?'

She shook her head. 'Here? No, of course not. You know the mailman does his rounds in the morning. I was at work.'

She adjusted the bath towel that had slipped down her breasts and gave him a questioning look.

'Why do you ask?'

He bit his lip, his thoughts swirling with questions. Should he tell her about the photograph? If so, how much? What possible good could that do? Would she dismiss it with a laugh? Or would she crumple in dread and worry? His mind made up, he forced a broad smile.

'I'm sorry, Kayla,' he apologized. 'It's been a busy day. I'm talking nonsense.'

She folded her arms across her chest and gazed at him pensively, a signal that she was not yet convinced.

'Are you all right? You seem overwrought about something.'

'No, I'm just tired,' he said with a mock sigh. 'I had a hectic day at the office. Like I told you.'

'And that's all?'

'Isn't that enough?'

She mumbled something incoherent before heading for the bedroom to get dressed.

For the rest of the evening he steered the conversation toward work and his father's birthday party. The next morning they telephoned Edward to wish him many happy returns.

'Another step closer to the end,' Edward grumbled. 'And you kids tell me to be happy.'

He didn't mean it, Jason realized. It was simply his father's attempt at humor, which often came across as dry as a desert gulch.

As was his wont, Jason followed Kayla toward the Pacific Coast Highway and waved at her when she stayed on Interstate 405. When he joined the congestion on the highway, he began to feel guilty. It was as if he were hiding something intensely personal from Kayla, such as an affair. This sort of cover-up went against his nature. They kept no secrets from each other. Trust and honesty were the cornerstones of their relationship.

I need to sort this out first, he thought; but deep inside a silent voice warned him that he was not capable of 'sorting out' this conundrum.

Blissfully, the morning at the office was free of interruptions from Barbara, Carol and Brian. Still, he found it hard to concentrate on his work. In his mind's eye he kept seeing the two Polaroid photographs. The first photo had simply inspired confusion. But with the second one, things had turned ominously serious. The only conclusion he could draw was that someone was out to threaten him, if not kill him.

Alone in his office, he placed the two photographs side by side on the desk in front of him and studied the images. Had they in fact been taken in the same graveyard? He searched for similarities and found several. The same row of small trees in the background was an obvious one. Behind the pyramid-shaped structure – whether it was a tomb or a sculpture, he could not ascertain – he made careful note of the same haphazardly placed gravestones jutting up through the tall grass.

He concluded that yes, the photographer – whoever he was – had shot the two photos in the same graveyard.

But *where* was that graveyard? And who the hell was the photographer?

Jason turned both photographs over and again studied the writing on the back. Then another, equally interesting question surged within him: *is this really a threat?*

What did the messages say, exactly?

You are dead. You think you're alive, but you don't exist.

If he put them together and interpreted them literally, the message said that he *thought* he was alive, but no longer was. It did not say someone wanted to kill him. It just said that his death was already a fact.

The message was bizarre, to say the least. But what really lay beneath it?

Jason recalled a heated discussion he had once had with a few friends from college. It had been one of those circular debates, lasting into the wee hours of the morning. Their favorite fuel for those pleasant, often nonsensical conversations had been Four Roses Bourbon with a few cans of Budweiser thrown in for good measure. Stu, who now worked for an IT corporation in Phoenix, Arizona, had considered himself quite the philosopher in those days.

That night he had questioned whether he was actually alive at any given moment. At the core of his argument was the phenomenon of time. Stu had argued that there was no such thing as the concept of 'now'. Everything one says or does is 'now' only after his brain has processed the statement, he had argued. And that process happens a fraction of a second after you actually say or do it. Our faulty senses therefore leave us constantly behind the times. So, in fact, we are completely unaware of what is happening in the real 'now'. Stu had finished his argument on a strangely upbeat note: 'Maybe I'm not even alive. Prove to me that I'm alive right now.'

Jason had never cared for these kinds of elusive philosophical pontifications and was usually the one who ended them.

He leaned back in his chair and stared up at the ceiling.

The two same simple but inescapable questions kept churning through his mind. Who had sent the photographs? And why?

It was another lost day at work and he decided to leave early and get home before Kayla. He struggled to keep his mind focused strictly on everyday matters, but found that impossible to do. After he arrived home, he showered and changed and greeted Kayla, who quickly followed suit. As they were about to leave the house for the birthday party, Kayla stopped short.

'Your father's present. You forgot it, didn't you?'

Jason bit his lower lip. 'Damn,' he muttered.

He stepped back inside and retrieved the nicely wrapped tool chest from the kitchen table. This kind of thing rarely happened to him. He was often the one who had to remind Kayla of what she had forgotten.

'You're distracted again, aren't you?' Kayla said as he backed the car out the driveway. 'So what's up?'

Is it that obvious? he thought dejectedly. One Polaroid photograph had not overly disturbed him. But the appearance of the second photograph had brought him close to the edge.

Again he considered telling Kayla about the pictures, and again he decided against it. They were on their way to a party. Telling her would ruin the evening for her. And if her evening was ruined, his father's would be too.

Later, he silently vowed. *I will tell her later.*

'I'm tired,' he said. 'The campaign for the Automobile King is taking its toll on me.'

It sounded like a hollow excuse, even to him. He had never excelled at telling white lies.

He was relieved when Kayla seemed sympathetic.

'You're busy at the office,' she stated, 'because you put up with a lot of fuss for a campaign for an uninspiring client who sells basically junk. I know how it is. Just hang in there a little while longer. Our vacation is coming up soon.'

He nodded, he hoped with sufficient enthusiasm.

'I can hardly wait,' he said from the heart.

They found Edward's house packed full of people when they knocked on the front door and Jason's father opened it. As they walked inside, Jason spotted a few familiar faces in the sitting room: family members, friends of Edward's, neighbors, a few people he knew from his hometown of Cornell. Clearly his father was enjoying himself. His smiles and laughter suggested that no one had yet had the bad taste to introduce the subject of Uncle Chris. But Jason felt confident it was only a matter of time before some social bungler broached the taboo subject. And he knew who that would be.

'Happy birthday, Dad!' Kayla exclaimed. She gave her father-in-law a hug and an enthusiastic kiss on the cheek. Jason grinned at his father's bemused reaction and then handed him the gift. Edward put it aside, promising to open it later after the party had died down.

They greeted the other guests, Jason mentally counting the people he liked and those he would rather avoid. The score was about even. *Let the party begin*, he thought without much excitement.

He participated in conversations, laughed on cue, fetched drinks for the guests, and passed snacks around. But there was only one thing on his mind: the photographs with their cryptic messages.

Trying to shake off such thoughts, he directed his attention to the exchange between Aunt Ethel and Kayla. Ethel, he was certain, was fishing for information. She had made it her life's mission to find out when Jason and Kayla would finally start having children. She no doubt thought she was being discreet about it, but she was about as subtle as a toilet full of unflushed bodily waste.

Apparently Kayla had had enough of that topic. 'We haven't decided yet, Auntie,' she said in no uncertain terms. 'We have all the time in the world.'

'But you're married, aren't you?' Ethel countered. 'You have been for two years. Maybe it's about time.'

In her own way, she was being delicate. Ethel was one of Edward's five siblings. She and her husband Hank had raised eight children together. Two of them, John and Ernest, were standing in a distant corner of the living room, as far removed as possible from that theater of action.

'There's plenty of time, Auntie Ethel,' Kayla said, her voice calmer and more patient. 'Jason and I are only thirty-one years old. Nowadays couples wait a while before having children.'

That is, if they start having them at all, Jason could hear her saying to herself.

He turned to Hank – six foot tall, good-natured Hank – and asked him how things were going with his business. He wasn't really interested; he simply wanted to stay clear of Ethel's awkward questions. He had a good notion, based on experience, of what subject would come up next. Ethel would invoke God and the sacred duty of all married couples to sow their seed and procreate.

Hank owned a thriving construction materials business. And he loved to talk about it. He took Jason's lead and launched into an animated monologue about all the things he had done to 'optimize his baby', as he referred to his company. Business was excellent, couldn't be better, he enthused. He finished his one-way dialogue with the same stale joke Jason had heard on too many occasions. 'Tell me, Jason,' he asked magnanimously, 'are Tanner & Preston in the market for new clients? In the construction business, maybe?'

Jason gave him the standard answer. 'Oh, you know, Hank, you're just too big for us. That's just the way it is.'

Hank grinned, patted him on the shoulder, and disappeared into the kitchen to refill his glass.

Jason found the rest of Edward's siblings gathered in a corner of the sitting room.

At seventy-four, Stephanie was the eldest. She had outlived her husband Frank, who had died three years earlier. She wore glasses that were much too big for her, with frames in the shape of butterfly wings. She often reminded Jason of Dame Edna, the showbiz transvestite, and she jabbered at least as much. The older the woman got, Jason observed, the less she seemed able to keep her mouth shut. Even now Jason was overwhelmed by an avalanche of well-intended words that went in one ear and out the other, as he stood there forced to listen to her.

She'll keep ticking for another quarter century, Jason reflected. *The undertaker will bury himself and his entire family before this dragon lady kicks the can.*

At fifty-six, Hilary was the youngest of his father's siblings. She didn't talk nearly as much as her sister, but when she did, it was to bemoan her real or imagined ailments. Jason couldn't remember ever having had a conversation with her that had not ended in a lamentation on her fragile health and her need to see a laundry list of physicians on an ongoing basis.

He turned to Eric and Ronald, the two brothers who looked remarkably alike. Eric had been an accountant. Ronald had spent thirty years working on a ranch. Both men were retired now. Despite differences in their choice of a career, they remained close and had plenty of things to talk about. Kayla chatted with them for a while until she saw her father-in-law acting as bartender and excused herself to go help him. Jason, eager to flee Aunt Stephanie's jabbering, went over to join her.

'Kayla and I will handle the drinks, Dad,' he said as he walked through the open kitchen door. 'You go socialize with your guests.'

'You're on, son,' Edward said as he walked back into the living room. 'Thank you.'

'Aunt Ethel was even more straightforward than usual, don't you think?' Kayla said as she deftly filled four glasses with various alcoholic mixtures. He and Kayla had always been of like mind when it came to having children. Their lives had consisted of three cherished beliefs: each other, their careers, and their freedom. Having kids would entail radical changes. Did they want that? Were they ready? Particularly in the last year they had discussed it for nights on end, without arriving at a clear decision. And since they could not reach a definitive conclusion, they agreed that they should defer the decision.

Jason felt an urge to tell Kayla, again, not to worry about his aunt: she was a broken record. But as he was about to speak to her, a mental image of the photographs intruded and he went mute.

Internally, however, he realized that in a sense his aunt was right. Parenthood was too life-defining an issue to postpone indefinitely. Truth be told, he wanted to be a dad. It was something he had come to accept about himself during the last few times he and Kayla had discussed the subject.

'Well,' he said at length, 'what *do* you think?'

She gave him a bewildered look.

'What is *that* supposed to mean?'

'She may have something of a point.'

'Huh?'

'Or not, or . . . well, you know, maybe. What do you think?'

'She has a point? *You* think Aunt Ethel has a point?'

He took a deep breath. What he said next could sentence Kayla and himself to a life of changing diapers, sleepless nights, and whatever else was involved in having a baby and raising a child.

'I think I'm ready now.'

He had blurted it out, come what may.

Kayla's eyes went wide. 'Are you serious?'

Jason nodded. He wanted to speak, but no words came. Kayla stared at him, searching for a clue to this sudden epiphany.

'What about you?' Jason asked hoarsely. 'Wouldn't you like to be a mom?'

Her eyes filled. 'You're asking me this *now*? Here? Great timing.'

'What's wrong with my timing?'

'Jason . . .' She groped for words. 'How would we organize things? With work? With everything?'

He chuckled. 'That's a long way off. I'm pretty sure we first have to plant the seed before we start worrying about things like that. Even then we'll still have nine months to prepare.'

A single tear rolled down Kayla's cheek. She made no move to wipe it away.

He came to her and wrapped his arms around her. 'You're right,' he whispered in her ear. 'My timing was rotten.'

'Doesn't matter,' she whispered back. 'Any time would have been fine. I love you, Jason. Deep down I've always wanted to have your baby.'

Raw emotion clogged his throat. 'I love you too, Kayla,' was all he could manage.

A little while later, the Sheehans entered.

'Mom! Dad!' Kayla cried out before her parents had a chance to congratulate the birthday boy. She was more cheerful than usual when she saw her parents, no doubt, Jason mused, because of their intimacy in the kitchen. Jason knew Kayla wouldn't be able to keep the good news to herself for long. Kayla quickly exchanged the latest news with her parents, and then Jason's father-in-law approached him with a big smile on his face.

She's told them already, he thought. *She really didn't waste any time. Is this really for public consumption?*

'How have you been, son?' Daniel Sheehan asked.

'Fine, Dad.'

'And what is it you do these days at that advertising agency of yours?'

'Well, it's not *my* agency, exactly, but I'm working on a campaign for a car dealership.'

Apparently Kayla had not shared their secret.

They left the party shortly after midnight. Many guests were still there, and, as expected, they all talked about Uncle Chris until the early hours. Of course, Aunt Ethel was the one who first broached the subject, much to Edward's dismay. The last thing he wanted was for the festive mood to fizzle out like a stale beer. On the other hand, raising the subject of Chris's death was understandable. The grief was palpable, and no one, least of all Edward, knew yet how to properly address it. It was like a shark swimming just beneath the surface, ready to strike and inflict pain at the least provocation. Kayla and Jason were two members of the family who preferred to keep their distance from it.

Besides, Kayla's mind was whirling with the decision they had made. It had unleashed floodwaters of pent-up emotions and expectations. And the fact that they finally *had* made a decision helped Jason forget about the photographs. Once inside the privacy of their car, she started gushing about all the things that would change once she became pregnant. Should they convert Jason's study into a nursery? That would involve moving his big desk into the living room. Maybe they could add a little space to the sitting room by stealing a few square feet from the porch. Wouldn't that be just the job for him and his father? Edward and Jason were both handy around the house, so a small extension should be a piece of cake for them, right? She then went on to describe some ideas she had for the nursery.

Jason listened to it all with a smile on his face. She was utterly absorbed in her inspirations, and Jason couldn't get a word in edgewise, nor did he want to. He would never dream of protesting. Once his wife had her mind set on something, there was no stopping it or changing it. And when her mind was set on something as glorious as creating a baby together, well, that made him so very happy.

Suddenly, two glaring headlights appeared in his rear-view mirror. The car approaching them from behind at high speed had its headlights on high beam.

'No bright colors,' Kayla was saying. 'We have to keep it light and quiet, because I'm told that's best for a baby . . .'

She stopped short, casting a worried glance in his direction.

'What is it, Jason?'

He peered into the rear-view mirror. 'I don't know. Someone's coming up my tail real fast, and he's got his high beams on.'

She glanced back.

'What *is* this?'

Those were the last words she uttered before hell erupted, as sudden as it was unexpected. The lights behind Jason's Buick grew brighter by the second and the car, already racing toward then, seemed to be picking up speed.

'Brace yourself!' he yelled at Kayla.

The car rammed into them, pushing Jason's Buick forward and sharply to the right. His safety belt locked hard, squeezing air from his lungs. He gripped the steering wheel and hit the brakes. The car spun around in a full circle. A row of trees appeared in the headlights, coming at him with blinding speed.

'Hold on!' he cried out, and crossed his arms in front of his face.

Kayla screamed. When the Buick crashed sideways into the trees, an air bag inflated from the steering wheel. Jason's head jerked backwards and he fought for consciousness as the world spun around him. He groped for Kayla, found her hand, and, a moment later, felt the heavy gray pillow material of her air bag. 'Lord Jesus, thank you,' he muttered.

She said nothing, just sat there, staring at him with wide eyes and open mouth. Then a sharp, caustic stench drifted over them. Jason recognized it immediately: the smell of fire. Smoke inside the car! He glanced over the top of the air bag: a jet of flame spouted up from beneath the hood.

He froze. Was he hurt? He felt no pain. He felt nothing at all. Kayla was screaming something at him, but strangely, he couldn't make out what she was saying. He could hardly hear her. An eerie sound like the chiming of old bells pealed in his ears. And dear Lord was he dizzy! It was as if he were experiencing the wildest roller-coaster ride of his life. But this was no thrill.

Flames from beneath the hood expanded, increasing the heat and suffering, and his sense of utter hopelessness. Still he couldn't move. Hell was breathing fire on him and smoke filled his lungs; yet he could do nothing. He was bound as though with chains.

Wild-eyed, Jason stared, mute, as his fate gathered strength, bore down mercilessly upon him, and claimed him for its own.

SIX
Fire

aughn is rummaging through the basket of kindling next to
the fireplace. This wood is dryer than the stack on the floor
beside the basket, but it's still damp. Outside it is cold and
wet, and the wood was hauled in not long ago. Vaughn picks up a
large bottle of methylated alcohol. He seems drawn to fire. More
often than Jason believes is necessary, he hauls spliced wood from
the yard to the living room. Also more often than seems necessary,
he lights a fire in the fireplace.

Jason hates fire. Its unpredictable crackling. The erratic dancing
of the flames. The stench of soggy, moldy wood burning. The awful
smoke. It makes him break out in a cold sweat. He is a guest here;
there is nothing he can say. At home it's different. There he won't
allow his own father Edward to light the fireplace. At home he
has the power to stop it, but not here. He only hopes that Sherilyn
won't notice how frightened he is. They have been dating for five
months now, and as far as he knows she is unaware of his terror,
his phobia.

Vaughn, Sherilyn's father, squirts some alcohol on the wood
inside the fireplace. With a practiced gesture he strikes a match
and tosses it on to the kindling. Whoosh! An unexpectedly tall burst
of flame leaps up. The bottle slips from his hand and lands in the
fire. It billows up and then erupts in roaring flames that threaten
the oak ceiling beams. Vaughn reacts instinctively. He steps back
and pushes his daughter away. Vaughn also grabs for Jason, but
misses.

Tongues of fire roll from the fireplace, consuming the Persian rug
on the floor in front of it. The flames surge toward Jason, surrounding
him. The world suddenly consists of nothing but the hellish fire; in
front of him, behind him and on both sides of him the flames perform
their ferocious dance of death. The fire quickly towers over him. He
stares at it, paralyzed. He cannot run. The flames are creeping

closer. Intense heat sears his skin. He can hear someone scream, and only then realizes it's his own voice. The first talons of fire are clawing at his body. He starts shrieking.

Then Sherilyn appears in front of him. Her face is blurry.

'Jason!' she calls.

He looks at her mouth, her face, registering her bewilderment and fear.

'Jason! Jason!'

Suddenly the fire retreats, crawling away from him like a man-eating lion into its lair. The flames dwindle to small tongues, climb back into the fireplace like a movie playing in reverse. He squeezes his eyes shut a few times and then opens them wide. He can't believe it.

Behind Sherilyn her father appears, looking bewildered and worried.

Jason looks around. There seems to be no damage. There never was an inferno. He stares at the fireplace and sees flames rising up a little higher because of the methylated alcohol, but that's all. He must have been hallucinating. He was the only one to see things that haven't really happened, reinforced with images from his recurring nightmare. The bad dream in which an enormous fire threatens to swallow him and from which he cannot escape. The dream that always drives him mad with fear.

Sherilyn knows nothing about this. Neither do Vaughn and his wife Francisca. Only his own parents are aware of it.

'Jason, you're sweating like a . . .'

The words catch in her throat. Sherilyn stares at him, her eyes wide. Jason sees incomprehension and horror in them.

'Are you all right, son?' Vaughn asks, concerned.

Francisca enters the room, drawn by Jason's screams.

Jason touches his face. Sherilyn is right, the sweat is dripping off him. His knees feel wobbly, his heart is pounding inside his chest. He wants to flee from here.

'Get him a chair,' Francisca says. 'Whatever is the matter with you, Jason?'

He has to say something. Three pairs of eyes are gazing at him in confusion. He searches for words.

'I thought . . . the fire . . .'

He had thought, no, he had felt *the flames coming for him. He*

was convinced he was going to burn alive. He could not escape.
He had been rooted to the ground.

Sherilyn wouldn't understand. So he says nothing. Sherilyn's
parents don't know what to make of him. In Sherilyn's eyes he sees
something else: distance, alienation. She doesn't understand this
Jason, he realizes. She no longer wants him. This sudden change
in him has shattered the image she had of her boyfriend. Jason is
trembling, sweating and white as a bed sheet. Right before her eyes,
he has shriveled up and turned into a pitiful nothing. Sherilyn doesn't
know this side of him, and it has visibly shaken her.

He realizes he is going to lose her, the result of her father acci-
dentally dropping a bottle of alcohol into the fireplace. In his mind's
eye, the flames roar up anew.

The rest of that evening Sherilyn barely says a word to him. She
doesn't seem to recognize him.

When he leaves, the kiss she gives him is perfunctory. He has
lost her already. Sherilyn, the first girl Jason Evans, sixteen years
old, has ever seriously dated, has no further use for a boyfriend
who is clearly so emotionally unstable.

SEVEN
Date of Death

The car door beside him was yanked open, and he gazed up at a look of utter panic staring down at him.

'Come on, Jason!' Kayla screamed. 'Get out!'

Matted strands of hair covered much of her face. Still he remained, as if transfixed. He stared at her as though he had never seen her before and had no idea who she was.

Kayla pulled on his arm, but the safety belt held him in place. Cursing, she reached across him and clicked it loose. Again she pulled on his arm. With a shift of weight, he fell out of the car on to the hard ground. He moaned in agony, but the fresh air seemed to finally lift the daze and revitalize him.

He looked at his car. Flames continued to sputter from beneath the hood and lick along the edges of the metal, but there weren't many of them and they were beginning to flicker out. Had the raging fire of his imagination ever really been a reality?

'We must get away!' Kayla cried. 'The car might blow!'

He scrambled to his feet, grabbed his wife's hand, and started running away as best he could from the Buick. When they reached the safety of the other side of the road, he paused, hands on knees, to catch his breath and calm his nerves.

He and Kayla were alone on Monte Mar Avenue somewhere between Cornell and Fernhill, in the desert heart of the Santa Monica Mountains. The car that hit them had not stopped. Jason had not the faintest idea what kind of car it had been. The question did not enter his mind, not even now.

The fire, his nightmare, did, however.

Much later, in the wee hours before dawn, they finally arrived home. After a quick shower, they went straight to bed, Kayla falling asleep almost the instant her head hit the pillow. But not Jason. He lay awake, unable to rest either his mind or his spirit. With an angry motion he tossed the sheets aside and stared up at the ceiling, his tortured mind awhirl.

The events of the night continued to plague him. He had used his cell phone to dial 911, and a police car had soon arrived at the scene. Two officers – Dillon, a tall, fair-haired man, and Herbert, somewhat more muscular and with a crew cut – had used a fire extinguisher to put out the last gasps of flames. They then questioned them.

Jason and Kayla had told the officers that another driver, perhaps someone who had been drinking, had crashed into the back of the Buick. No, they couldn't provide any details about the driver or the make of car, or even its color. It had all happened in a matter of seconds and at breakneck speed; they had been blinded by the glare of high beams, and it was dark outside. After taking careful note of the facts, the police officers insisted on taking them in the police cruiser to the emergency room at Barlow Hospital. A brief check-up by the physician on duty revealed no serious injuries to either Jason or Kayla. Afterwards Dillon and Herbert had kindly given them a ride home, with a promise to conduct a thorough search for the hit-and-run driver.

They had talked for a short while on the drive home. Tomorrow, he would call the insurance company to have the Buick towed away.

'If it's totaled, maybe I should call Tommy Jones,' Jason had quipped, but Kayla just shook her head, finding no humor in that statement. It didn't sound very funny to Jason, either.

She had said nothing about the way he had sat frozen with fear after the brief fire in the engine. She knew him and was thus well acquainted with his fear of fire. Who had rammed their car? Someone who had had a little too much to drink, Kayla kept insisting. She had no doubts, although Jason certainly did. And his doubts were centered on the two Polaroid photographs of which Kayla still knew nothing. These doubts were the reason he could not relax and sleep.

At length he slid from the bed, went downstairs, switched on the porch light, and walked outside. The cool night air felt good on his face, and on his bare chest and arms. There was almost no wind. Crickets and other insects had long since launched into their pleasant night-time orchestra. A cloud hid a thin sliver of moon. The sky was no longer tar black; it held a slight yellowish tinge that slowly spread to a deeper blue. The countless stars overhead and the night sounds from the woods made him feel melancholy. His thoughts drifted back to Stu's philosophies about the non-existent present. But then the flames from his Buick assaulted him, erasing the possibility of any other mental image. When he finally went back to bed, it was to no avail. The blessed oblivion of sleep continued to taunt him.

As he lay in bed, he heard sounds in the house: rumbling and clattering drainpipes, groaning wood. *Or was it crackling?* Was that the sickly smell of fire he sensed?

Jason froze. At length he slid out from under the sheets and darted out the bedroom door. What *was* that? Something glowing in the hallway? His fingers shaking, he searched for the light switch. The light went on, revealing no plumes of smoke, no crackling flames, nothing.

Sweat trickled down his face. A wave of nausea washed over and through him. He reacted instinctively, running from the hallway into the living room and switching on the lights there. Then he ran into the kitchen and then into the bathroom. He even ran outside on to the back porch, but he found nary a flicker of flame there, either. *Of course not*, his mind chided him from somewhere deep inside.

Calmer now, he circled Canyon View from the outside, dressed in nothing but his underwear.

The fetid smells of fire and death slowly faded away. Until he smelled nothing. There was no fire, no cause for alarm.

He clasped his hands behind his neck.

Don't let this get to you now, Jason, he thought. *Stay calm, trust your common sense.*

By now, shards of morning sun were intruding upon the eastern sky.

Jason went back inside to find the door open from the living room into the hallway. As he walked through it, he spotted something on the doormat inside the small entrance hall. He stooped to pick it up. It was an envelope. His heart sank and he felt a surge of nausea in his intestines.

It was a manila envelope, of course. The blocky handwriting that he recognized stated only his name. No address, no stamp.

This envelope had been hand-delivered.

But when? Had it been here when he and Kayla returned from the hospital? He didn't think so because he would have noticed it.

Whatever it was, he held it in his hand now.

Jason stared at the envelope, dreading to open it. Finally he did. As he tore it open, his fingers were trembling.

It contained another Polaroid photograph, but this image was different from the other two. Instead of another graveyard he saw a single letter on a gray sandstone wall – a weathered wall, with irregularities, cracks and lichen. A strange wall . . .

Then it suddenly hit him. He *was* looking at a gravestone. The stone filled the entire picture, and on the gray background, like graffiti, a single graceful red letter stood out.

M

The red curly M consumed a good part of the gray background. Jason quickly determined that the letter had been superimposed on to the photograph. Not hard to do for someone who knew how to do it. Jason could have done it in a heartbeat.

He turned the photograph over.

There it was, the handwritten text.

August 18th, your date of death

EIGHT
An Old Dream

The next morning Jason called Brian Anderson, and Kayla called Patrick Voight. Both men responded with shock and concern. Jason and Kayla tried to reassure them that everything was all right, the accident could have ended a lot worse.

Kayla drove Jason in her Chrysler to Felix Auto Repair on City Terrace Drive. Together with chief mechanic Ron Schaffner, they surveyed the damage to the Buick. The grille was a mess, the fender had become partly detached, and the headlights were shattered. The hood was open and pointing up in a slight buckle; along its edges, the familiar aluminum shine had been defiled by streaks of charred black.

Scratching his ample beer belly, Ron spat out a wad of chewing tobacco and said in his usual sharp nasal twang, 'We should be able to fix her for you, but it's gonna take a while.'

'OK, Ron, thanks,' Jason sighed. 'Do your best, that's all I can ask. You know I have faith in you.'

Jason followed Kayla home driving a loaner car, a Tommy-cheapie Chevy Aveo. Once back at Canyon View, they received a visit from the local police captain. Guillermo Caiazzo had an Italian name and looked the part – complete with a dab of Armani aftershave, as Kayla was to later comment with a satisfied smile that made Jason jealous. Dressed snugly in a pinstriped tailored suit, he stayed for half an hour taking copious notes. As it turned out, however, there was not much more either Jason or Kayla could tell him than they had not already told Officer Dillon and Officer Herbert. In what seemed like a flash after they had first noticed the bright headlights of the other car, the Buick had been rammed off the road and the other driver had kept on going. Nodding in understanding, Guillermo said he planned on searching for trace evidence on the Buick and at the crash site.

Jason said nothing about the photographs either to the police captain or to his father. Kayla kept giving him worried glances, as if sensing he was withholding an important piece of the puzzle from her. But she didn't say anything about it, thinking, perhaps, that he was preoccupied with the fire that had erupted in his car's engine. She knew that there was nothing she could do about his fire phobia.

That night, in bed, while Kayla lay asleep and there were no distractions, his fear took flight. He wondered, again, what the pictures meant and who had taken them. He had a suspicion – growing into a conviction – that the person who had delivered the last photo was also responsible for the accident. He or she had rammed his Buick and then in the resulting confusion had sneaked up to the house and slid the third picture into the mail slot of his front door.

If that were true, then the accident had been no accident. It had been a deliberate assault.

Other Polaroid photographs might be waiting in the wings. And additional onslaughts.

Is someone going to kill me on August eighteenth?

Was that when this would all end? Did he have only one more month to live?

He could no longer keep the photographs a secret from Kayla. He had to confess everything to her. But he was afraid to do that. Something still held him back.

At some point in the middle of the night, Jason found himself in a darkness devoid of stars. From the corner of his eye, he spotted the glow of a fire. Where was the door? He couldn't find it. His heart was pounding and rivulets of sweat were trickling down his back. He looked to his right and left. Flames were all around him! Was it a funeral pyre? He opened his mouth to scream, but no sound came. A blistering heat seared his face and burned away his skin. There was no way out. Flames towered over him, closing in on him. The pain, oh God the pain . . .

Uttering a hoarse cry, he sat up with a jerk and gasped for breath. *It's not real!* he struggled to assure himself. *I'm not trapped, there was no fire, I didn't get burned. It was a dream, a nightmare.*

'Jason?' He heard Kayla whispering beside him, her voice a study in controlled fear. 'God Almighty, Jason, what's the matter?'

He wanted to answer, but his teeth were chattering, his body was shaking as if from a winter blast. He rubbed his sweat-smeared face. Or were those tears? Yes, they were tears. Sweet Jesus, he was bawling like a baby!

Kayla wrapped her arms around him.

'Jason, *say* something. Talk to me,' she pleaded.

He took a deep breath, tried to suppress his uncontrollable sobbing. His head felt as though it might burst.

'I had the dream again,' he whispered in agony.

She gazed down knowingly, as if expecting this. 'You mean the nightmare?'

He nodded. 'Yes, the nightmare.'

'No doubt it was induced by the accident.'

He shook his head. 'No. You don't understand. It was *the* nightmare. The same one I've had before.'

Kayla massaged his back and his trembling slowly subsided. She looked deep into his eyes. 'About a fire, and you can't get away?'

'Yeah, that one. I'm in a dark place somewhere. It's night and I can't see anything except the fire. It's all around me. It's crawling closer and closer, closing in on me. It's like I'm tied to a stake or something. I'm trapped, and I can't move. All I can do is wait until the flames consume me and I burn to ashes. Then I wake up.'

Kayla swallowed. She wanted to say something to convey love and sympathy, but no words came. Jason put a hand on her cheek and saw the glint of unshed tears in her eyes. Suddenly he was no longer shaking, and he felt all the more guilty for the suffering he was putting her through. And she didn't even know about the photographs.

He sank back on to the pillows. The last time he had had this nightmare was more than four years ago, soon after they had met. He had no recollection of when the dreams had first started. As a small child, he had experienced the dream several times. In the twenty years since then the fire had often intruded upon his sleep, sometimes several nights a week; and then nothing for months. Occasionally the terror surged within him in broad daylight, like that time in Sherilyn's house. His love for Kayla had released him from the horror of the dreams four years ago. For good, he had assumed.

His fear of fire had remained, but it was less intense than before.

Still, the thought of a fire raging out of control was about the only mental image that could bring him to the verge of panic. Burning candles, campfires, or the bonfires of Halloween, it didn't matter. Jason Evans hated all varieties of fire – just about anything that could burst into flames – and avoided them whenever he could. Other memories floated to the surface. In his parents' home, when he was young, he had never wanted his father to light the fireplace, not even during the bitter cold of a winter night. Edward had ignored his objections at first, but after his son suffered through a few dramatic nights filled with nightmares he had accepted the fact that the hearth would remain forever empty of wood and paper. In Canyon View they never lit candles, and Jason had convinced Kayla that they didn't need a fireplace.

Even though he had tried to deny it at first, he came to realize that his fear was irrational. There was even a scientific term for it: pyrophobia, an exaggerated fear of fire. That term had become embedded inside him. Why it had, he had no idea. He had never been involved in a fire, and nothing else could be tied conclusively to his terror. He had asked his parents if perhaps they could recall some event from his childhood, something that could help to explain his pyrophobia. An incident he did not recollect, maybe. Could his subconscious past hold the key to his recurring nightmare?

But his parents had been unable to offer anything substantive. When he had fallen in love with Kayla, he had ended his search for clues. He was too happy to be obsessed with anything beyond making her happy.

During the last four years he had led a normal life; the flames torturing his mind seemed to finally have been extinguished. For four years it had worked. But now an anonymous photographer had cruelly inserted his sinister sickness into the joys of Jason's life. Jason had to find out who this person was and what message he was attempting to deliver. He felt like he didn't have much time.

August eighteenth was just around the corner.

NINE
Dead Ends

On Friday they both returned to work, as they had agreed to do. As soon as he walked in the agency's front door, Jason was besieged with questions and had to relate all the gory details of the accident to his co-workers. His account was so riveting, they hung on to his every word. After they finally dispersed to their work stations, he summoned Carol Martinez into his office and asked her how the divorce proceedings were going. Carol told him that Bruno had left her and that her lawyer would be filing divorce papers imminently. This would all be over soon, she assured him with a smile. Jason returned her smile and squeezed her hand.

'I'd like you to look into something for me,' he said in what he hoped was a casual tone. 'This, to be precise,' he added as he pointed to the image on his computer screen.

He had scanned and saved the third Polaroid photograph to prevent Carol from seeing the message written on the back. 'I can email it to you. It's a weird, doctored photo. There's a letter M in a stone that is probably a grave marker. It may have held a name that was brushed away by Photoshop and replaced by the letter M.'

He looked at her calmly, as if what he was asking of her was a simple favor. 'Please continue,' she said, leaning in and studying the photograph. 'What exactly do you want me to do?'

'I was wondering if you could extract the layers of the image, to get the original name on the stone to reappear. If ever there was one,' he added.

'I can try. Where did you get this photograph?'

'It arrived in some spam,' Jason lied. 'Just out of curiosity, I wondered whether you could determine the original name. You're far better at this sort of thing than I am.'

He could see that she was flattered.

'I'll have a look at it,' she said. 'Go ahead and email it to me.'

He did, immediately after she left his office, although he didn't hold out much hope she would uncover anything of significance. Only the original sender's computer contained the individual layers the picture had been made with in Photoshop. And even so, he couldn't be sure there *had* been a name in the original photograph.

But it was worth a try.

In the meantime, there was something *he* could try. Googling the key words 'grave with pyramids' produced a lengthy text about an Egyptian pharaoh. 'Grave + pyramid' resulted in thousands of links involving ancient Egypt. He tried a few other combinations of words, but this approach was getting him nowhere. Not that he was expecting anything useful. Finding something concrete using this method would be like finding the proverbial needle in a haystack.

Carol appeared in the open doorway. She reported that her analysis had turned up nothing.

Dead ends.

The promotional campaign for Tommy Jones was by now in draft form, thanks to good work by Tony, Barbara and Carol. Their last brainstorm session had gone surprisingly well. Everyone had been focused, and one person's idea had been fleshed out, reinforced and enhanced by another's. Nothing else needed Jason's attention today. He was free to start his weekend early, something that was most convenient at the moment.

Jason was acquainted with a man whom he considered to be a genius with computers. If Lou Briggs couldn't find any leads in the photographs, no one could.

Jason punched in Lou's number. At the third ring, when Briggs answered in his usual wheezy voice, Jason asked if could stop by.

'Sure,' Lou said, chipper as always. 'When?'

Jason glanced at his watch. It was only three thirty. Although expected to stay in the office until at least five o'clock, right now he could not care less about what he was supposed to do.

'Could I come right over, Lou?'

'Sure. See you when you get here.'

In his Aveo – the Buick would be in the shop for a few weeks, according to Ron Schaffner's latest update – Jason left the downtown office building and drove to North Hollywood, where wide asphalt streets were flanked by low-rise buildings with eye-catching signs and miles of garish billboards. Turning left on to Burbank Boulevard, he entered a middle-class residential neighborhood. He parked the car in front of a whitewashed wooden house, the most striking feature of which was its two asymmetric roofs. The second inverted V had been added on at a quarter-turn and was leaning against the first.

A year ago, Lou had contacted Jason through a web forum they had both visited from time to time called ipyrophobia.com. In describing his life-story in an email to the forum, it turned out that Lou had incurred serious scars following a horrific house fire.

Jason had responded to his email, offering his sympathy and his support. As time went on, they had exchanged additional emails. Then one day he was inspired to pay a visit to Lou. His self-described 'serious scars' turned out to be an understatement, and at first blush Jason had felt a spasm of revulsion toward the man. Lou, bald and skinny, looked more like a skeleton than a full-bodied man: he no longer had ears, a nose, lips, or eyelids. He was also confined to a wheelchair. Severe muscle spasms made it impossible for him to walk any distance. He was the same age as Jason, but his raw, splotchy skin made him look decades older.

Lou, who did not have many friends or relatives and lived in virtual isolation, said that the Internet had saved him. He was making a decent living with investments and stocks, and the financial crises that had ruined many of his contemporaries had not touched him. In certain circles he had acquired some fame as a guru of Wall Street. It proved to be an ideal situation for him, since he never had to meet anybody face to face, and still the money poured in.

After his initial shock at Lou's appearance, Jason had become increasingly involved with the man's life and had started paying him regular visits, often on a weekly basis. Over time he became more and more impressed with Lou's mental acuity. The fire may have claimed much from him and much of him, but it had taken neither his intelligence nor his wisdom. Lou always seemed to have a piece of solid advice or a good story with which to cheer Jason up. On one occasion he had even helped Jason with his work by offering a creative and useful idea for a campaign – although even the genius of Lou Briggs had not come up with anything for the Tommy Jones campaign. On another occasion Lou had fixed Jason's personal computer after a virus seemed to have devoured everything on his hard drive. But usually they talked about mundane things, and Lou always managed to make Jason feel better about life before he left. The only subject that remained largely taboo was the pyrophobia they shared.

Lou had told Jason that he had been burned because a gas pipe had exploded inside his family home when he was seventeen years old. Within moments, the house had become a towering inferno. Although he had been severely injured, he had survived the cataclysm. Not so his parents. From that point on, overcome by grief and emotion, he had been unable to continue his story. The memory of the tragedy was too painful for Lou, even now.

The subject of fire was therefore not one he was inclined to talk about. If the subject came up, Lou's face twitched, causing his scars to become even more prominent.

Jason rang the doorbell and the door clicked open. Lou had installed remote controls for nearly everything inside his house, including the door. Sitting in his wheelchair, the frail, disfigured man greeted him jovially. Jason returned the greeting and walked into the living room where he found a cream-colored couch, upholstered chairs in the same color, a glass coffee table and two white cupboards on an immaculate, sand-colored tile floor. In addition to a flat-screen television, the room contained three large computer screens, placed side by side on a long, whitewashed wooden table in front of a window overlooking a small backyard typical of homes in the area.

Jason sat down on one of the chairs and placed his three Polaroid photographs on the coffee table. Lou picked them up and studied each one in turn.

'I'll come right to the point,' Jason said. 'I'm here because of the three photos you're holding. You're probably wondering why I brought them to you.'

'Yeah, but I have a hunch you're about to tell me,' Lou responded, absently rubbing his right hand.

Jason started talking. He was completely frank about everything that had happened to him since Monday. His eagerness to tell Lou every detail related to the photographs surprised Jason, since he had yet to tell Kayla anything about them. But he knew and trusted Lou, whereas he feared Kayla would be unable to cope and would fly off the handle. While Jason was talking, Lou slid a bottle of beer across the table toward him and took one for himself. Jason gratefully swigged from the bottle.

'What it comes down to,' he concluded, 'is that I don't know what this all means or what I should do about it. My apparent date of death is August eighteenth, or at least that's what the person who sent me the photos wrote on the last one. And it could very well be that this same person rammed my car and pushed it off the road. He also claims that I'm already dead, that I only *think* I'm alive. When is he going to strike again? When will the next picture arrive? Are Kayla and I being watched? What can I do?'

Before Lou could respond, Jason said, an edge of exasperation in his voice, 'I came here because I thought maybe you could extract something from the photographs. The second Polaroid has a tomb in it. If I could identify that tomb, I'd know which cemetery this is. And I'm convinced that the M in the third picture was put there in Photoshop. I'd sure like to know what is really inscribed on the headstone.'

Lou picked up his bottle of beer, drank deeply and gently laid it back on the table.

'Why don't you start at the beginning? Give me those photos. I'll slide the third one into my scanner.'

That sentence sequence was quintessential Lou. He never let himself be fazed by anything. He simply acted. Jason handed him the three photographs. Lou slid the picture with the M under the lid of his HP, and then opened a program on his computer; not Photoshop, but some other tool. Lou had an extensive collection of software.

'So what do you think of my story?' Jason asked.

'It's fierce,' Lou said simply.

'You can say that again,' Jason sighed.

'Who have you talked to about this?'

'You're the first one I've told. Even Kayla doesn't know.'

'Why not?'

'You know about her problem. And we just had that whole affair with Chris. And now this . . .'

He shook his head.

'But I'm going to tell her. When the time is right. I know I have to.'

'Why don't you go to the police?' Lou asked.

'I had cops over at my place just yesterday, because of the accident. An Italian detective by the name of Guillermo. A wannabe stud, if you ask me. Kayla liked him, I think. He asked . . .'

Jason caught his breath as the third Polaroid appeared full screen on Lou's monitor. From what he could tell, the M had been smeared on to the headstone with red paint.

'He asked all kinds of questions,' Jason went on after a moment, 'but because Kayla was there with me, I kept my mouth shut.'

'There's nothing stopping you from going to see him now.'

Jason rubbed his chin. 'No, you're right.'

'Look,' Lou said, motioning toward the screen, 'I've managed to separate the layers.'

Jason glanced up and saw that the grave marker had been separated from the red M. The letter now sat beside the stone on the screen.

'Christ. How did you do that so quickly?'

'I'm good,' Lou grinned. 'I'm really good.'

All that was visible on the gray stone were traces of erosion, lichen, cracks and scratches.

'I had hoped . . .' Jason started. He cleared his throat. 'I had hoped that there would be another name underneath the M. The original name on the headstone.'

Lou shook his head. 'This is the only layer I can peel off. This is all there is.'

'Are you sure?'

'I could fiddle around with it some more, but yeah, I'm pretty sure.'

Jason sighed. Lou turned his wheelchair around and gazed at him intensely.

'What did *you* think? That your own name would be on it?'

'No,' Jason responded quickly, as if to emphasize that the very thought of it was ridiculous. Except, he was not at all convinced it *was* ridiculous.

'No, of course not, but . . .'

Then he decided, what the hell; he'd confess what was on his mind. 'I've had a few days to think about it,' he said. 'On the one hand, this may be a threat. On the other hand, that's not how it's phrased. I'm supposedly dead, and apparently I died on August eighteenth. From that perspective, these messages could be interpreted as statements of an accomplished fact. And since grave markers have names on them, I thought . . .'

Lou gave him a pensive look. 'I see,' he said, nodding. 'That would be my thought as well. Technically, as you know, the photographer could have erased the original name, but there's no way to tell without the source files. Or maybe he used a piece of blank stone for this image.'

Jason rubbed his chin thoughtfully.

'So I should try to find the original images that were used to make this photograph. That's what you're telling me, isn't it?'

'Yes,' Lou said. 'Better still, the actual headstone.'

Jason nodded in agreement. 'But that means I'd have to find out which cemetery this tomb is in. I've done some research, but I've come up empty so far.'

'Want me to help find it for you?' Lou offered.

'I would, Lou. Thanks.'

He got up and started pacing back and forth.

'Let's take a step back. So you agree with me that I should interpret these messages literally? But I assure you, I'm very much alive.'

Lou smiled as he rubbed his bald head. Because he had no lips, his teeth already looked unnaturally large. His smile therefore made him appear more macabre than friendly.

'I can see that,' he asserted.

'And the accident? It was a close shave, and it could have ended a lot worse. If the photographer was driving the car, he certainly is not acting as though I'm already dead. In fact, he's trying his damnedest to make sure I *am* dead.'

Lou shrugged. 'I can't explain this either, Jason. If you ask me, your first step is to find that cemetery. I'll get right to work on that for you.'

When Jason returned home, he took two aspirin to relieve a headache and sat down in his hanging chair on the porch to wait for Kayla, who was later than usual. Maybe she was catching up after missing work yesterday.

No other manila envelopes had arrived in the mail. Not at Tanner & Preston's and not at the house. Kayla came home and told him about having to put in overtime compiling appendices for the annual report. In turn, he shared with her his progress with the Tommy Jones project. They did not discuss the car accident. As if by unspoken agreement they had decided to put that nightmare behind them.

They heated a frozen dinner, watched television for a while, and went to bed early. The night was uneventful. No dreams, no fire. He craved sleep, and sleep is what he got. The next morning he woke up at nine, a rarity for him. Kayla was outside, smiling as she puttered around in the garden. The sun stood high in a cloudless sky; this morning death and fire seemed not part of their life.

With the good life continuing on Sunday, Kayla again broached the subject of children. The words she used were as warm and excited as her expression, and the prospect of soon starting a family of their own embraced them in a tight emotional bond. They decided to take it easy that day. Jason spent time in front of the computer, and Kayla relaxed on the porch hammock to read the book she had started.

Later, as the afternoon was quietly slipping into the shadows of early evening, he still hadn't summoned the courage to tell her about the Polaroid photographs. The day had been perfect, and he was loath to upset her. The photos and handwritten messages would affect her deeply because they would stir up mental visions that were best forgotten. Her issues with her previous boyfriend Ralph bore an uncanny similarity to what was happening to him now.

As it turned out, however, Kayla forced him to confess. At eleven o'clock, just before retiring, she suddenly stormed into his study. He was dressed in a bathrobe and sitting in his desk chair, still scouring the Internet for the pyramid-shaped tomb. He had tried several times during the day to dredge up a web image of the structure, hoping at the same time to uncover the name and location of the burial site where it was located. But his efforts had proved fruitless.

'What's *this*?' Kayla suddenly cried out. She was standing in the door to his room, dressed in a sheer, short white nightgown, and her voice was laced with anger.

In her right hand she held the three photographs.

TEN

Confession

Jason slowly rose to his feet, a grim expression on his face that matched her own. Her eyes flashed disgust; she was glaring at him as though she had caught him *in flagrante delicto* with another woman.

'Where did you find those?' he asked her quietly.

'In your pants,' she said in no uncertain terms. 'I wanted to run the washer before I went to bed. What's going *on*, Jason Evans?'

Adding his last name usually signaled that she was *really* angry. He would have to remain calm and proceed carefully. 'I've been meaning to tell you about them,' he said somewhat lamely. 'Come, sit down.'

'I don't *want* to sit down!' she fumed.

He walked around his desk and put a hand on her shoulder. She brushed it off.

'No! Explain this first!' she yelled hoarsely, waving the photos before his face.

He started talking, struggling to keep traces of fear and doubt from his voice. He needed to keep as much fat from the fire as he could. At the same time, he wanted to kick himself for keeping this secret from her for so long. That, and the fact that he had forgotten to take them out of his pocket and hide them somewhere safe when he had undressed and put on his robe.

The time for subterfuge had passed. He had to come clean – for her and for his peace of mind. So he told her everything to date, including his visit to Lou Briggs, his own attempts to determine the location of the cemetery, and how he had tried to deduce a name from the headstone in the third photograph. His main defense for not telling her was that he didn't want to worry her.

Kayla listened to him, her eyes seemingly growing larger with every sentence he uttered. A range of complex emotions crossed her face. After he finished his story, she said nothing for several moments.

'So it could be a threat,' he finished, 'although the words don't indicate that, exactly.'

Kayla took another look at the photographs and the messages. Then she looked up at him. 'Do you have enemies, Jason?' she asked tentatively. 'I can't imagine that you would or who they would be, but *do* you? Could there be someone who'd want to hurt you? Somebody who is that angry with you?'

Her anger remained, but slowly it was morphing into concern for him.

Jason shrugged. 'Beats me, Kayla. I didn't think I had any enemies.'

'But what in God's name is all this supposed to mean? Who would do such a thing?'

'I haven't a clue.'

'Why would anyone want to see you dead?'

'I'm not sure that they do,' Jason insisted. 'It's what I told Lou. The words don't expressly imply a threat. They just say I died on August eighteenth, and that I'm not really alive.'

Kayla again studied the photos and their cryptic messages. She crossed her arms and flicked her thumb across her forefinger, as if playing with an invisible cigarette lighter. It was a nervous habit of hers. 'And you think the accident was no accident?'

'What do *you* think?' he asked her.

She waved that away. 'Why haven't you reported this to the police?'

'Lou asked me the same thing. But I can always do that later. I'm not sure what I'd be reporting. As I keep saying, there is no explicit threat. Maybe the accident *was* simply that: an accident. I have no proof that it was anything more than that. Who knows? Maybe this is just some freak trying to scare me. If so, he has succeeded.'

'Me as well,' Kayla added. She stared ahead. 'What do we do now?'

'Good question,' he sighed. 'What does the sender want us to do? Every road I take to try to make sense of this has led to a dead end. I need to figure out which cemetery the photos were taken at, but that's another riddle. I haven't been able to find anything, and I haven't heard from Lou yet.'

'You own two Polaroid cameras yourself,' she remarked.

He did indeed. An ancient, nostalgic model 95B and a fairly new TL234 12,0 megapixels. Just recently he had sold his TL031 on eBay.

'Yes, I do. What's your point?'

She shrugged. 'You're a Polaroid fan. You even joined one of those online clubs. But Polaroid cameras aren't exactly hip any more. They're passé.'

'Says you.'

'Yeah, says me. Think on it: why weren't you sent digital images?'

'I don't know, Kayla. Maybe that's a message in itself. Or do you think that these photographs were sent by one of my Polaroid buddies? Jack, maybe? Ricky? Shaun Reilly?'

Kayla shifted her gaze from him and then shifted back.

'Why didn't you say anything to me about this?' she asked bitterly.

'I told you. I didn't want to worry you. I needed to think about it for a while before I discussed it with you.'

Suddenly, something inside her seemed to snap. She shuddered, and the photographs slipped from her grasp and fell to the floor. She started to cry.

'Not again,' she whispered through the tears.

Jason came to her, his hands on her hips.

'I'm not Ralph,' he said softly.

She pressed her face against his chest.

'You're not dead,' she sobbed. 'You can't die. You *can't.*'

'I'm not going to,' he said, with more conviction than he truly felt.

'Don't leave me,' she begged him, sniffling.

'I will never leave you,' he said firmly. 'We'll get through this. You and I will get through this together and we'll grow old together. And we'll be good parents too, I promise. I'm not going to die – at least not anytime soon.'

He picked up the photographs from the floor.

'But in the meantime we have to deal with this. I . . . *We* have to try to understand what the messages mean. Help me, Kayla. Let's do this together.'

She took a few deep breaths and looked up at him, her eyes glistening.

'*Of course* we'll do this together,' she stressed. 'Just promise me you won't keep secrets from me again. Never again, do you understand? Don't do that to me.'

He held her face gently in his hands.

'Together. You and I. Together we will figure this out.'

ELEVEN

Torches

When Kayla slid behind the steering wheel of her Chrysler Sebring sedan the next morning to set off for work, her face looked drawn. Her chic brown jacket and matching skirt did nothing to boost her appearance. And the sun washing over her smooth caramel skin served only to emphasize her pale complexion.

Even so, she was a beautiful young woman. She was just not the type to take advantage of her natural assets, such as her sea-blue eyes set in the perfect symmetry of her face. Kayla wanted to be judged by her performance, not her looks. She would never admit that her alluring physical appearance had sometimes opened doors for her, but of course they had. Jason smiled at her and waved goodbye as she drove off.

That morning, they did not discuss the photographs either before, during or after breakfast. He did not want to cause a scene by broaching the subject again. And he assumed that because she was unable to talk about Ralph, she was unable to come to terms with this new horrifying development.

Ralph Grainger had been Kayla's fiancé before she met Jason. She would have married him and perhaps even had children with him if the man hadn't suffered a premature and tragic death. She had been with him when it happened, in the tent they shared while climbing in the Rocky Mountains bordering Nevada and Arizona. He had suffered a cardiac arrest just a few weeks before his twenty-sixth birthday. Kayla had been in deep shock. Ralph's death had seemed a mystery, but then a post-mortem revealed that he had been born with a deficiency in his pulmonary heart valve. For most of his truncated life he had been walking around with a time bomb ticking inside of him, and not a single doctor had correctly diagnosed the problem. Had that problem been caught in time, Ralph would still be alive. Doctors could have replaced his defective valve in open-heart surgery. It was not a life-threatening procedure; the risk of complications was small. Ninety-nine percent of patients were discharged from the hospital after only eight days. Ralph should have been one of them. Unfortunately, congenital defects are not normally detected during routine medical exams.

Since then, death had reared like a monster in Kayla's mind. She just couldn't seem to cope with it. Often, when a family member or friend died – such as recently with Uncle Chris – she fell into a deep depression that could last for weeks.

Ralph's heart attack was one of the few things Kayla never talked about, despite Jason urging her to discuss it to help bring closure to her. She had let something slip once, something that placed Ralph's death in a strange light. It still wasn't clear to Jason exactly what she had meant, but apparently Ralph had predicted his own death not long before it actually happened. He wished he knew more details, especially now.

He tried to think about other things on his way to Tanner & Preston, but his brain would not cooperate. Foremost among the sea of questions plaguing him was where in God's holy name the cemetery in the photographs was located. At first glance it looked like countless other cemeteries in the United States. It could just as likely be in California as in Maine. Random guesswork wouldn't help. His Internet research had yielded nothing, and Lou – to whom he had talked briefly over the phone yesterday – had so far come up empty.

His head was saturated with questions and void of answers as he followed the Pacific Coast Highway, the azure blue ocean on one side and the pleasant green of the Malibu hills on the other. He didn't understand any of it. He was staring ahead as he navigated by rote through the rush hour traffic.

His mind wandered back to his recurring nightmare that suddenly had surged back into his consciousness. Just as all the times before, he could not recall a single event from his past that could explain his pyrophobia. It was simply a part of his nature, in the same way that some people are afraid of heights and others are scared of open spaces. For as long as he could remember, the dream symbolized what he feared most: being trapped by raging flames, unable to escape, having to wait for the inevitable searing pain and a horrible death. As an icy shiver crept down his spine, he caught his breath. Pulling the car off the road and stopping on its grassy shoulder, he forced himself to inhale deeply and exhale slowly, several times.

Cars sped past him. In the distance, beautiful Santa Monica beckoned. He saw pavilions on the beach and teenagers roller-skating, the more adventurous of them taking a dip in the bracing ocean water. Overhead, a yellow sun shone brightly from a cloudless turquoise sky. Another typical day in the good life of southern California.

But he wasn't feeling well. Not well at all.

Something that had happened a long time ago reappeared before his mind's eye.

He is running, zigzagging between trees, branches scraping his skin, tree bark grazing painfully against his elbows. The torches! They are chasing him like terrible beasts with burning eyes. Everywhere was the stench of scorched earth. He leaps over a felled giant of a tree and barely manages to duck beneath a thick branch.

He is gasping for air. He cannot go on. Desperate now, he jumps over a thorny bush and lands on the hard forest floor. He crouches down on his knees, making himself as small as possible. The glow of the fiery sticks approaches. Then they are floating beside him. The smoke scratches inside his throat. The heat is torture. The stinging smell of the fire dazes him.

Suddenly he hears voices. Behind the torches. Shrill, yelling excitedly.

'There he is! There! Jason . . .'

He draws up his shoulders, wraps his hands around his head and tries to become even smaller, hoping they won't see him. But it's too late. The torches draw together in a circle around him. In their glow, he can now distinguish boys' faces, those of Victor Pringle and Terry Boxall. And behind them Gavin, David and Peter. Victor is grinning wickedly.

Get the fire away from me, *he wants to scream, but his throat is incapable of uttering anything beyond a whispery, wordless squeal. He hardly notices the tears coursing down his cheeks.*

Gavin and Peter yank him up, drag him along. He is their pris-

oner now. They're taking him to their camp; the hunters have caught their prey.

The rest of that evening Victor and his friends torment him. Victor tells everyone who will listen that Jason Evans cried like a baby when he was found. Finally, Jason is the first to crawl into the tent.

Summer camp can be a nightmare, but the core of the bad dream is still to come. After he falls asleep, he goes to another dark place, where there is another fire.

It whips out its fiery claws at him. He starts awake and can't go back to sleep, doesn't want to. Across from him in the tent, Victor and the others are fast asleep. They don't know of his fears, nor do the camp counselors.

Nor does his father, when he returns home to Cornell a few days later. Jason looks Edward in the eye and sees resignation there. Even a holiday camp with his classmates is too much for Jason. Simple things like playing hide-and-seek in the dark send him into a panic.

But it's not about the dark. It's the flaming torches.

If they hadn't been brandishing the torches, everything would have been fine.

His mother urges Edward to cut their son some slack. She's protecting him, like she always does; in his mother's eyes he can do no wrong.

It helps. The nightmare leaves him in peace after he returns from camp. Not that he has shaken the bad dream; little Jason knows that would be too much to hope for. But at least he can sleep in peace – for a while.

TWELVE
List

That Monday morning, July twentieth, Jason invested several hours tweaking and improving the promotional campaign for Tommy Jones. But his heart wasn't in his work. He wasn't fond of the Automobile King to begin with, but today he hated him even more than he had thirteen years ago as he watched his red Plymouth Road Runner being towed to the scrap heap.

He asked Brian for his feedback on the proposal. His boss recognized its strong points, but also its weak points.

At eleven o'clock Jason convened a team meeting with Barbara, Carol, Donald and Tony to discuss Brian's criticisms. Carol kept everyone focused and Barbara made some sensible suggestions for small changes here and there. But no one had substantive changes to recommend.

At noon, Brian asked Jason to join him for lunch with Derek Eccles, a public relations representative for electronics giant Kaufman. Brian referred to such outings as 'PR lunches'. Brian liked to pamper his best customers with lunch or dinner from time to time, convinced it was the most effective way to keep them as customers. After lunch Jason made a few phone calls and wrote several emails to keep a few current projects on track. The biggest problem that day was rejected text for a brochure touting Sunset Pleasure Paradise, a small chain of outlets that made beach pavilions. First he had to take an angry phone call from the client, and then take up the matter with Tony, the copywriter in charge of the project. Jason knew plenty of copywriters who would hit the roof if their creations were dismissed in such a perfunctory manner. But not Tony. He simply shrugged. 'Some you win, some you lose, and some are rained out,' he grunted matter-of-factly, and went back to the drawing board.

Jason then called Kayla. He needed to know how she was doing. And he just wanted to hear her voice. They exchanged some small talk, without addressing the issue that was aggravating emotional wounds.

It was nearly three fifty when he put the phone down. Every business item that required attention today had been seen to, so he had time on his hands to ponder the accident, the photographs, and who might have sent them. There was no doubt in his mind that this person knew him. In that case there were quite a few possibilities. But who on this earth would want to kill him? Or simply scare him witless with morbid messages?

Something else ate at him. If he had died on August eighteenth, why had he received those Polaroid photographs *now*?

Why not two years ago? Or five years ago, for that matter?

Maybe because at that time I wasn't dead yet.

It was a bizarre feeling to think about his own demise in the past tense, as if it had already happened. He was *alive*.

But that meant he had to assume that someone was planning to kill him on August eighteenth. Or did it?

He needed answers, but how to get them? Jason decided to go outside and take a walk, to clear his mind before again considering the facts. As he left Roosevelt Tower and started walking along Wilshire Boulevard, he reviewed the facts of the case for the umpteenth time.

The photographs said what they said. If he interpreted them literally, then he could interpret them only as obituaries. The sender was addressing him, writing about him, as if he were dead, a corpse. The person in question was therefore someone who hated him enough to want him dead.

Who hated him that much? Jason stopped and put his hands behind his head, knotting his fingers together. Time to draw up a list, he thought. If he did that, what would it look like? Who were his enemies? He thought hard, but no names or faces came to mind. *Come on Jason*, he berated himself, *you can't really believe you have only friends out there. That's an illusion, surely. Everyone has enemies.*

Then who? Which names?

Suddenly he received an inspiration, as if somewhere inside his mind the lid had been pried off a cesspool. Well, well, so even *he* had made a few foes along the way. And he couldn't blame them all on his fear of fire, which had cost him a few friends and his break-up with Sherilyn Chambers. But he had made many mistakes before; bad mistakes; he was no angel. Once he opened his mind to such reminiscences, his bad decisions and moments of weakness came bobbing to the surface.

The first people he thought of who might still have a bone to pick with him were Tracy and Carla.

His heart suddenly felt leaden. He had opened the door to a Pandora's box that contained some of his worst memories. It was almost like voluntarily sticking his hand into a wasps' nest.

He had not talked to Tracy in years. The last thing she had screamed at him was that men were not to be trusted, and he was the cad who had taught her that. What if he called her? What would he say to her?

Trace! Hi, I was curious about you. Are you still on a-bottle-per-day plan? Or doesn't that cut it for you any more? And by the way, did you happen to stop by a mailbox, driving to and from the liquor store the other day? With a manila envelope, maybe?

No, that would be a bad idea.

In his mind, he replayed the manifold scenes of his eighteen months with Tracy. She had been his most serious girlfriend at Cal State Northridge. Fair-haired, slim, attractive, lively, intelligent. The world had been her oyster. She gave all indications of a great career in her future. But booze had interfered and messed up everything. What made good people walk into these kinds of traps with their eyes open wide? He hadn't noticed at first that she was an alcoholic – yes, she drank a lot at parties, but so did everyone else. When her cheap Limestone Creek bourbon and her rot-gut brand of Russian vodka started appearing on the counter within easy reach, she had become hammered almost every night. In her rare moments of sobriety, he had tried talking to her, to no avail. In the end he had suggested Alcoholics Anonymous, and that had been like waving a red flag at a bull. Shortly after that, with nothing left to prop up their relationship, it had caved in.

Goodbye, Tracy Dufresne.

The next person on his list was Carla Rosenblatt. He had met her while working for his first employer, DRW Advertising. Jason had been a traffic manager there for fourteen months when Brian Anderson invited him to dinner one night. DRW and Tanner & Preston had cooperated on a number of projects, and Jason had succeeded in impressing Brian. Over an exquisitely tender rib-eye steak Jason was offered a job at Tanner & Preston, for quite a bit more money than he was making at DRW. Even though he had been happy in his current job, the generous hike in pay had convinced him.

Carla was an assistant art director for DRW and was even more ambitious than Jason. Before he transferred to Tanner & Preston they had had several arguments about starting a family. She usually brought up the subject, to emphasize the point that she wanted to have her cake and eat it, too. She wanted children *and* a career. She implied that she had no intention of cutting back on her hours, and that her work was more important to her than being a mother. He suggested they postpone the decision for a few years, but that didn't satisfy her. *I don't want to wake up one day and realize I'm thirty-five years old, only to find you no longer want this.*

And then he had switched to Tanner & Preston. His boss at DRW, Walter Murphy, had sworn that Jason's decision to change jobs would not reflect badly on Carla. But soon after Jason left she was bypassed for a promotion to art director, a position she had coveted for years. At the same time, DRW cut back her involvement in important projects. Somewhere down the line she was informed in no uncertain terms that if she wanted to advance her career, she had best apply for a position in some other firm.

Carla blamed Jason, of course. He was flying high at Tanner & Preston, while she was in danger of crashing and burning. Couldn't he pull some strings for her with *his* boss?

He couldn't, nor did he want to. He had had his fill of her moaning and nagging. He couldn't deny, however, that he had improved his position at her expense, and that realization had bothered him.

A nasty break-up ensued. With Tracy it had been a relatively brief process and he had moved on. With Carla it was months before they finally went their separate ways.

She had done well for herself in the end. Steve, a former co-worker at DRW with whom Jason had remained in touch, had told him she'd had a healthy baby girl the previous spring. Jason had not received a card, of course. The baby's father, Steve had further told him, was an obedient stay-at-home-husband. And Carla had secured a new and demanding job.

Jason sighed and wondered who might be next on his list of personal enemies. He remembered Jordan Avins, the man who had taught him the ropes when he first started working for Tanner & Preston, but who had been fired six months later for stealing company property. Not money or anything major; a pen here, a paperknife and printer supplies there. One night, perhaps to mollify his conscience, Jordan had confided in Jason that he was a kleptomaniac. So his stealing had been a compulsion more than petty theft. Avins, five foot two and insecure, had begged Jason not to tell Brian. He didn't have any friends, he said. There was no one else he could talk to. Jason had kept Jordan's thievery to himself for several weeks. To make the man feel more at ease, Jason had told him about his own irrational fear of fire.

But when items kept disappearing, Jason felt compelled to inform their boss. Brian gave Jordan a verbal thrashing and – at Jason's request – gave him one final chance to mend his ways. But it made no difference. Within forty-eight hours an expensive calculator had disappeared, and when Brian confronted Avins with the theft, Avins insisted that Jason be present when he was officially fired. During his exit interview, the poor man had pleaded with Jason with his eyes. *Jason, my friend, I can't help myself. Please, I beg you, make Anderson understand.* But there was nothing Jason could do; Jordan Avins had had his chance and he had blown it. When Jason watched him walk out the front door for the last time, he knew he had gained another embittered enemy.

Jason shook his head, turned around, and found himself staring into the dark eyes of a skinny young man who had crept to within six feet from him.

Just then, another doorway into the past opened. Doug Shatz! Doug had been just as slender as this skinny boy, and he had the same sour look on his face.

Open your mouth! Let's see your grin, your teeth!

If Jason could see the chipped tooth, he would be convinced that once again Doug stood in front of him, fifteen years after they had last met.

A dark cloud seemed to pass over the sun and envelop the young man in shadows.

He did grin, but he didn't open his mouth. Then he turned away and ran off without uttering a word.

As Jason watched him go, he felt a painful cramp in his stomach. The boy had looked so much like Doug. Could it be that—?

He didn't finish the conjecture. Of course it hadn't been Doug. This boy was about sixteen, and Doug by now was long past that age. More likely, the boy had intended to pickpocket him or mug him, and Jason had turned around in the nick of time.

Cars drove past on Wilshire Boulevard, always a busy thorough-fare. Jason felt sunshine prickling at the back of his neck as the skinny boy disappeared around the corner of a building. His thoughts, however, remained firmly focused on Doug.

Dick Shevelow had taken Doug in tow for a while.

A calm and gentle guy, Dick had decided while attending Cal State Northridge that he wanted to work in the healthcare industry. Doug Shatz became Dick's first 'patient', along with Dick's pal

Mark Hall. Doug was a highly gifted young man, but he was also pathologically disturbed, socially awkward, unpredictable and outright violent at times. He had trouble keeping his temper, and if there was a fight somewhere, Doug was often in the middle of it.

Mark Hall and Dick tried to help him get his act together, and even Jason had offered his help. He had come to deeply regret that decision, in part because in trying to help Doug, Jason had confided in the skinny young man about the things that troubled him, including his pyrophobia.

Some weeks later, a small fire broke out in a girls' dressing room. It was no big deal, just a lot of scared girls and some damage, and no one got hurt. But afterward, there was talk about the fire being intentional and that Jason, so obsessed with fire, was an arsonist. He was called in by the school principal, who demanded to know if Jason had started the fire. Indignant and shocked, Jason had denied the charge vehemently. The principal had let him off the hook, but suspicions remained. The real arsonist had never been caught, but every time he looked in Doug Shatz's sour, dark brown eyes, and saw the chipped tooth whenever he grinned, Jason suspected who had falsely accused him.

A year later, more trouble erupted at the college when a coed was raped. Maria – who had a long, impossible to remember Spanish last name – claimed she didn't know who the perpetrator was. Jason, however, had a strong hunch who had done it. He won Maria's trust, and after meeting with her a few times, she admitted that Shatz had been the one who had raped her. But Maria was terrified of him. He had threatened to kill her if she ever told anyone. Jason managed to talk her into reporting Shatz, and Shatz was arrested. He confessed, and that was the last time they had seen him at Cal State.

Jason was responsible for landing Doug Shatz in prison. Since then, Doug had seen the inside of other detention facilities, a fact confirmed for Jason by Lou Briggs. Doug was one of the few people Jason knew who he believed was capable of murder.

Could Shatz have something to do with the photographs?

Tracy. Carla. Jordan. Doug. So yes, there were more people than he initially thought who had cause to do him harm. These same four individuals knew about his anxieties. Nonetheless, he could not imagine any of the four sending him the photographs.

Back to square one, Jason mused. He still had not the first clue in solving the mystery.

Dejectedly, he walked back to Roosevelt Tower. During the elevator ride up to his floor, in the blink of an eye, his thoughts linked Doug Shatz's madness to another instance of insanity, even further back in his past.

Noam Morain.

THIRTEEN

Noam

Noam was the older brother of Robin, Jason's teammate in Little League. By everyone's estimation, Robin Morain was the best player on the team and Jason was second best. Batting third and fourth, they had been the driving force behind the Red Sox.

Robin had suddenly quit the team. At first, his coach and teammates were flabbergasted. Then word got out that Robin's brother Noam had become seriously ill and had been rushed to the hospital in a coma. Although he had recovered in a physical sense, his brain had suffered badly from the illness. Initially Jason hadn't believed it, until he accompanied Robin to the mental ward to which his brother had been admitted. Noam told them he was being followed around by a ghost that walked through walls. A phantom dressed in black chased him wherever he tried to flee. Noam called him the black horseman, and he had an elaborate theory about it. He was, in fact, convinced that the man in black was one of the four Horsemen of the Apocalypse, from the Book of Revelations in the Bible. Noam claimed that he therefore must be one of the four plagues: War, Famine, Pestilence, or Death. Jason had never understood which of the four powers Noam believed his tormentor to be, but did it matter? Noam saw him, heard him, and was receiving orders from him to mutilate himself. He had cut his wrists, hung himself and stuck his fingers into an electrical socket. The horseman also whispered to Noam who his enemies and who his friends were.

That probably explained why he could be so aggressive toward some people. Noam meekly did whatever the specter ordered him to do. His psychiatrists shrugged it off. They claimed that such behavior was the natural consequence of schizophrenia. If anything, it was a miracle that he had managed to survive these repeated incidents of self-mutilation. Noam Morain had slowly deteriorated. Jason had last seen him many years ago. His friend's brother was still institutionalized then, heavily medicated to keep his psychoses in check.

On one occasion, during a visit from Jason and Robin, Noam had suddenly jumped up from the chair he was sitting on and stared intently at Jason. His eyes shone with insane brilliance as he pointed a trembling finger at Jason and screamed, 'Where are you? You're not here!'

He had never reflected much on what Noam had meant by that outburst, but now, twenty years later, he did.

You're not here.

At the time, he had dismissed the words as the ravings of a disturbed young man.

Only now did he realize that Noam, in his own way, was perhaps trying to tell him something important.

You're not here.

You don't exist.

Two short sentences, with practically the same meaning. Jason suddenly remembered the outburst as if it had happened only yesterday. In his memory, Noam had stared right through him, straight into his soul.

Jason left the elevator and surveyed the open-air office complex. Everyone was engrossed in his work, except for Tony, who was leaning back with his hands clasped behind his head, staring into space.

He walked into his office and sat down. Had Robin's brother seen something within Jason that normal people couldn't see? There was only one way to find out. He had to try and contact Noam again. Where would he find his address? He wondered whether Morain was still alive. He sat down and opened his email software. From an early age, he had been meticulous in updating his address books, both in paper and digital formats, at home and at work. Within seconds, he found phone numbers for Robin Morain and his parents, but not for Noam. He couldn't remember what had prompted him to remove it. Maybe the event he had just remembered had been such a shock for him that he had decided to delete the number and never to visit his old friend's brother again.

After college, he and Robin had lost track of each other, as people often do after college. Sad, because they had always gotten along so well. But such is life.

He tried Robin's number, to find it was no longer in service. Then he tried the number for Robin's parents. To his relief, Jeannine answered. Jeannine was pleasantly surprised that Jason called. No, she hadn't forgotten him, what *was* he thinking? Her husband Douglas had passed away some years ago, she told him. Robin was doing fine, however. Two years ago he had married a girl named Maggie, a redhead who worked in childcare. They were living in San Diego now, and Robin worked for SunTrust Banks.

When Jason asked her how Noam was doing, Jeannine replied that he was doing just fine. In the late nineties he had been trans-ferred to a facility in Anaheim, where he lived with other former patients. He could take care of himself – with some help, admit-tedly, but all in all he was getting by better than many people expected.

Jeannine wanted to know everything about him. He told her a bit about his life and said that it was great in all areas. If she had asked him that same question a few days earlier, his answer would have been an honest one.

Jeannine sounded as if she hadn't changed a bit. Unless he begged off, he would wind up on the phone with her for an hour. But after fifteen minutes, she surprised him by asking him if he wanted Robin's phone number.

I'd rather have Noam's, he thought, but then he would have to tell her why he wanted to talk to her eldest son. Besides, there was no harm in calling his old friend first. She gave him Robin's busi-ness number and extension, as well as his home number. He thanked Jeannine, hung up, and punched in the number for Robin's office.

The door opened a crack and Carol and Tony peeked around the corner. When they saw him on the phone, they waved goodbye. He stole a glance at his watch. Quarter to six already. He hoped Robin was still at work.

'Morain,' a deep voice answered – a change from the throaty, piping voice of the prepubescent boy he had once known, but a voice Jason nonetheless recognized.

'Robin! It's Jason Evans.'

There was silence. Jason waited.

'It's been a long time, Robin. Remember me?'

The silence stretched before Robin responded somewhat pensively.

'Jason? Is it really you?'

'None other. A couple of years older, but still the same. Surprised?'

'You might say that. How are you?'

'No complaints. I just spoke to your mother – she gave me your number.'

'Ah, and to what do I owe the honor?'

'I'll get to that in a minute. Man, it's great to hear your voice again. I still remember the days on the Red Sox.'

'We were the best,' Robin chuckled. 'It's amazing to talk to you again after all these years. Do you play sports these days?'

'No, not really, I can't seem to find the time.'

'Tell me about it,' Robin said. 'I keep meaning to start up again, perhaps playing in a softball league, but I keep postponing it. I should, though. I'm developing kind of a spare tire.'

'A spare tire? You?' Jason smiled at the thought. 'You were the skinniest of the bunch.'

'Not any more I'm not. How about you?'

'Can't say I'm that svelte myself any more. That's what age does to you.'

They dove into their shared memories. It was almost as if they had last spoken to each other a week ago. Each filled in the other about his life. Half an hour passed before Robin asked what had prompted Jason to call again after all these years.

'I'd like to talk to Noam, Robin. Could you give me his address?'

'Noam?' Robin repeated. Jason could hear the bewilderment in his voice.

'Jeannine tells me he's living by himself now,' Jason said.

'With some assistance, yes,' Robin said. 'He can't manage on his own. Why do you want to talk to him? What do you want from him?'

'Look, I . . .' Jason paused. 'To be honest, I need Noam's help.'

'Help? From Noam? What for?'

'It's hard to explain,' Jason said. 'Kind of a complicated story.

It's because . . . He used to say some pretty funny things, didn't he?'

'Noam says funny things all the time,' Robin responded. He hesitated. 'Although they're not always so very crazy.'

Jason frowned. 'What do you mean by that?'

Robin coughed. 'Well, the staff in the home where he lives tells me that he says things sometimes that turn out to be true. That he has an uncanny sense of what people are about. I have that same sense myself. He got one of the psychiatrists fired because the bastard couldn't stop touching his patients. His *young* patients, if you know what I mean. Girls as well as boys, it didn't matter. No one knew about it, except for Noam. No one had told him – the patients were too frightened to say anything to anybody – but he knew anyway. Weird.'

'It sure is,' Jason concurred.

'Carina, one of the nurses who works with him, was very sad just recently because she had lost a relative. Noam told her that her loved one was still with her. He said that the deceased relative was right there in the room talking to Carina, and then he told her what this person was saying to her. Personal things that Noam could not possibly have known anything about. He scared the shit out of Carina, but she did admit that everything he had said was true.'

Jason fell silent for a moment. 'So is he psychic or something?'

'You'd think so after hearing these things. He's told me several times that I would "leave with red". Maggie does have rather red hair, and I did leave my old home and move to San Diego with her, so . . . Believe what you want, but I think you're spot-on.'

Jason cleared his throat. 'When we were kids, Noam said something that shook me pretty hard. I remembered it just now, and I need to know more about it. Robin, I know this sounds strange, but it's important to me. Especially after what you've just told me.'

'So what's this about?'

'Not like this – on the phone, I mean. It's too personal and too complicated. I'd love to get together with you one of these days, like we used to. We really should. And the sooner the better.'

'And that's all you're going to tell me?'

'We'll grab a beer soon, and then I'll tell you all about it,' Jason promised.

Robin gave a loud sigh, signaling his frustration.

'There's one thing I will share now,' Jason said, in an effort to convince Robin of the urgency of his request. 'I'm being harassed. Not by Noam, don't worry; but I think he may be able to help me.'

'This is very mysterious, Jason. You're making me curious, and not a little concerned.'

A brief silence ensued.

'OK. I trust you,' Robin said at length. 'What would you like to do? You want to call Noam?'

'I'd rather go see him, actually. He's living in Anaheim now, right? That's an hour's drive for me, tops.'

'OK, but be careful how you approach him, Jason,' Robin cautioned. 'If he feels threatened or even uncomfortable, he'll clam up. That often precedes the beginning of another bad spell, when his episodes return.' Another pause, then: 'Tell you what. Let me give him a call first.'

'Thanks, buddy.'

Robin called back ten minutes later. He had talked to Noam, who had said he remembered Jason well. A visit would be fine with him. Robin gave him Noam's address and directions on how to get there. The phone call with Robin ended in a promise to get together soon.

Jason stood and stretched. It felt good, finally being proactive instead of just waiting passively for the next shoe to drop. He called Kayla and told her he'd be home late because of a meeting. He said he had to run, and hung up before giving her an opportunity to ask what kind of meeting it was. Was it a lie? Yes and no, depending on one's perspective. He thought about what she had said. *Don't ever keep secrets from me again.* He was breaking his promise already.

An hour later he met face to face with Noam Morain. In Jason's memory, Noam had been Superman: muscular, very strong, a granite disposition. But at the time Jason had been about half his size. The man sitting at a rickety table – the only piece of furniture in the spartan room save for two chairs and a plain bed – appeared shriveled, a shadow of his former self. Where once he had possessed a mop of black hair, his scalp now looked withered and barren.

Strands of poorly cut and lanky gray hair fell across his ears. His skin appeared sallow, unhealthy, wrinkled. Everything about him was bloated, obese and shapeless. He had put on a good fifty pounds.

Had the black horseman inside his head transformed him that much?

'Noam Morain?' Jason asked, as if meeting a stranger for the first time.

The man smiled. When the corners of his mouth turned up and curled slightly, Jason caught a brief glimpse of the old Noam. That was how he had always smiled. Maybe his body resembled an ill-fitting, oversized coat, but this was definitely him.

'Yes,' he confirmed.

Jason pulled up the other chair and sat down.

'Hi, Noam. I'm Jason Evans. Do you remember me?'

Noam nodded.

'How have you been?'

The man shrugged. 'Fine, I guess.'

'That's good to hear, Noam.' Jason's gaze shifted around the room as he collected his thoughts. When his eyes again locked on Noam's he said, 'Robin told me you were doing well.'

'Yes,' Noam said. 'I am well, very well, thank you.'

Jason tried to conjure up the image of how this man, in the throes of some terrible madness so long ago, had screamed out that he wasn't there.

And his eyes – he stared right through me. That was the worst part of it.

Noam's eyes looked lifeless now. He was pitiful, nothing more. Jason decided not to beat around the bush. The staff had restricted him to half an hour with Noam.

'Noam, do you remember that I used to visit you before? When I was little?'

He smiled and held his hand up to his chest to indicate that he had been quite a bit shorter in those days. Jason wasn't expecting much, because he suspected that Noam's memories would be spotty at best. Maybe coming here had been a bad idea, but now that he was here, he was determined to make the best of it.

'When you were little,' Noam said.

'When I was little,' Jason agreed.

'When you were little . . .'

Jason waited. He thought he could see a tiny flame flare up in Noam's eyes.

Noam chuckled. 'I remember. I'm good with faces. Your face is different now, but I remember you.'

'That's good, Noam. I used to visit you sometimes, didn't I? With Robin and your mom.'

'Yes, you visited.'

'And I liked to visit you, liked talking to you . . .'

Noam nodded.

'But you know,' Jason continued, 'there's something I've been wondering about.'

Jason felt like he was talking to a child – which, perhaps, he was. He took a deep breath. 'One day when I visited you, you said something.'

He tried to catch Noam's eye, but the man was staring at the table.

'You said . . . I wasn't there,' Jason said. 'You asked me where I was. I was with you that day. We were face to face like we are now, but still you said I wasn't there. As if I was somehow invisible. Do you remember?'

He expected Noam to say no. And then what? He wouldn't have a clue what to do next.

To Jason's surprise, Noam replied, 'Yes, you were playing hide-and-seek. You always do. Why is that?'

Jason blinked. 'I was playing hide-and-seek?' He leaned forward, closer to the withered man. 'What do you mean, I was playing hide-and-seek, Noam?'

'I enjoyed it very much. And I'm doing fine now.'

'Noam!' Jason urged. 'Can you hear me?'

'I like it here. I have a pet, did you know that? I have a cat. Her name's Joshi. She should be around here somewhere.'

'Noam . . .'

'She's black, with white spots. Would you like to see her? Let me call her, and—'

'What did you *mean* when you said I was playing hide-and-seek?'

'She's a very pretty cat, and so sweet,' Noam continued happily, oblivious to the questioning.

'Listen to me, dammit!' Jason cried out.

The effect was immediate. Noam's eyes clouded over. The spark inside them flickered out and a shadow crossed over his face. It was exactly what Robin had warned him about.

'Noam, I'm sorry I yelled at you. Please tell me, what did you mean?'

Noam turned away and gazed at the wall.

'Noam, please, I'm sorry.'

No response. Jason stood and put a hand on Noam's shoulder. 'I'm really sorry I upset you, buddy.'

Noam cringed and remained mute.

'You're not going to talk to me any more, are you?'

The man just sat there and stared, at nothing.

'Me and my big mouth,' Jason mumbled. 'I got what I deserved.'

Noam kept staring at the wall, unruffled.

'OK,' Jason sighed. 'If you don't want to talk any more, I guess I'll be going. My apologies again, Noam.'

He walked to the door, opened it, and turned to look back at the broken man sitting in the chair. 'I'll be back, Noam, and this time I won't wait fifteen years.'

Jason walked out of the room, and was about to close the door behind him when he heard a noise. It sounded like fingernails violently scraping along a blackboard. He froze. He heard the sound again, and it sent shivers down his spine.

He had a chilling thought: *the black horseman, a ghost walking through walls.*

But Noam was behind him, sitting quietly in his chair. He was not the one making the scratching noise.

He had another thought, an even darker one.

The plague is death. My *death.*

Slowly, very slowly, he turned around.

He was staring straight into Noam's face, which had turned toward him.

Suddenly Noam appeared normal, not at all confused. The difference was in his eyes; they were clear now, strong. In those few moments Jason could see the Noam he knew from before the man's battles with schizophrenia.

Calmly and lucidly Noam said to him, 'What was it that came in the fire?'

Jason was stunned. 'The fire?'

Noam nodded and turned his head to stare mutely at the wall again.

'What fire, Noam? I don't understand . . .'

But Noam appeared lost in the quagmire of his private thoughts.

'Noam?'

He sat there like a statue, seeming enthralled with the wall.

Jason took another stab at getting through to him, to no avail. Noam did not move or say anything. The scratching noise had ceased. In the deathly quiet Jason left the room and closed the door gently behind him.

He walked outside to his borrowed Aveo and sat behind the wheel. His head was spinning from the effects of that bizarre conversation.

You're not here. You're playing hide-and-seek. What was it that came in the fire?

He didn't have a clue what it all meant – or if it meant anything at all. Perhaps it was just the ranting of a madman.

'What was he talking about?' Jason heard himself ask, nonetheless.

A thought entered his mind.

Ask Mark Hall.

Now *that* was a thought. As a psychotherapist, Mark was the perfect candidate to delve into Jason's mind and find . . .

Whatever was in there not firing on all cylinders.

Over the years Mark had repeatedly offered to help Jason with therapy, to tackle this pyrophobia problem together. But Jason had always declined, kindly but firmly.

Could the time be right, now? Maybe lying down on his couch would finally offer some new insights into his recurring nightmare and the flames that kept threatening to engulf him in his dreams.

Jason drove off, but a few miles down the road he stopped. He grabbed his cell phone and consulted the contact list until he found Mark Hall's number. Without allowing further thought to intrude on his resolve, he pushed the buttons. Mark's wife Laura answered. She and Kayla had become good friends, and the two women often went out together. Jason was in no mood for a lengthy chat with her, so he just asked her whether Mark was home. Luckily he was.

He heard her calling for him, and several moments later he heard the familiar voice.

'Jason!'

'Mark, I'm glad you're home.'

'Happy to hear that. What's troubling you?'

That was typical of Mark. Always cutting right to the chase.

'I need your help.'

'As a friend or a therapist?'

'Both.'

Moments of silence ensued.

'You know about my nightmares,' Jason continued.

'Yes,' Mark acknowledged.

Of course Mark knew. With his professional background, he was an expert in diagnosing and analyzing Jason's nightmares. He knew even more about them than Kayla, and was eager to help Jason overcome his terror. Jason had always refused his offers of therapy. For a long time he remained in denial, and in truth, he was not keen on the idea of being one of his friend's patients.

Jason recounted his story about the Polaroid photographs and their messages. He told Mark about the detective work he had done so far to unearth the identity of the photographer – including his recent meeting with Noam Morain.

'Ever since the accident, I'm having the nightmare again,' he said, adding, 'after many years of sleeping like a baby.'

Mark hadn't interrupted him while he spoke. When he had finished relating the facts as he understood them, silence clung on the other end of the line.

'Jesus,' Mark said finally.

'You can say that again. I just wish Noam could help me. Listen, Mark, what I want to know . . . what this is about . . . is his question to me.'

'Go on,' his friend said.

'I have no idea what he means by "what came in the fire". Maybe it has something to do with my nightmare. The way I experience it, I'm surrounded by fire, and I'm alone. I don't know if this is a lead, but it couldn't hurt to analyze the dream a bit more.'

'OK, I understand what you're saying,' Mark affirmed. 'But are you sure you want to do this with me? We've discussed this subject before, and you've always kept your distance.'

'I'm sure, Mark. The last thing I want is to see some therapist I've never met. I want *your* help, and no one else's,' Jason stated with a resolve he did not feel.

'Don't worry, I'll do my best for you,' Mark said. 'Let's compare schedules. When would suit you?'

'You're the one who's probably booked solid. When could you find some time?'

'I'll make time for you. My last patient of the day usually leaves at five, which gives me an hour or two for paperwork before I go home. So I'm available to see you any day after five. Just tell me when you'd like to stop by.'

Jason suddenly realized how tired he was. The long day, this emotional roller coaster, was starting to take a toll. He rubbed his eyes.

'How about tomorrow?'

'It's a deal. I'll see you tomorrow at five.'

He was home by ten thirty, convinced that this day had lasted three days. Jason filled Kayla in while he tackled his reheated dinner at the kitchen table. She frowned when he told her that he had gone to see Noam, but said nothing about it. She *was* pleased to hear that he had talked to Mark.

'Mark is an expert, he is down-to-earth, and he knows everything about your anxieties,' she said. 'You two have talked about them often enough. I'm glad you're going to see him.'

She bowed her head. When she raised her eyes back to his, he saw the glint of unshed tears in them. 'You gave me such a scare last night.'

'I'm sorry,' he said.

'I'm really afraid,' she said. 'The only thing I'm holding on to is that the last photograph arrived three days ago, and there's been nothing since. I pray that's a good sign.'

'I'm scared, too,' he confessed. 'And of course I realize all this stirs up some terrible memories for you.'

She nodded. 'Yes, it does.'

He hesitated, but then decided to finish what he had started.

'Kayla . . . I would like to talk about that.'

'I don't,' she countered at once as she got up from her chair.

'What happened inside that tent?' Jason asked her.

'Don't,' she pleaded. 'Please don't go there.'

'He said he knew he was going to die, right? What—'

'No!' she cried out. 'I want nothing more to do with that occult stuff. Not now, not ever!

Occult? That was a word he had seldom heard her utter before.

'Kayla, we're married,' he tried. 'For better or for worse, remember? Why is this subject taboo?'

'*You're* doing the same thing.'

Jason did not respond. She had a point.

'There's nothing to talk about,' she said, ending the discussion.

He sensed this was one of those rare times when she wasn't being totally honest with him.

'My mother also died many years before her time,' he plowed on. 'She was older than Ralph, but forty-seven is still too young. I can talk about *that*.'

'Please, just leave it alone,' she said testily. 'Do you hear me?'

He nodded slowly. There was more to Ralph's death than met the eye. He was aware of the official medical explanation, but he also knew that it wasn't the whole story. Whatever had happened that day, it had rendered Kayla incapable of addressing death and the grieving process. Jason wished he knew what secrets she was keeping from him. But tonight was not the night to unravel those secrets.

Jason let go of his thoughts about Ralph. It was enough, for tonight, that Kayla agreed with his decision to solicit Mark's help and that she would be joining him for the first session.

FOURTEEN

In the Fire

Jason arrived outside Mark's office at five o'clock sharp. Kayla got stuck in traffic, so it was another fifteen minutes before they went inside together. Mark greeted them warmly. While he offered them a seat and poured out three cups of coffee, Jason looked around the office, noting several more awards hanging on the wall since the last time he was here. Certificates and diplomas adorned the olive green wall behind the mahogany desk. Business was good for Mark; he ran his practice with dedication; and he seemed fulfilled professionally. He complained about his receding hairline from time to time, feigning jealousy of Jason's full head of hair that was untouched by gray or white. But that was about all he ever groused about.

Mark put the coffee down and sat down across from them.

'All right then, let's talk,' he said.

The silence stretched to many moments as each side waited for the other to serve the ball. Then Jason leaned forward and said, 'Mark, I told you everything on the phone. And as I indicated to you then, I think it would be best if you're the therapist in this session, not my friend.'

'Don't worry. I'll be the therapist,' Mark said, tapping his right knee with two fingers. 'But I was hoping I could be both.'

Jason nodded. 'OK.'

'Let me see those photographs,' Mark said. 'You did bring them, didn't you?'

Jason took the three photos from his briefcase and handed them to Mark, who studied them attentively.

'You've tried to find this cemetery, have you?'

'I have. And I have also tried to separate the layers in the doctored picture. But so far I have come up empty on both counts.'

'You could go to the police,' Mark suggested, echoing Kayla's and Lou's advice.

'There's still time to do that, and most likely I will at some point,' Jason said. 'But keep in mind that this photographer has done nothing illegal – yet. He has sent me photographs with messages written on them. Insane messages, to be sure, but hardly illegal messages. He doesn't threaten to kill me. According to him, I'm already dead, and I have been since August eighteenth. And since there is no evidence that he is responsible for our car accident, I really have nothing on him that would interest the police. Oh, by the way, the police inspector, Guillermo, called today. He's taken a good look at my Buick, which as I told you is in the shop for repairs. He found nothing suspicious. At this point he can only assume it was a hit-and-run accident. So it looks as though the police can't help me. I'd rather continue my own investigation.'

Mark nodded and rested his chin on his hands.

'What I'm here for . . .' Jason started.

'Is your recurring dream,' Mark finished for him. 'Because of Noam Morain's remark.'

'It all comes back to his pyrophobia,' Kayla added. 'By the way, Mark, is this a rare affliction?'

'Not really,' Mark assured her. 'There are many types of phobias, and fear of fire is one of them. It's not as common as a fear of spiders, for example, or mice, or heights, or enclosed spaces. But I wouldn't call it rare.'

'Where do these anxieties come from?' she asked.

'From as many places as you can imagine. For instance, what are *you* afraid of?'

'*Spiders.*' She almost spat out the word. 'Merely thinking of a tarantula gives me the shivers.'

'I see. And why are you scared of them?'

'I'm afraid one of those hideous creatures will bite me!'

'Precisely,' Mark said. 'The same goes for all people with exaggerated fears. They worry that what they fear will harm them.'

'What about claustrophobia?' Jason said. 'Why does someone panic in a small space? What's so dangerous about that?'

'They don't necessarily have to be *small* spaces,' Mark explained. 'A person may experience claustrophobia in a movie theater. Claustrophobia can often be traced back to an unpleasant experience in childhood. Agoraphobia is similar in a way; patients fear that they won't be able to escape from wherever they find themselves. And the list goes on and on. There's always a reason why someone suffers from anxiety attacks.'

'And pyrophobiacs?' Kayla pressed.

Mark stood and pursed his lips. He gazed pensively at Jason. 'It's no different. My suspicion is that you experienced something dreadful in your youth that involved a fire. Or smoke or extreme heat.'

'My nightmare . . .' Jason said.

'I'd wager these certificates you see on the wall that your nightmares are induced by some experience you've had,' Mark reiterated.

Jason shrugged. 'As far as I know, I've never *had* a traumatic experience with fire. You know that, Mark. And Kayla, so do you and so does my father. It's not like we haven't discussed this topic before, I've thought about it often enough, and believe me, nothing in my life, to my knowledge, could be causing my phobia.'

'Hang on, not so fast,' Mark said. 'First you'll need to convince me that your past is as unblemished as you seem to think it is.'

'Alright,' Jason sighed. 'If that must be done, so be it. How does this work?'

'There are several methods,' Mark said. 'But you know . . . I'm not entirely convinced that what you have *is* a phobia. At least, not in the normal meaning of the word. Phobic people have a hard time functioning in society. Jason, you mentioned claustrophobia earlier. I had a patient once who suffered from it so severely, he was afraid to step into an elevator. He couldn't drive a car, he never closed the door when he used the bathroom, and he got out of bed four times a night to make sure he could still open his bedroom door. At the same time, he had to go to work each day. And he couldn't tell his boss, because that could have ended his career.'

'How awful,' Kayla said quietly.

'This patient was constantly keeping up appearances that nothing was wrong. He had excuses for everything. He claimed he would rather use the stairs instead of the elevator because climbing the stairs was a healthier option. He used the same excuse for riding his bike to work rather than driving a car. But his anxieties kept getting worse, and he ended up here, in my office. Keeping up this charade for so many years had exhausted him.'

'And then what?' Kayla asked. 'How did his therapy go?'

'At my suggestion, we did hypnotherapy, which as you know is a keen interest of mine. I don't believe in medicating patients and I have my doubts about neurolinguistic programming. With hypnotherapy the patient is induced into a trance-like state – or relaxation, if you prefer. It helps the patient to see things that lie beneath the surface of his consciousness. During his sessions we discovered that the man's father had abused him and that his mother used to lock him up in a tiny closet. He gradually retrieved these memories that he had repressed for a long time. You can imagine how shocking an experience it was for him. When those memories returned from some recess deep inside his brain, he burst into tears. First he became very emotional, and then he became angry. But at least he now *understood* his anxieties. After that, he did better.'

Jason said nothing. Kayla gave him a sideways glance.

'As I said, I'm not sure that what you have is a phobia, Jason,' Mark mused. 'In general, people with phobias find their anxieties becoming increasingly disruptive. This is not the case with you, right? Ever since you've been with Kayla, you've hardly mentioned them.'

Jason nodded. 'I've taught myself a few . . . let's call them "game rules". Every night I check to see if the stove has been turned off, and if the appliances have been disconnected. I'm extra careful when the weatherman predicts thunderstorms. That kind of thing. But it's not always on my mind. You're right, it used to be much worse. I've been doing better the last couple of years, because of Kayla.'

He put his hand on his wife's knee.

'Everything was fine until I got those photographs,' he said softly. 'But you think I must have repressed or forgotten some incident?'

'Possibly. That's what we're here to find out,' Mark said. 'I'm going to help you reach a trance-like state and lead you into your dream. We'll start slowly and see what we discover along the way. Don't expect success right away. You may experience blockages, and it may take several sessions to break through them, assuming we can break through them at all. Neither of us can control a process like this, once it's under way.'

'OK,' Jason said. 'When do we start?'

'Whenever you want. We can do this some other time, or we can start right now.'

Jason looked askance at Kayla. 'I see no point in waiting.'

'You're sure?'

Jason nodded.

'OK, then I suggest you lie down on the couch,' Mark said.

'On the couch?' Jason said hesitantly.

'That doesn't mean you're a patient. Not like my other patients. But you'll find it easier to relax lying down – and relaxation is key in this sort of therapy.'

Jason shook his head. 'I never expected to see the day I'd be lying on a therapist's couch.'

'Things change,' Mark countered. 'Again, don't get your hopes up about this first session. It's just a start.'

'Understood,' Jason said.

'Are you comfortable?' Mark asked several minutes later.

Jason nodded. 'Getting there.'

Mark's gaze traveled across Jason's body. 'You could loosen your belt a notch, if you want to,' he said. 'It may help you relax.'

Jason admitted that yes, his jeans were a bit tight, and loosened his belt. When Mark asked him again whether he was comfortable, he felt he was.

'Close your eyes, Jason.'

He did, but in truth he wasn't fully relaxed yet. He could imagine Mark and Kayla both watching him as if he *were* a patient. In his mind he was one, no matter how much Mark had tried to reassure him to the contrary. At the moment Mark was not his bar buddy. He was his psychologist.

'Tell me what you hear, Jason.'

He heard a truck rumbling by in the street. A siren wailing in the distance somewhere. He became aware of the sounds of footsteps and unintelligible mumbling from people outside Mark's door. A chair, Mark's or Kayla's, creaked. She coughed. He knew all her little sounds. He considered saying this, but instead he answered, 'I hear all sorts of things.'

'I want you to concentrate on the sounds you hear coming from inside you,' Mark said.

'From inside me?' Jason asked, confused.

'Yes. The beating of your heart. The blood in your veins. Imagine it is the sound of the ocean, and your heartbeat is the sound of a beautiful old clock. You once told me that your father owns an antique wall clock that you love.'

He pictured the eighteenth-century clock in his parents' house. Small and elegant, its mechanism encased in an oaken cabinet with a mahogany veneer. When he was a boy, his mother had let him wind the clock while she smiled down at him. She remembered her always smiling at him. His mother . . . His dear mother . . .

In his mind's eye he saw her standing beside the clock as if she were still alive. A warm, sensitive human being made of flesh and blood, not yet claimed by death. He had always been the apple of her eye, and she had spoiled him in every way possible. If he wanted something, he simply needed to tell her what it was and it was his. God, he suddenly realized how much he missed her.

'Talk to me, Jason,' Mark said. 'Tell me what's going through your mind.'

'I'm at home, in my parents' house. I'm looking at the clock. My mother is there. She's smiling.'

'That's good, Jason, very good. Now look around. I want you to be in a good place. The place where you feel most comfortable. Near that clock, or someplace else; it doesn't matter. Where would you like to be?'

He looked around, and realized he *was* somewhere else. Green treetops swayed overhead; nearby he saw the centuries-old bole of a giant tree. He stood on the steep sandy trail toward Saddle Peak.

'I'm in the Santa Monica Mountains, where Kayla and I often go hiking.'

Saddle Peak was their favorite place in the mountains. Sometimes they climbed to its summit to enjoy the panoramic vistas and the blue of the Pacific. If they arrived early in the morning, they often found fog clinging to the rocks like a cool blanket.

Near this old tree they had made love one summer, hidden within the tall grass. But because Mark was present, he said nothing about this gold-framed image in the photo album of his memories.

'OK,' Mark continued, 'breathe in the air deeply, listen to the birds, look around, feel it, Jason.'

He *did* hear leaves stirring, birds chirping, a cascading waterfall nearby. There was no other place like this on earth. No place where he would rather be.

Then he heard Mark's voice.

'What are you doing now?'

'Lying on my back,' he said drowsily.

'Would you stand up for me?'

He complied, rising up from the tall stems of the grass.

'Now I would like you to go somewhere else. Someplace where there is fire. But before you do, listen closely: you can return here any time you want, to the Santa Monica Mountains. All you have to do is snap your fingers and you'll be back here, where you are completely safe. Do you understand?'

'Yes,' Jason said, or thought he did; he wasn't sure. Mark's voice reached into him like the voice of an invisible deity.

'I want you to start moving now, Jason. Start walking. Very carefully, very slowly. And remember, you can go back anytime you want. Just snap your fingers.'

Jason peered ahead. He saw no fire on the forest path.

'Where are you now?' Mark asked.

'In the same place. I don't know where to go.'

Again, he couldn't tell whether these words were part of his thought process or whether he was actually speaking them.

'Take your time, Jason. Take all the time you need. This is your place, you can always come back here. Just walk somewhere. Anywhere.'

'I'm not sure . . .'

Jason started walking. About fifty yards ahead, the path veered sharply to the right and disappeared from view. Straight ahead he saw a patch of tall thickets, with pale gray mountain peaks rising up behind them.

The thickets seemed to be beckoning him. The closer he got to them, the more clearly he saw that the plants formed a broken wall of green. There were openings without branches or leaves, big enough to walk through.

Black holes.

Without thinking, he walked straight into one of the holes. As he did, the sun disappeared. It was as dark as night. He was surprised, but he stumbled on.

In the darkness ahead, flames suddenly clawed up furiously, like distorted red-hot fists. Now he did stop, his heart pounding hard. The fire seemed to sense his presence, because the flames started crawling toward him like snakes hissing at him, licking at him, surrounding him. This was a nightmare. *The* nightmare. Jason screamed.

Several things happened at once. The first was a realization that he was not alone. Something or someone was hiding inside the fire. Something that was using the flames as camouflage. He knew instinctively that it was there, but he couldn't see it – not yet. The fire was hiding it.

The second was that the deity was calling his name.

'Jason!'

And another voice he knew very well: Kayla's.

'Come back, Jason!'

He listened to their voices. It was vitally important to listen to them and to leave this place, this blaze. He thought about going back. He *wanted* to go back and then—

And then Mark's office reappeared in his vision. There were no flames in the room, no searing heat. The heat he felt was inside him. He was drenched in sweat.

Kayla was crouching beside him. Behind her stood Mark.

'What happened?' she asked, nearly as upset as he was. He wanted to talk, but his voice failed him.

'Let him catch his breath first, Kayla,' Mark said in a stern voice.

'Could I have a glass of water?' Jason managed.

'Coming right up,' Mark said.

A minute later, Jason downed a glass of water in nearly one gulp.

'I never want to go through that again,' he said, his voice quivering.

'Go through *what*?' Kayla cried fearfully.

He told them what he had seen, the words coming in fits and jerks.

'Mark?' he said after he had finished. 'What do you make of this?'

'It's too soon to jump to conclusions. We'll have to—'

'There was something *with* me,' Jason interrupted in a gruff voice. 'I wasn't alone. Something or someone *did* come in the fire.'

'It seems that way,' Mark said. 'But we'll leave it for next time. Calm down, try to come to grips with this first.'

Jason shivered. 'If there *is* a next time.'

'What do you mean?'

'You heard me.' He averted his gaze. 'The nightmares are bad enough. This time I felt like I was really on fire. I don't ever want to go through it again.'

Something *had* been hiding in the flames. Of that he had no doubt whatsoever. What sort of thing could exist, survive, inside an inferno like that?

FIFTEEN
Fire Spirit

During the next two days Jason tried to avoid thinking about the session in Mark's office. Whenever he closed his eyes he worried he would have nightmares, but blessedly they failed to materialize. At work, the days seemed to grind on endlessly. But at least he received no additional manila envelopes.

On Thursday afternoon, after work, he stopped by his father's house. He found him busy in the shed preparing for next winter, when he wanted to have the wood siding on his house replaced. Jason waited until Edward had carefully trimmed a board to size with a circular saw and had put the wood aside. Sensing his son's presence, he turned around.

'Thanks again for the toolbox, son,' he greeted him good-naturedly. 'I'm really pleased with it.'

'You're welcome, Dad, I'm glad you like it.'

They went inside for an ice-cold Corona. In the living room, Jason stood staring at the antique wall clock for a while. It had been there for as long as he could remember. Just as he had on Mark's couch, he imagined himself as a little boy, when his mother was still alive, remembering her sweet smile.

He felt privileged to have had two very special women enrich his life. One of them was Kayla, and he prayed that she would stay with him for eternity. The other had been Donna, his mother. She had died on the twenty-seventh of June, nine years ago – taken by inoperable cancer at much too early an age. She had been diagnosed with the illness in November of the previous year, and for several months after that diagnosis she had lived a perfectly normal life. If Jason hadn't known better, he could have sworn that the cancer did not exist, let alone be running rampant inside her body. Before June, her weekly chemotherapy session at the hospital was the only thing that indicated everything was not as it should be. At the time, Edward and Jason had prayed that they would at least have Christmas with her.

But in early June Donna's health had deteriorated rapidly. Until the end she had remained resilient and loving, no matter how awful her pain and suffering she had to endure in those final days. She had already lost so much weight, and her wasted body was weakening further by the day. Jason and his father kept vigil by her bedside until she drew her last breath, and then both of them had collapsed in tears.

His mother was a good Catholic with strong religious beliefs, but not to an extreme. When her son brought home girlfriend after girlfriend, she had never said anything against it. Donna understood that Jason had other interests besides the church – even though, to make her happy, he rarely skipped the weekly masses presided over by Father Abraham. Donna had been president of the local Bible society, a rare phenomenon in liberal California. But she had given it her all and had recruited a healthy number of new members.

His father had never been much of a churchgoer either. Until he retired he had been a production supervisor for a manufacturer of farming equipment. As such, he was more interested in machines, tools and gadgets than in religion.

Donna showered her family with love, particularly her son Jason, who never understood why she of all people had been the first to go. It was as if she had been rewarded for her good work with a brain tumor. It made no sense.

And it went a long way toward proving Kayla's point. Death *was* a monster.

Jason felt a stab of sadness at the memories and the injustice of it all. After Edward joined him in the living room, they finished their beers and chatted about the birthday party – one that his father had enjoyed immensely. Of course, Jason told him nothing about the photographs. What good would it do? Edward wouldn't have any answers either, and Jason would only be burdening him with worry.

As he drove home through the green of Malibu, he felt alone. And it wasn't just because of his mood; he *was* alone on this stretch of road. Even this close to the frenzied metropolis of Los Angeles, on some smaller asphalt roads surrounded by olive and oak trees, you could still imagine yourself to be either the last man on earth or the first man to discover this fair land.

But in truth, he was neither.

He was *not* alone.

He had had company, with whoever was in that fire.

The vision from the hypnosis returned, unbidden. The fire that had surrounded him had been terrifying. That in itself was nothing new. But something mysterious had been hiding inside the fire. Certainly he had never experienced that vision before.

It was alive. The fire was alive.

Now he wondered, because of his session with Mark, whether the fire had *always* been alive – from the first time his recurring nightmare had encroached upon his sleep those many years ago, until the last time in Mark's office.

If Mark and Kayla hadn't called him back, maybe he could have seen more of what had been there with him, camouflaged by the flames.

Was it looking at me? Did it sense me? Does it know me?

Intriguing questions with no answers. And the only way to get answers was by taking the same road again.

The same road that led into the fire. The thought tortured him and made him break out in a sweat.

Although he discussed it with Kayla, he had already made up his mind. Only one man could shed light on these matters. One man he trusted enough to let him poke around inside his mind. That man was Mark.

Jason decided to take the plunge. He had taken the first step. The second one was inevitable, however terrifying it might prove to be. Going to the dentist to have his wisdom teeth extracted was nothing compared to this prospect.

Kayla listened to him with mixed feelings and said she would do anything to have a future without fear. She stood quietly beside him as he called Mark.

Jason made an appointment for the next day, Friday, again at five o'clock. When he went to sleep that night, he was convinced the bad dream would return.

I have no worries, he kept telling himself in an effort to stay calm and composed. But this was an outdated mantra, because he most definitely *did* have worries. If he denied them, he'd be fooling only himself. But first there was another night to get through. Jason turned off the light, prepared for the worst.

When he woke up the next morning he had slept through the night, without incident.

Late the following afternoon, when they met together with Mark in his office, the tension was palpable. For Jason and Kayla this was to be expected. What gave Mark away were his little coughs; he always coughed when burdened with stress. Jason was reminded of a midterm exam at Cal State, when Mark got under the skin of his classmates, coughing and clearing his throat so often, he had to be taken into another room to finish the test alone with a hastily summoned professor as a private proctor. Jason hadn't been there, but had believed the stories. Yes, Mark was cool and collected most of the time, but when he felt uneasy, his seemingly unshakeable equanimity could turn into a spate of coughing.

The reason for his nervousness today he left undefined. A psychologist, Jason believed, was supposed to radiate knowledge, empathy, confidence and security at all times. After all, *he* was the professional, with the authority that came with his lofty position.

Jason suspected – or hoped – that Mark's tension was based on nothing more than his wish to help an old friend. What if these sessions led nowhere? What if all they did was make Jason even more confused? If he were Mark, those would certainly be questions he would ponder.

He had resolved to stay in control of his emotions on this day, come what may.

Mark asked him to lie down on the couch again. Jason did so and tried to relax. As he had before, Mark asked him to journey to a place where he felt safe.

'But don't go to the Santa Monica Mountains. Pick somewhere else this time. Where else do you feel safe?'

He remembered the salt plains in Utah where he had once visited with Bill Hallerman, an old friend from college. They had spent that summer driving around in Bill's rusty Buick – about the time Jason had first become acquainted with Tommy 'the Automobile

King' Jones – and chasing girls. Together, they had burned their share of rubber on the snow-white plains.

Then he heard Mark's voice seemingly from somewhere far away, like a voice coming over a telephone line asking whether he was ready to return to Saddle Peak, where the fire was.

He stood there in Utah, on the endless white salt, in clear view of jagged mountain ranges in the distance. He felt calm, at peace, safe. He and Bill were sole rulers of their vast domain and it felt good.

He didn't want to leave there.

He had no desire to return to the fire in the Santa Monica Mountains.

But then, reluctantly, his mind started wandering back to *that* place. Getting there was no effort at all; in no time he was walking on the steep mountain trail again, retracing his steps.

When he saw the patchy foliage, he felt a surge of fear and anxiety. This time he knew what lay beyond it. It was a gateway into horror and he was afraid to continue. But he had no choice. Beyond the green foliage lay the secret to his recurring nightmare.

As if an echo from a faraway place he heard Mark asking him where he was.

'I'm back before the wall of leaves,' Jason answered.

'Continue on,' Mark said.

'I don't know . . .' Jason said hesitantly.

Mark told him that he didn't have to do it, that they could do this some other time if he didn't feel up to it now, it was no big deal.

'I have no choice,' Jason argued. 'I'll never be ready for this, but it needs to be done. Better to get it over with.'

'Are you sure?' Mark asked.

Jason thought for a moment, considering the alternatives.

'Yes,' he said. 'I'm sure.'

'OK. Keep going. You can come back any time you want. It's easy. Just snap your fingers. All right, Jason?'

Jason repeated that he was going for it and started walking tentatively toward the wall of foliage. As before, he walked into one of the black holes and found himself in the deep black of a moonless night.

He paused a moment, gathering his courage. Not that he felt

brave. Quite the opposite. He was here reluctantly, against his will. He could think of many other places he'd rather be. Very *different* places.

Mark? he said, or thought.

There was no answer. Silence permeated his mind.

Mark!

Still nothing.

His connection with the real world was Mark, and that connection seemed to have been severed. He now had no lifeline to that real world.

He glanced at his right hand.

All I have to do is snap my fingers and I'll be back. Piece of cake, I can do that.

He decided not to go back yet, because all he saw was darkness, as if he were in an underground basement with no lights on. Jason felt his way forward like a blind man and wondered when the pyre would appear. Just as the thought entered his mind, the fire suddenly burst to life.

He realized that he could *will* the fire from his nightmare into existence. Was that strange? No, he thought, because he was only taking a trip through his own brain. This night was a crevice inside his mind, just like Noam Morain had caverns inside his soul, forever haunted by a horseman dressed in black.

He wasn't really in the Santa Monica Mountains; he had gone nowhere. All he had done was fashion a path inside himself. He was more fully aware of this reality today than he was the last time.

All right. If I haven't traveled outside my own mind, and I can think things, just think them, I might as well let the rest in, and see what happens.

The flames lashed out at him as if they were truly alive and could sense him and even see him. It was at once both astonishing and agonizing. Still, he struggled to suppress a surge of terror. The fire undulated toward him and made a circle around him. Horrified, he watched the circle form as the heat slashed at his face like a hot steel blade of a knife.

He could escape by snapping his fingers – or he hoped he could. Mark had promised him that, and Mark was his trusted friend. But what if nothing happened when he did that? What if he found himself still here, trapped within an inferno?

But this isn't real. It's all in my mind. I don't need to be afraid – this is an illusion.

The clarity of his thoughts surprised him. There was no panic, not yet.

Then he realized that, once again, he was not alone. There was something inside the fire. He didn't know it, hear it, or see it – he could just *feel* it. If he had the courage to stay he would see it; if he could just not snap his fingers and not believe he would be burned alive. He just needed to *wait*.

Despite himself, he felt a scream gathering force deep within him. His fear was trying to possess him, and it was fast gaining the upper hand.

The flames crawled closer and nearly touched his feet. The imaginary knife of heat felt as though it would slice his face to ribbons. He couldn't hold out much longer; no one could withstand this torture. He held the thumb and forefinger of his right hand together. One snap, just one, and it would be over.

Show yourself. Damn you, show me who you are. You're here, I know it. Show yourself, I want to see you!

Slowly the fire changed shape. He watched with morbid fascination as a figure seemed to materialize from inside the inferno. Was it just an illusion? Squinting, he peered at a flaming area that seemed to be moving. Then, to his horror, it stepped out from the flames and came toward him. The creature had a head, arms and legs, and it was burning like a torch. Flames enveloped its body from head to toe. It had no face, or at least no face Jason could discern. Flames covered it entirely. He stared at it, aghast. Was it a spirit? A fire spirit? He did nothing, powerless to act, even when the apparition stretched out a burning arm toward him. Fiery fingers came ever closer to him.

The scream tore past his vocal chords and out his throat. He toppled backwards. His thumb found his index finger and he snapped them together.

SIXTEEN
Mawkee

He could still see the creature from the flames as the blurred contours and shapes inside Mark's office came slowly into focus. He was trembling in the transition from one realm to the other, but at least he no longer felt the pain of the scorching fire.

Kayla's hands were wrapped around his right wrist, her eyes wide and fearful as she crouched down beside him. Mark stood behind her. He was saying something, but Jason couldn't hear him. It was as though he had gone stone deaf.

Slowly, ever so slowly, sound began filtering back into his world. The phone rang, but Mark didn't answer it.

Hey, answer the phone, he wanted to say, but he could not. His lips seemed frozen in place. Nor could he get up. He felt as though a truckload of bricks was piled on top of him. Then, finally, Mark's voice reverberated through the haze. '. . . that you're OK, Jason. Speak to me. Are you OK?'

'I'm back,' Jason said in a shaky voice.

He told them what had happened. When he explained how the fire had taken shape and turned into a figure, a walking firebrand, his breath caught in his throat. He described in detail what he had seen. Expressing how he had felt during the course of events proved more challenging, however. He could convey the pure terror he had felt only in diluted form. If their positions had been reversed, if Kayla had been surrounded by imaginary spiders, he would not have been able to fully comprehend her horror either. Empathy only reached so far.

His words sounded hollow even to him. For the life of him he couldn't come close to expressing the panic that had gripped him during the hypnosis.

'So there really *was* something in the fire,' Jason concluded, his voice soft yet resolute. 'Or the fire turned *into* something. I don't know which.'

'That's scary,' Kayla said in a small voice.

Jason looked at his friend. 'What do you make of this, Mark?'

Mark rubbed his chin thoughtfully. 'This is just the start of our analysis, Jason,' he said. 'It does appear to be some kind of repressed experience, or a series of experiences. The images you describe are symbolic of something. Of that I am certain. We'll have to wait and see. But you've made excellent progress in this session. In fact, I think you've made a breakthrough. You managed to keep in control of yourself. You never forgot where you were, and how to break the trance.'

'Thanks. But where do we go from here?'

'I always like to compare these sessions to peeling an onion,' Mark said. 'The first layer has come off, but you have yet to reach the core. You need to go back a few more times. Peel off one layer after another. It won't be pleasant, but I'll help you, if you want.'

'If I continue with this, I'd only do it with you,' Jason answered.

'I agree,' Kayla said.

Jason reflected for a moment. So far, what he had done had inspired more questions than answers. What was that fire in his vision? What in God's name *was* that burning creature? And what, if anything, did all of this have to do with the three photographs and messages?

Mark was right. This process might very well resemble the peeling of an onion. But Jason believed Mark was wrong about one thing. With every layer that came off, more questions arose, adding additional layers to the onion.

The session had exhausted him, and he would have given a lot to take an aspirin and get some sleep. Assuming he was free of dreams about the fiery creature.

'Could we call it a day?' Jason asked.

'Good idea,' Mark agreed. 'And I think it's best if we wait a few days before picking up where we left off. Trying to force these things often backfires. How about we meet again next week, same day, same time?'

'OK,' Jason said. 'Let's do that.'

After they said goodbye to Mark, Kayla drove them home. Along the way, she kept glancing askance at him.

'I'll be all right,' he assured her, more than once.

'Yes, you'll be all right. Everything is going to be fine.'

Neither of their voices held much conviction.

Back at home, Kayla turned quiet and contemplative. Jason, in turn, couldn't dismiss the creature and the fire from his mind, try as he might. As if by rote, he retrieved a bottle of Pinot Grigio from the fridge. The label offered no clues about its quality, but he remembered its price: $4.99.

'You get what you pay for, right?' he murmured, opening the bottle and filling two glasses.

'Come, let's enjoy the fresh air for a while,' he told Kayla. She agreed and together they walked outside to Canyon View's back porch.

Kayla sat beside him on the old sofa, and he put his arm around her shoulders. For a while they both just sat there, enjoying the peace and panorama.

'Jason?' she said finally. 'Do you want to talk?'

He managed a smile. 'Sure. Shoot. What do you make of all this?'

'I think . . .' she started, and then shook her head. 'I just don't know.'

'Same here.'

He pulled her close. He needed his wife now more than ever. She smelled of lilac flowers, a sweet scent that carried with it blissful memories.

He had met her more than four years ago during a business dinner. Brian Anderson had asked him to come along for another one of his outings with clients: Joe Daniels and Alvin Smith from Weinstein Productions, one of the larger television producers in the glamorous City of Angels. It had been a pleasant and commercially successful evening at The Duchess, a classy restaurant on Sunset Boulevard. But that evening Jason's attention was diverted toward the waitress who served their table. When she took their orders, he had complimented her on the artful way she had done up her hair, even though he had never been in the habit of complimenting waitresses. But he sensed immediately that she was different from other waitresses and from other women he had known. Different in every sense of the word. When she asked him later what had drawn her to him, he told her it was her sexy, husky voice.

While eating their entrées he had received a phone call and excused himself from the table. He stood in a corner of the restaurant with his cell phone pressed to his ear, with her looking at him from a distance. He had to suppress an urge to walk up to her and say, 'Where have you been my whole life?' Corny, yes, but that's how he felt.

But he was just not that bold, and the magic would have ended there had he not forgotten his credit card. As they were walking back to their cars after dinner, Jason patted his shirt pocket and discovered he had handed over the company's Visa card and signed the bill, but had neglected to retrieve the card. He bid the others goodnight and hastened back to the restaurant. At first Kayla seemed surprised to see him again, but then had helped him find his card. She appeared flustered, claiming it was her fault. He had wanted to tell her it was alright, it didn't matter. But what he did, instead, was place his hand over hers.

Their eyes met. Then she had placed her other hand on top of his. Her eyes shone, and without having to exchange a word, they had become inexorably connected to each other in mind, body and spirit.

The next evening he returned to The Duchess for dinner. By himself. After that, one thing led quickly to another.

As it turned out, she had studied at Heald College, an institute that trained executive secretaries. After backpacking through Europe for six months, she was now trying to find a job. But finding the right job hadn't been easy, which explained why she was waitressing.

There'd been Ralph too, of course. The first time they had gone out for a drink, she hadn't mentioned him. On their second date, she broached the subject. Over the years Jason had learned more about Kayla's erstwhile fiancé, but never the whole story. After Ralph died, she had traveled to Europe, her trip paid for partly by her parents and partly with the money she had earned working in diners and bars.

It wasn't long before he started spending more nights at her place than his own house, which was under construction. Twenty months after the business dinner at The Duchess they became man and wife. They were very much in love and saw no point in waiting longer. That sunny, springlike day in February had been unforgettable. And in the meantime, as icing on the cake, she had landed her current job at Demas Electrical; a job she loved.

By now they had been married for almost two and a half years. During all that time they had never experienced any serious problems. Except on that day in April when she lost her maternal grandmother and then, just four months later her maternal grandfather.

Losing these loved ones had broken her heart. In November of that same year, Rose Salladay, a long-time friend with whom she had often enjoyed a game of squash, was killed in a traffic accident. That tragedy depressed Kayla for months.

A more recent setback had been Uncle Chris's passing. Naturally, how he had died had been the major shock. In the first few days after his death, Kayla had cried constantly, unable to be consoled by Jason or anyone else. At the funeral she hid her puffy, red-streaked eyes behind a pair of large sunglasses. Jason had imagined it would be quite some time before she could come to terms with her grief, so he was pleasantly surprised when, soon after the interment, she had managed to move on with her life. He had not dared ask her why she seemed to be handling it so well this time, fearing that his simple question would open up sore wounds. Maybe, he thought, a death in her immediate family or group of friends was more traumatic for her than the death of a relative stranger.

Whatever it was, death upset her, and that was putting it mildly. He had his fear of fire, and she had *that*.

He woke up to a diabolical crackling. His bed was on fire. Tall, furious tongues of fire shot up around him and Kayla, who remained asleep. A searing heat wafted into his face. At the foot of the bed a figure burned brightly: the fire spirit. In utter panic he could think to do one thing: snap his fingers. When he did, nothing happened. The flames remained, and so did the creature. This was no nightmare, and it was no hypnosis; this was *real*.

A tormented sound erupted from the fiery creature, like the roar of raging flames. Or was it a wailing, growling whisper?

Mawkee . . .

That hissing sound seemed to emanate from the sweltering fire.

The thing lumbered closer, it was on the bed now, crawling toward Kayla and him. The heat was terrible. Still the raging flames hid the creature's face.

It was very close now, lifting a burning hand, about to put those flaming fingers on his face, or in his eyes, about to—

A piercing scream erupted from Jason's throat.

And he woke up. Again.

And he saw no creature, no fire – nothing, anywhere.

Beside him Kayla sat up, stiff as a board, staring at him.

'Another nightmare,' he said with a shiver, before she could speak. 'One hell of a vivid one, this time.'

Mark did not close my mind off properly, was his first thought.

His second thought was: *Mawkee?*

However the word was spelled, it contained the word 'key'.

The key to what?

He dropped back on to the pillow and wiped his sweaty brow with this hand. Again, the fire had only been inside his mind. He had suffered through many nightmares, but this was the worst one ever.

SEVENTEEN
Saddle Peak

The next morning Jason needed two aspirin to help quell a throbbing headache. He knew not what to do about the nightmare, or what to make of it. He had been so sure that he was awake at the time, but obviously he was mistaken. It seemed that he was growing increasingly less able to distinguish delusion from reality. In that case, he had all the more reason to worry. Be that as it may, he had to move on. He had work to do and a wife to protect. He called Lou Briggs.

'It's not going so well, Jason,' Lou reported. 'I still haven't found the pyramid. I'm starting to sense that the tomb is the creation of some graphic artist and was superimposed into the image, as was the letter M.'

'Just keep trying to find that graveyard, Lou, please,' Jason urged him before hanging up.

Minutes later, as he stood in the shower with hot water running off him, his thoughts drifted back to the thickets on the trail ending at Saddle Peak. Why had the gate into his nightmare been in that precise spot? He had thought he had nothing but happy memories of the place.

A sudden urge to go there welled up inside him – not to see it from a prone position on Mark's couch, but with his own eyes. He needed to see the actual foliage there for himself.

He shared his thinking with Kayla.

'That's a good idea,' she said. 'I'll come with you.'

He briefly considered calling Mark, but decided against it. After all, it was Mark's weekend off. Better to just go out there and have a look around.

After a quick breakfast they walked out the front door of their home into a California summer dawn. Even at this early hour, Fernhill was basking in the heat of a July sun. Although Jason had been living in the town for just a few years, he felt at home here. The village nestled between the mountains was a refuge of peace and tranquility compared to Los Angeles, just twenty-five miles away.

They drove off in Kayla's Chrysler, crossing Fernhill's very own 'Beverly Hills', a neighborhood that owed its nickname to the large number of artisans, artists and writers who had taken up residence there. Most of these people were from Los Angeles, and they had flocked here in the hope of finding creative inspiration. Jason glanced at the mansion of sculptor David Mayne, who had made a name for himself in art circles; next to it was the impressive home of Richard Hawthorne, the suspense novelist. These two men sported the only famous names in Fernhill; the majority of the other artisans were Hawthorne wannabes – although, according to Jason, these sycophants and artistic hangers-on were 'canneverbees'. He remembered something and chuckled softly, despite the tension and misery of the moment.

'Private joke?' Kayla asked.

'I was recalling the garden party at Hawthorne's last year.'

'Oh, that.' She didn't find the memory amusing. 'How could I forget? It was *so* embarrassing.'

Honored to have been invited to the private party, Jason had bought a new Armani suit for the occasion. Later, when Kayla was returning from the bar with two glasses of white wine, she tripped on a cable for the garden lights, spilling the contents of both glasses down the front of his expensive suit. His immediate reaction was anger, but his anger quickly faded when he saw his wife's face turning beet red.

It didn't take long to drive the eight miles toward the dirt lot at the foot of Saddle Peak. From there, it was a climb of about three miles to the thick of the foliage. The path continued farther up for a few more miles before it branched off, giving hikers a choice of trails to take, each with its own name. Ocean High Trail was their favorite.

They weren't the first visitors today: a few cars were already in the lot. After exchanging their Top-Siders for hiking shoes, they set out.

During their walk, each remained engrossed in private thoughts, and the silence between them was as palpable as it was unusual. As they approached their destination he felt a chill, despite the warm California sun.

Ahead they saw the tall grass where they had made love near an ancient oak tree.

And *there*, a few dozen yards farther up the trail, where it made a sharp turn, were the thickets. He stopped.

'And?' Kayla prodded.

He took a few more steps, his reluctance mounting, as if he were inching toward the side of a cliff. When he reached the bushes, he found that they were just foliage; nothing more. Leafy canopies, branches, tree trunks, growing from perfectly ordinary forest soil. He was almost afraid to touch the plants, but at length he managed to carefully push some of the branches aside and sniffed them, like a house cat on its first foray outside.

There were bare patches between the bushes – what he had been thinking of as black holes. Although the thickets looked exactly as they had during his session with Mark, he was now unable to determine which of the openings he had walked through to find, first, a strange darkness and then a hellish fire.

'Funny thing,' he mumbled.

'What?' Kayla asked.

'I don't know where it is.'

'Where *what* is?'

He retreated a step and clasped her hand. 'This is the place, all

right. This was where I went during my session with Mark. But
. . .' He squeezed her hand. 'I don't know what I did next. I went
through somewhere, through one of these openings. But which one
was it?'

None of the holes in the foliage formed a passage into another
realm. On the sandy ground beneath the bushes were dry bracken,
dead leaves, gray pebbles and a few rocks. That was all. Kayla said
nothing.

He looked up, tuning in to his senses. He heard twittering birds,
the quiet rustle of leaves and the caress of a soft wind as he breathed
in the sweet smells of the forests. Nothing else came to mind.
Nothing at all.

But still . . .

Still the fire was sizzling somewhere. Inside him.

He turned to Kayla. 'Something *did* happen to me.' Even though
the words came from his own lips, they held no meaning for him
yet. 'Inside me . . . something has died.'

Her face tightened and she gave him a cold stare. It was a look
he had never before seen in her eyes. He realized what was going
through her mind – too late. He had said something very, very wrong
– something she did not want to hear.

'I didn't mean I'm not alive . . . I don't know what I meant,' he
said tentatively. 'I'm sorry. Forget what I said.'

He looked beseechingly into her eyes. She averted her gaze and
pulled back her hand.

'If you're done here, can we go?' she said coldly.

'I think I'm done, yes.'

She turned her back to him and started walking back down the
pathway. He waited a moment, and then followed her, pondering
what he had said. No, what had come out of his mouth. *He* hadn't
said it. It was . . .

It came from somewhere inside me, but it wasn't me.

Another shiver crawled down Jason's spine.

But what hurt him was Kayla.

She was stalking away from him at an ever more rapid pace.

The atmosphere between them hadn't improved by the time they
arrived home. Kayla walked straight into the small study and, from
the living room, Jason heard her talking on the phone. It was obvious

she needed to blow off steam by chatting with one of her friends. He left her alone, and sat down in the hanging chair on the porch to think. After half an hour he went back inside. Kayla was still in the study, but no longer on the phone. She was just sitting there, staring off into space.

'Hey,' he said cheerfully. 'I'm here on a peace mission.'

He clumsily waved a half-clenched fist, mimicking a white flag of truce. 'Can we talk about this?'

'We can always talk,' Kayla snapped.

'Good. What will it take to make this right?'

Just like that her anger melted away like an ice cube set out under a hot sun. Her voice assumed a beseeching tone.

'Jason, I want to help you,' she said. 'You know I do. I think it's a good thing that you're trying to make sense of your nightmares, no matter how awful they are. But one thing is certain: you *are* alive. You exist. I see you standing here, and you're no ghost.'

He grinned. 'Not a ghost? Are you sure?'

'Huh?' she said, taken aback.

'Shouldn't you check? To see whether I'm really all flesh and blood?'

She smiled at that. Finally. He had not seen her smile for too long. Her eyes softened.

'OK,' she whispered, extending a hand. 'Let me check you out.'

Later, lying naked side by side on their bed, she again brought up the events of the last few days.

'There seems to be something you've repressed,' she began. 'That's what Mark said. I wonder . . .'

'What it is,' he finished for her.

'Yes. And this fire thing . . .' She shook her head as if in denial. 'This *creature*, as you call it. What is *that*?'

'I haven't a clue,' he said. 'In my dream last night I heard this sound. Mawkee. *Key*. What key?'

He turned toward her and circled her right nipple with his fingertip. 'And still, I keep insisting that I was never actually *in* a fire,' he said absently. 'So where did my phobia come from? And why are my dreams suddenly getting weirder?'

'It could be something else,' she said.

'Like what?'

'What's your earliest memory of fire?'

'Jesus, Kayla, how should I know?'

'You don't necessarily have to have been inside a fire *yourself*,' she continued, growing convinced of her own interpretations. 'Maybe you were a witness, saw the victims; people who died in a fire. It's a possibility, isn't it? Maybe the fire and that thing you keep mentioning have something to do with that.'

'I see where you're going with this.'

'*Did* anything like that happen? Could that be it?'

Jason searched his memory. Then he shook his head. 'Not as far back as I can remember.'

'Still, you *must* have had a horrible experience with fire,' she pressed on. 'Everything is pointing in that direction. Maybe it happened a very long time ago. So long that you've forgotten it. Or you've shut the memory out.'

Again he searched through his memories. 'I can see why it would be reasonable to think so. You know what, let's get this straight once and for all. I'll call the one person who should know.'

She frowned as he swung his legs over the side of the bed, sat on the wooden bed frame and picked up the phone. He dialed a number, and the phone was answered almost immediately.

'Hello?'

'Hello, Dad, it's me,' Jason said. 'Everything all right?'

'Excellent, son. Tyler and Roger are on their way over. They should be here any minute.'

'That's great. Where are you guys headed?'

'Nowhere. We're going to have a beer. More than one, I suspect. And we're probably going to play some cards.'

'So it's an afternoon with the guys,' Jason said.

'That's right. Keeps me young,' Edward quipped.

'Good for you,' Jason said. He breathed in, preparing to get to the point. 'Listen, Dad, I want to ask you something. We've talked about this before, but I need to make sure. It's about my . . . well, you know how I hate fire.'

'Yeah?' Edward said, his voice lowering. This was not his favorite subject.

'I've asked you this before, I know. But I'm going to ask you again.' He took a deep breath. 'Dad, have I ever been through anything that might explain it, a long time ago? Have I ever been up close to a big fire? Could I have seen something that, well, gave me a scare? A hell of a scare?'

'Come now, son,' Edward said. 'If that were true, I would have told you about it. Your mother and I used to worry so much about this ah . . . you have a fancy word for it. What is it?'

'Pyrophobia,' Jason whispered.

'That's it. Has it come back?'

'It's never really gone away,' Jason said, keeping his tone light. 'I was just wondering how on earth it might have started.'

Edward sighed audibly. 'Jason, please believe me, if I knew anything of the kind, I would have told you about it a long time ago.'

'OK, one more try, then. Have you ever heard Pete McGray say something about it?'

Edward said nothing for a few seconds. In the silence, Jason could sense that his father was not happy that he had involved Pete in this. But he had no choice. He had to look under every stone, from every angle.

'No, son, I've never heard him talk about it either. Believe me.'

Jason leaned back and brushed a lock of hair from his eyes. 'I understand, Dad. I just needed to hear that confirmation one more time.'

He ended the conversation.

'That was a no,' he told Kayla. 'Dad doesn't have anything new to add, either. Not that I had expected him to.'

'Then what *is* going on?' she murmured. She shook her head. 'Maybe it doesn't matter and you should just tuck it away and stop thinking about it.'

He seriously doubted if that would be possible.

Until several days ago he had been Sunday's child. It had been smooth sailing all the way. He was blessed with a good brain and good looks, he'd had a happy childhood, he had always gotten good grades in college, and he'd found a nice job and a loving wife. Nothing had veered off course. Nothing at all.

My past appears to be clean, he thought. *No scorch marks there.*

Except that perhaps his assumption was wrong. More and more, he was beginning to think it was.

The night was balmy, young and full of promise. He tasted her soft mouth, and his lips roamed from her slender neck to her full breasts, down to her tight belly and beyond, where his tongue explored her most intimate parts. She moaned softly, pushed herself up a little and draped her arms across his shoulders. He kissed her, she smiled seductively and lowered herself back into the pillows. He entered her and thrust deeply, closing his eyes with the ecstasy of it all. When he gave her a loving gaze, he was surprised to see her grinning. The familiar dimples on her cheeks remained, but the sparkle in her eyes had become a dark flash, as dark and forbidding as the underworld.

A gray, ashy spot appeared on her right cheek. Flakes of skin started peeling off and he detected the acrid stench of smoke. Her left cheek caught on fire. Then, her right cheek. Bursts of flame erupted from her mouth, as from a dragon. Fire smoldered in her hair; flames crept along her arms, her upper body and her legs.

Jason recoiled in shock. The fire was consuming her. Blinding panic gripped him. But in the next instant he realized that this couldn't really be happening. Kayla was disappearing, and he sat staring at a creature that consisted of nothing but furious flames. Flames that should be setting the whole room on fire, but didn't. Kayla, alone, burned. Nothing else. But she wasn't Kayla any more; she was the fire creature. Had he truly made love to that demonic thing?

The creature reared up. Blazing arms reached out for him, and from the heart of the roaring flames he heard the hissing again, making the same awful heart-wrenching sounds as in his previous nightmare.

Mawkee . . . Mawkee . . .

The creature of fire crawled toward him. He scrambled back in abject horror and fell off the bed.

He started awake.

He flailed his arms. He was still in bed; he hadn't fallen out. Beside him Kayla slept peacefully. It was night, dark; there was no fire. It had been a dream, another horrendous, ghastly, satanic dream.

His heart was racing. He felt beads of sweat coursing down his face. He was gasping for breath. And he smelled the stench of burning flesh.

Jason could still vividly picture the flames, hear that awful voice echoing in his ears.

It took a long time before his breathing finally evened out and his heart rate returned to normal. Beside him, Kayla slept, the very image of serenity and innocence. He crept outside to the porch, sat down in his hanging chair and buried his head in his hands.

They hadn't discussed his anxieties since yesterday afternoon. They had gone out to dinner at the Malibu Palm and had enjoyed a wonderful, intimate dinner together.

When they went to bed, he had been happy and tired, and convinced he would get through the night without incident. But no such luck.

His despair gnawed at him. That very first Polaroid photograph had ignited a chain of events that had branched off in strange scenarios and perilous pathways. Now it was focused on his anxiety over anything to do with fire. It was a very old terror, from the time he had been a little boy.

Then he remembered something else.

Something that hit him like a steel fist.

EIGHTEEN

Mapeetaa

At three o'clock in the dead of night, Jason sat wide awake on the porch. He arose from the chair he was sitting on and walked inside the house to his study, where he flicked on the light and opened the twin doors of his oaken cabinet. On the top shelf was a box he had kept with him every time he moved, because its content spoke directly to his past.

Jason placed the box on his desk and stood staring at it. The silence in the room calmed him. He was at peace, at least for the moment. At length, he opened the box and removed a powder-blue photo album containing his childhood pictures. This album he placed next to the box. Then he removed a number of notebooks from the box, along with more photos and sheets of paper with writing on them. As a little boy, he had enjoyed drawing almost anything. Now he searched for his old drawings and found them. Immediately his brief period of inner calm abandoned him.

The subject of many of the drawings involved a fire of one kind or another. A house going up in flames. A burning tree. A blazing sun, even.

He had to admit, looking at the drawings after all this time, that he had not been endowed with an artistic genius. The drawings were crude, abstract, *childish*.

His obsession with fire, however, had clearly started at a tender age.

One drawing had a number of graves in it. Headstones, sticking up from the ground at odd angles, maybe in some cemetery. He put the sheet of paper on his desk and flattened it. More flames, capturing the gravestones in a big red cloud that was intended to represent a fiery glow. The middle headstone had a word inscribed on it, scribbled in his youthful hand.

Mapeetaa

That was what he had remembered. This drawing, with this word in it.

He dragged his fingers through his hair, and massaged his temples. *Mawkee. Mapeetaa.*

The words were different, but at the same time similar. 'Mapeetaa' was a word he had written himself, a quarter of a century ago.

What did this mean? Where had it come from?

Suddenly, in his mind's eye, Uncle Chris appeared, the man who had fooled them all. He had never told anyone that he had been diagnosed with incurable cancer; he had also hidden the fact that he was suffering from depression as a result of that diagnosis. Most importantly, he had said nothing about the pain that was fast becoming too difficult to bear. He had ended his life by hanging himself, and all he had left was a note. Jason would have tried to help him, but Chris had never given him a chance. He had given *no one* an opening to offer him any type of emotional or physical support. Now Chris appeared in his mind, alive and kicking, and about twenty or thirty years younger. His beard was not as full or long back then, and his hair not as gray. And it bore no resemblance, as yet, to Santa Claus out of costume.

Chris' lips were moving, he was saying something, but Jason couldn't hear him. Still, he thought he knew what word Chris was mouthing. It shot up forcefully from Jason's memory, like a dolphin beneath the ocean surface propelling itself upward for a graceful leap into the air.

In the bedroom Kayla woke up to find Jason gone. It was Sunday, usually not a day for him to be up and about at the crack of dawn. She yawned and stretched leisurely, gathering her courage to leave the comfortable warmth of the bed. At length she got up, donned a housecoat, and went in search of Jason.

She found him in the study at his computer. She made a show of picking up the clock from the oak desk. 'Five past eight on a Sunday morning,' she said, as if in a mock reprimand. 'You're supposed to still be in bed. Any chance you getting up so early involved making me a cup of tea?'

He smiled at her. 'Cup of tea, coming right up.'

Leaning in, she kissed his stubbly cheeks. She then peered at the monitor. 'What're you doing?'

'Research,' he replied.

'What kind of research?'

'You're way too curious for this early in the morning.'

'That's your fault. You're making me curious.'

'How about I fill you in over breakfast. Is that a plan?'

'Sure.'

Over a vegetable omelet and French rolls he told her about waking up during the night and not being able to go back to sleep. And then something had suddenly hit him: a new and enigmatic word. He did not mention to her that the reason he had awoken was because of a bad dream he had had in which she had turned into a living torch while he made love to her. He also kept to himself both the mystery of his drawing he had uncovered and the memory of his Uncle Chris, mouthing the same weird word that Jason had seen on the drawing. He desperately wanted to avoid any topic that could send her spiraling down a slippery slope of depression. More and more, it seemed, this mystery of his was taking on elements of the occult.

'What was that word again?' Kayla asked.

'Mapeetaa,' Jason replied, in the same tone of voice he believed that Chris would have said it. 'It starts with an M. Just like in the picture. And it also sounds like the word Mawkee.'

'What you mean is, the M on the headstone could stand either for Mawkee or Mapeetaa? What *is* Mapeetaa?'

'I don't have a clue. At least not yet. It sounds enigmatic to me.'

'Almost like an Indian god or something.'

'I thought the same thing at first. But not according to Google. "Mapeetaa" doesn't get a single hit. But it would be stranger still if it didn't mean anything.'

'Sure, it probably means *something*. But what?'

He shrugged. 'You want another roll?'

When he offered her the bread basket, she took a croissant.

'What, Jason? What does it mean?'

He selected a roll for himself, cut it open and spread some jam on it. 'Like I said, Kayla, I haven't the faintest idea. That's why I was Googling it. I have to start somewhere.'

She gave him a questioning look.

'And this word "Mapeetaa" simply occurred to you all of a sudden?' she asked.

'Yeah, it did.'

Was he lying? On the one hand he wasn't, because the word had spontaneously come to him, like a lost treasure washed up on a beach. On the other hand he could not deny that he himself had used the word a long time ago.

'Although I'm starting to doubt the spelling now. I wonder why . . .' He stared at her pensively. 'Maybe it's spelled a different way.'

Kayla filled her glass with fresh orange juice. 'To be honest, I had hoped we wouldn't have to discuss this whole mess for a while.'

He could tell she meant it. From the bottom of her heart. Kayla wanted to plan ahead. Have children, be happy, live a normal life.

His face assumed a dogged expression. 'I need to know, Kayla,' he stated emphatically. 'Otherwise I'll never have peace of mind. That's why I can't let it go.'

No, he thought to himself, he could not let it go, no matter how she felt about it.

After breakfast, Kayla cleared the table. Jason returned to his study, probably, Kayla thought, to Google some more.

She opened the sliding doors to the porch. There was no need to use the key, because, once again, Jason had forgotten to lock the doors. She put the dish towel out on a porch chair to dry and took a moment to gaze at the panorama before her in the light of the morning sun. She heard an excited voice coming from somewhere to the right and, curious, walked to the corner of the porch to inspect. The voice turned out to be that of their neighbor, Allan, who was fighting with a garden hose that stubbornly resisted his efforts to untangle it.

Smiling, she turned around and went back inside. 'Mapeetaa.' She said the word out loud to herself. It had a menacing ring to it.

She spotted the calendar on the wall and saw the note she had written to herself there. This morning she was scheduled to go jogging with her friend Simone. They had met when they were both waitresses at The Duchess, and had since become close.

Kayla had forgotten all about their plans. She considered calling Simone and canceling. But that thought she quickly dismissed. Here in the house the worry mill would keep right on turning with the same concerns and questions. She needed a break from that worry. She needed some fresh air.

It wasn't just Jason. She also reflected on Ralph, who, in his own way, had been just as fascinated with death as Jason.

Ralph had been obsessed with his body and health. He never touched anything but the healthiest products, refused to stay in the same room with people who were smoking, and was fixated with staying in shape. Skipping even one evening at the gym made him edgy. Sometimes he had spells of gloom that life was too short, much too short. She had always waved such thoughts away. *Yeah, we only live for eighty years or so. So what?*

It had never been funny to him.

'I'll never get that old, Kayla,' he had said to her during one of his solemn episodes. 'I'll be gone long before then. In fact, I'm not going to live much longer.'

She had repeatedly told him to stop freaking her out with such gloom and doom. After Ralph's cardiac arrest, she had often thought about his prophetic words and talked to people who had had similar experiences. In the process Kayla had heard some remarkable stories. The one that continued to stay with her involved Matthew Henson, a member of one of the self-help groups. He had told her about his girlfriend, Claire Simpson.

It had been a classic case of love at first sight. Two soulmates, destined by fate to meet one day. He was deeply in love with her, and she with him, and nothing seemed to be standing in the way of their happiness. Within five months after they first met – he was twenty-five at the time, she three years younger – they had decided to get married.

That should have been the blissful end of the story, but something changed. Claire started acting strangely. She needed Matthew to tell her how much he loved her, over and over again and at the oddest moments – when he was in a meeting, for example, or hanging out at a bar with friends. She would call him up, demanding confirmation of his love. The first few times it had seemed romantic, but soon it grew old. Whenever Matthew asked Claire why she was acting in this bizarre manner, she never gave him a satisfactory answer. The only thing she kept repeating was that she *had* to.

When she fell ill and things didn't improve, they called in a doctor. He couldn't find anything wrong with her and suggested she get herself checked out at a hospital. Then things started spiraling downhill. Claire was diagnosed with a rapidly growing cancer mass inside her frail twenty-two-year-old body. The doctors couldn't cure her and told her she had three to six weeks left to live. As it turned out, she only had five days.

Matthew was devastated. He had spoken often with Claire in the final days and hours before she died, and they had said everything that needed to be said.

Kayla had asked Matthew if Claire had had a premonition of her own death.

Matthew had nodded his answer. In her last days, Matthew said, Claire had told him she loved him, but that 'he' had always been stronger. Matthew had asked Claire who she meant by 'he'.

Kayla would never forget what Claire said next, according to Matthew.

I have to go back to God. He wants me to return.

Those words confirmed that Claire had known she was not going to live much longer.

Just like Ralph, dead before the age of thirty, not much older than Matthew Henson's Claire.

But what if Ralph's heart condition had been diagnosed in time? Then what?

Would everything have turned out all right, or would he have died of something *else*?

The same questions applied to Claire's cancer. Had it truly been inevitable that she 'returned to God' so soon? If her cancer had been cured, would some other disease have claimed her?

Kayla had concluded that while we are all terminal, we will all die eventually, the concept of predetermined death was not one she could readily accept. Since then, every time someone close to her died, the old wound of Ralph's death was torn open in her again. Every time that happened, it left her devastated.

But she was also convinced of something else. People who sent death an open invitation were tempting fate.

She felt that way in the first terrible months after Ralph died, and she still did.

Had God called Claire Simpson to Him while she was in the prime of her life?

Would God do such a thing?

She refused to believe it. God simply did not micromanage to that extent.

Ralph's death could have been prevented if some doctor had found the problem with his heart valve in time. Claire would still be alive if her cancer had been diagnosed earlier. That was Kayla's simple down-to-earth reasoning, and she believed it passionately. Anything else was nonsense – superstitious, occult nonsense.

To make matters worse, Kayla thought she may be partly to blame for Ralph's death. If only she had made him get regular check-ups. She could have made him go see a doctor, who could have referred him to a specialist, and then . . .

And then Ralph would have lived and she would be married to him now. There would be no Jason in her life.

She sighed at the thought, not for the first time. Whatever the future consequences of her non-action, she could not deny that she had never insisted that he get a medical check-up. Because he had always appeared to be in such excellent health, she had taken his somber words with a grain of salt. More accurately, a shaker of salt.

She wasn't to blame, that much she understood, but still she felt somehow guilty. She could have done more, pure and simple. And she hadn't.

And now Jason. The photographs *were* enigmatic. His night-mares *were* troubling. The burning figure was simply terrifying and added a flavor of the occult that she despised. Ever since she had discovered the three photographs, she had been trapped inside a nightmare of her own. All she wanted was to wake up to the start of a new day, a bright blue day, without any of the darkness that had settled over her life. Was that really too much to ask?

She leaned against the kitchen counter, drained in body and soul.

Perhaps the day would look brighter after her run with Simone. Right now Canyon View felt more like a tomb than a home.

Kayla had gone out jogging with Simone, on a date that had been set some time ago. Getting her mind off things for a while would do her good, she had said, and Jason had agreed. After she left, he went back to researching what the mysterious words 'Mapeetaa' and 'Mawkee' could mean.

Absently, he recalled when their friend Rose Salladay had died. After the funeral Kayla hadn't left the house for weeks, and all his efforts to comfort her came to naught. One day, when he had tried to tell her that no matter how tragic Rose's death might have been she shouldn't let it get her down like this, Kayla had nearly gone berserk. 'You can't dictate how I should feel, Jason Evans!' she had screamed at him, just before hurling two porcelain teacups against the wall, shattering them. Ever since, Jason had trod carefully around the subject of death, and gradually he had come to understand what lay at the core of Kayla's angry reaction. Rose had only been thirty-three years old, and her death had been so *unfair*.

Jason drummed his fingers on the thick desk. Outside, through a window, he saw the peaks of the canyons tinged with a pleasing bluish-gray hue. His gaze roamed around the room to the luscious house plant, the only thing livening up the confined space. It had a complicated Latin name Jason couldn't remember, so he simply called it the reed plant.

Then he looked at his screen.

He typed: mawkee.

Several thousand hits for that word came up. He leafed through the pages. Mawkee was a name of someone from New York, an Arabic name, a river, a song by some band. He clicked some of the links, but found nothing that had any direct meaning for him.

He tried other spellings.

Next, he typed: mapitaa.

Google didn't recognize that word. Then: mapita

For that word he received 4,130 results, most of them on Spanish-language sites. He clicked through a few of them. Apparently Mapita was a mountainous area in Argentina and also a region in Spain. There was another Mapita in Guinea, and Google also found a pharmaceutical company by the same name.

Jason heaved a heavy sigh. He wasn't getting anywhere.

Mawkee. Mapeetaa. Mapitaa. Mapita. M.

What now?

The photographs were on the desk beside him. He picked them up and studied them intently, paying special attention to the last one delivered. He peered at the letter M like a magician staring at a top hat just before the rabbits come jumping out.

He was trying out all kinds of sounds even remotely similar to the word Mapeetaa. Suddenly he froze. Something was bubbling up from the depths of his subconscious mind.

It was *not* Mapeetaa.

Jason got up and paced around the study. Then he sat back down and typed out two words: mount peytha.

He hit 'enter' and received 200,000 hits that informed him about Mount Peytha City, a town in the desert of Arizona, on the state line with Nevada. He knew this town; he and Kayla had been near there just last year, on the way to Las Vegas and the Grand Canyon. It was halfway between Interstate 15 going toward Vegas and Interstate 40 going toward Flagstaff. They had skirted the town, deciding not to stop there. So Jason had never actually been there.

He clicked the first link, **mountpeythacity.com**, and the official site appeared on his screen. Information from local authorities, a link for tourism, the airport, panoramic shots of the surrounding area. He clicked through the site wondering, *Is this it?*

He felt a strong urge to go there, as if a voice inside his head was yelling at him that yes, this *was* the place.

M. Mawkee. Mapeetaa. Mount Peytha. They were not very much alike, although each word had phonetic similarities to the others.

He bit at his lower lip.

Mount Peytha City. What about it? What happened there?

Another part of his mind threw a bucket of ice water on his feverish thoughts.

Hang on, you've never been *to Mount Peytha City.*

No, he hadn't. He had heard of it, but that was all . . . or maybe when he'd been eighteen, the time he and Bill Hallerman had been partying in Utah. He had done other things besides partying – a pair of full, cherry-red lips belonging to some girl named Sonja flashed beguilingly in his mind. What had been her last name?

Jason tried to remember, to no avail. Probably just as well, she thought.

Maybe the first time he had ever noticed the name Mount Peytha City on a map had been during his holiday in Utah with Bill, although he was convinced he had never actually been to the town.

But now the name of the town was pulling at him, and he needed to go there. It took a conscious effort to not grab the car keys.

He gripped the armrests of his chair.

What's with *that place? What's* wrong *with you?*

He covered his face with his hands and desperately tried to create some semblance of order in his churning thoughts.

I need *to go to Mount Peytha City.*

The feeling remained. But why?

Because there's something I need to find there.

It seemed to make sense. He picked up his children's drawing again. The burning graves. The word 'Mapeetaa' on one of the headstones.

My God, is that where the cemetery is?

It was almost like an explosion inside his head. Until this moment he had thought the graveyard could be anywhere in the world.

But then a dose of common sense kicked in. Did he really think he knew? Or was he just *hoping* he knew? Or was he imagining things? He had no idea, just the feeling that he was a puppet whose strings were pulling him along in a maelstrom. Or maybe it was some kind of epiphany. What if . . .

What if he found the graveyard in Mount Peytha City? And the headstone depicted in the third photograph? One thought inevitably linked to another. In the Photoshop-less reality there could be a stone without an M, but with the name of the deceased. What was that name?

You are dead. You think you're alive, but you don't exist.

And that could indicate . . .

That my *name is on that headstone.*

The belief that he had touched upon a wondrous revelation left him as quick as it had arisen. He was back where he had started, because this was ridiculous. He was *alive*. And if it were up to him, he would stay that way for many more years.

Another explanation surfaced.

Jason let it come, very slowly, until it formed a clearer picture.

He took a deep breath, got up, crossed his arms and pressed them to his chest. He was experiencing terrible stomach cramps. He ran outside and leaned across the porch railing, retching. Slowly his nausea eased.

He stared up into a clear azure sky. Sunlight glittered in his eyes. He didn't avert his gaze but let himself be dazzled by the white sphere in the sky.

Suddenly Jason understood how he could have died.

NINETEEN
Plans

Kayla walked in the front door at four thirty. After a pleasant run with Simone, she had decided to stop by and visit her parents. She looked calmer than she had earlier in the day, and seemed more like her old self.

Jason had spent the last few hours in the kitchen, his favorite place indoors to think. Which is what he had been doing while grilling chicken, boiling potatoes and cutting up vegetables for a salad. When Kayla came in, he was just whipping up a chocolate surprise for dessert.

Her eyes lit up when she noticed his culinary creations. Her smile turned into a laugh when he proposed having a bath together before sitting down at the dining table.

'You're on, sailor,' she gushed.

He drew the bath and opened a bottle of wine. Not a cheap one this time, but a good Chablis, imported from France. After they had settled themselves in the steaming water, he raised his glass to her.

'Thank you,' she said. 'To what do I owe all this pampering?'

'To the fact that I love you.'

'I love you, too, Jason. But please tell me the *real* reason for this divine treat.' She held her wine glass in one hand and as she rubbed some flowery soap on her apple-shaped breasts and her shoulders and neck with her other hand, she sighed the way she did during other, more intimate moments.

'The real reason?' he said. As he sat there watching her ministrations, he felt the familiar stirrings in his loins. 'You think I have a hidden agenda?'

Her gaze wandered down his body. 'It's not so hidden any more, is it?' She looked up, smiling. 'I don't think anything, Jason. I *know* you have a hidden agenda. I know you that well.'

The last time he'd used this trick to get his way hadn't been long ago, when they had been unable to agree on where to travel for their vacation. She had wanted to explore the Cascade Mountains in Canada. He had preferred Utah. Their last bath and dinner session had decided that they would visit Utah this year, and Canada the following year. *Blackmail me all you want, but* that's *what we're going to do*, she had told him firmly.

'Am I that transparent to you?'

'I'm listening, Jason.'

He nodded and started talking. Calmly he told her about how he had thought of Mount Peytha City. Maybe he had been mistaken with that strange word 'Mapeetaa'. Although he had never been to Mount Peytha, he now felt a strong urge to visit the desert town. Maybe he would find something of value there.

'Like what?'

He cleared his throat. 'This Mapeetaa *didn't* just enter my mind out of the blue.'

Quietly, as if this were a small matter, he told Kayla about the drawing. She let him finish, but the expression on her face was not welcoming.

'In other words,' he concluded, 'it could be that Mapeetaa refers to Mount Peytha City, and that's where the cemetery with the headstone in the third photograph is located.'

She hit the edge of the tub with the flat of her hand; flakes of suds flew up.

'So now we have another new thing – this drawing. You're still a man with secrets, Jason Evans.'

'There was no reason to show you. It's not like it's cheerful for you to look at.'

'A cemetery in flames? No, thanks,' she sulked.

Jason wiped a streak of foam from his nose.

'But you're right of course,' he said. 'I need to put all my cards on the table. So that's what I'm doing.'

Kayla groaned. 'OK. Supposing, just supposing, you're right about Mount Peytha City. What do you think you'll find there?'

'Hopefully this particular grave, like I said.'

She leaned across to him and carefully placed her wine glass on the tile floor. For days now, he had missed the cheerful sparkle in her eyes that made her so irresistible to him.

'And what do you think is so important about that grave?'

Jason knew he was treading on thin ice. This was not a subject Kayla wanted to discuss. But he needed her support. He didn't want to proceed without her.

'If you read carefully what's written on the photographs,' he started cautiously, as if he were crossing a floor covered in glass splinters and any misstep would cause agony, 'then I may have an explanation. I could be wrong, but it's a possibility. If we don't think of something, we'll get nowhere. I *did* think of something. So please, keep an open mind and listen to me.'

'I'm listening,' she said in a steely voice.

'Past lives,' he said.

Her eyes went wide. When he remained silent, she said, 'Now *that's* pretty far-fetched.'

'Kayla, try to bear with me,' he continued. 'It's not unheard of in cases of pyrophobia. Believe me, in the last twenty years I've read quite a bit of material on phobias. I found more of those kinds of stories on the Internet today. One of them was about an eight-year-old boy who was afraid his house would burn down. In other words, my life story in a nutshell. This boy also got edgy whenever someone lit so much as a candle. But he underwent regression therapy, and during that therapy he went back to a past lifetime. In that life he was twelve, and he described a wooden house. One night he woke up and smelled smoke. The house was on fire. The boy, or the child he was then, tried to get out, but he couldn't. He was trapped and perished in the flames. After this session the boy knew where his anxieties had come from, and that made them go away.'

Jason paused.

'Another account involved the mother of a five-year-old son. He kept talking about "before, when he was big". The child, whose name was Tyler, said that he had been called Doyle "before" – meaning in another life. At some point, when his mother sat Tyler down and talked to him about it, he described a battlefield where men had shot his fellow soldiers.'

Jason gazed intently at Kayla.

'Tyler went down on his stomach and copied the stance of a soldier about to shoot a gun. He stretched back his left leg, drew up the right and said that he had his "finger around the ring", meaning the gun's trigger. After that he'd been "winged", or hit by a bullet. He had suffered a lot of pain, his heart had started racing, and his fear had almost choked him. Then the soldier had arrived, the one who had cut short his previous life. "I still had my finger around the ring, but this man came toward me. I wanted to move, but there was too much pain. He shot me, and then I was dead," Tyler said. When the mother asked him what happened after her son had taken his last breath, he cheered up. "Then I grew inside your belly and my heart started beating again".'

Jason took a sip of wine to lubricate his parched throat.

'Since Tyler could not supply dates and places, his mother went to see a regression expert. He thought Tyler could have been a soldier during a conflict on the Mexican border around the year 1880. Tyler, as Doyle, could have been part of a government force fighting a rebel army, but the superior strength of the rebels had been underestimated. His memories had left Tyler with certain anxieties. His mother said her son recoiled in fear if one person were to crawl toward another person in any sort of threatening way. This probably had to do with the way he had been killed when he was Doyle, she thought. Trapped there on the ground, terrified and in terrible pain, he could only lie there waiting for the final, inevitable shot.'

He looked at Kayla and said, 'Who knows, maybe it *is* that simple. If reincarnation is real – and there are billions of people who think it is – then we have the possibility that I lived in a previous life, and that maybe I died in a fire.'

Kayla rested her head on the edge of the tub as she blew suds off her hand.

'You don't really believe in these things, do you?' she asked at length.

'I never said that. I know that *you* don't believe in them.'

'You're right. Why do we need to start dragging in past lives? Who says there aren't other, perfectly down-to-earth factors at work here? What would a psychologist say about this? What would Mark say?'

'I asked you to keep your mind open to other possibilities.'

'Excuse me for being a skeptic and not accepting with open arms what I believe to be pure bullshit.'

'That's taking the easy way out, Kayla.'

'You're doing it, too.'

He bit his tongue. No fighting. He didn't want this to turn into an argument.

'I admit there's a hole in my theory,' he said.

She scowled at him. 'Do tell.'

'Without the photographs, we wouldn't be having this conversation. But how could the photographer know if I did have a past life? And how would he or she know the exact date of my death? That's impossible. I don't believe it for a second.'

'So, no past lives?' Kayla asked, with a hint of hope.

'I haven't finished yet.'

'Oh.'

She couldn't hide the disappointment in her voice.

'It's the only theory I have, and I'm not ready to throw it under the bus yet. I still want to go to Mount Peytha City. I have to see the place for myself.'

'I knew you'd want something from me,' she said.

He held his tongue, embarrassed.

She continued, 'You're going to ask me to come with you. And if you don't, or if you don't want me to come, that's almost like leaving me.'

'You're overreacting, Kayla. I'm not leaving you; that is the very last thing I would ever want. But yes, that is what I wanted to ask you. Come with me. Please?'

She glared at him. 'Do I have a choice? You're going, no matter what. And if I'm not there with you, I'll feel even worse.'

Kayla was silent for a moment, staring at the wall behind Jason's head.

'But I do have one condition.'

'Name it.'

'After Mount Peytha City, if the nightmares continue, you go back to Mark. But maybe they'll go away if you forget about this whole mess. They had gone, remember? They're back now only because of the photographs, right? I'd much prefer if you'd just sit tight and do nothing for a while. The photographer, whoever the bastard is, seems to have stopped what he was doing. Maybe you're right and this wasn't meant as a threat to your life. He's lying low, thank God, so we could do the same.'

'Sitting tight and doing nothing will get us nowhere, Kayla. Besides, maybe something *is* going to happen on August eighteenth.'

'Sometimes problems go away if you ignore them. You've told me so yourself, on more than one occasion.'

'You're calling the guns on to my own position,' he demurred.

'And what is our problem here?' she continued, unperturbed. 'Someone is saying you died. That's insane. Yet despite that, you want to set out to look for that cemetery . . .'

She peered up at the ceiling, as if the answer to the enigma resided up there. 'How can I explain this? I'm worried you might be sticking your hand into a hornets' nest, and that awful things will happen as a result. You might set something horrible in motion. Who knows? I want to get on with our lives. Just *move on*. Will you promise me you'll try that?'

'Of course, I'll try.'

'*Promise* me.'

'I . . .' He gazed into her blue eyes, begging him to please say yes.

'I promise,' he said.

She rested her head back against the edge of the tub, into the cloud of white suds. 'And you really haven't been to that town before?'

'No.'

'Well, I find all this very peculiar.'

'So do I,' he confessed.

'When do you want to go?'

'Soon. Not tomorrow, but the day after.'

'How should we arrange this with work?'

'We'll take off three days, but leave open the possibility that we'll need four days. That will give us the weekend if we need it.'

'You're in a hurry.'

'Kayla,' he started, more calmly than he felt, 'I just *can't* postpone this.'

She sighed. 'How long would this trip take?'

'Three days. One day to drive there, another day to look around, and then we drive back the third day. If we take the rest of the week off, that gives us Friday as a buffer, should we need it.'

Kayla eyed him cautiously. 'And that's the whole story? Have you been doing anything else this afternoon, besides concocting incredible theories and making me dinner?'

'Guilty as charged,' he admitted. 'I've been searching the Internet for information about Mount Peytha City. Apparently, it's a charming place. Lots of water sports. It's right by the Colorado River and Lake Mohave, and near Laughlin, Nevada. They call that place Little Las Vegas. And ah . . .' Jason coughed. 'It has one large graveyard. I have the address. I couldn't tell you what it looks like, because there's no website for it, and the undertaker couldn't paint me a clear picture.'

She straightened up abruptly. 'The *undertaker*?'

'Yes,' he said, gazing at her sheepishly. 'I'd meant to bring that up. This afternoon I called Cleigh Abbeville's Funeral Home. I found it in the Yellow Pages. I spoke to the funeral director and told him I was working on my family history, that my genealogic research had led me to Mount Peytha City, and that I was hoping to find the grave of a relative there. He left me with the impression that he gets those kinds of phone calls all the time.'

'Jason, stop beating around the bush,' Kayla admonished.

'OK,' he said. 'I've made an appointment to see him. He's expecting me – us – Wednesday morning at eleven.'

'Jeez, you really haven't been sitting still,' Kayla said wryly. 'Wednesday? That means that yes, we do need to leave here on Tuesday. What do you want to ask this man? What was his name again?'

'Cleigh. Chuck Cleigh. It's a family company. He said something about a son he's training. I'm not sure what I'm going to ask him. I think we should see the graveyard first. Maybe I shouldn't have called him until after we get there, but what's done is done.'

'And that's it?' she asked.

'Basically, yes.'

She nodded. 'So this may be over on Wednesday. You will have completed your investigation, and we can move on.'

As she said this, her body language spoke volumes. He put both hands on the edge of the bathtub.

'You don't believe a word of this, do you?'

She shook her head no.

'Listen,' he continued. 'It's possible I'm a long way from being done before August eighteenth. Maybe Mount Peytha is just the beginning. I could promise you all kinds of things, but I have only a few weeks to go, and no idea of what's in store for us. Kayla, I need your *support*, dammit.'

His last utterance had been too harsh, and he regretted it instantly.

Again she shook her head. 'I'll go with you, I'll support you, and I'll behave. But after our little escapade to this pit-hole of yours, this sort of nonsense is over and you're going back to Mark. Or you talk to the police, if any new threats arise. If you love me, listen to *me* for once.'

She spoke in a voice of granite, and Jason knew she meant it.

Kayla had drawn a line in the sand and if he crossed it, he would do so at his peril.

Then he had a thought, or maybe a little voice that spoke into his ear. It said he was going to lose her. He was going to lose everything he had.

He tried to silence the little voice.

He woke with a start and glanced at the glowing red numbers on the digital alarm clock – it was 2:12 a.m. His head was cluttered with hazy thoughts that collectively made no sense whatsoever. Beside him Kayla slept.

Jason got out of bed and sat down in his chair on the porch. When would he finally get another full night's sleep? It had been days. As the bouncing balls inside his head finally settled down, he gazed out into the balmy darkness, listening to the familiar sounds of the crickets and other creatures of the night.

Everything had changed. In Jason's mind, his old life was over. He was standing on the threshold of a new existence.

TWENTY
Mount Peytha City

T he drive was just shy of three hundred miles. The day before, on Monday, Kayla had arranged to take three, maybe four days off from work. For Jason it had been a little less comfortable, compliments of that wretched Tommy Jones campaign. He was forced to stand on his contractual right to use his allotted vacation days at his discretion. Enduring his boss's displeasure he accepted as part of the deal.

Interstates 10 and 15 took them to Interstate 40, straight through the hot, stifling Mojave Desert. After they passed by the town of Needles, it was only another twenty miles on Highway 59 to Mount Peytha City. They had lunch in a small town called Ludlow. Besides a rusty gas station and a small, ramshackle grocery store – with a sign out front proclaiming IF YOU DON'T SHOP HERE, WE BOTH LOSE MONEY! – Ludlow featured a Wendy's, a Kentucky Fried Chicken and the Desert Rest Steakhouse. Kayla and Jason opted for the steakhouse. After their meal they got back into the car and drove on across a shimmering tarmac past sun-bleached land with desert sand, dry shrubs and cactuses, waving reed grass, blown-out truck tires, garbage dumps and one trailer park after another clinging to both sides of the road.

'What have you discovered about Mount Peytha City on the Web?' Kayla asked.

'It was founded in the nineteenth century by an eccentric pioneer named David Laurel,' Jason explained. 'He started a postal service and stuck his nose into everything. For that reason the locals started calling the place Laurelville, much to David's satisfaction.'

'Modest man,' she remarked.

'You might say that. In those days, Laurelville was popular mainly with prospectors,' Jason continued. 'Apparently there are quite a few abandoned gold mines around the area. But the good times didn't last. What little gold there was played out, forcing the prospectors to move on to other stakes. With them went the town's lifeblood. Laurelville became a ghost town. That was around the start of the twentieth century. Coincidentally, the old cemetery is the only thing remaining of Laurelville. And that old cemetery abuts the new one.'

'Sounds cozy. Nice place for a wedding trip.'

'For tumbleweeds, maybe.' Jason chuckled at his turn of phrase, then continued. 'Eventually, Laurelville got back on the map as Mount Peytha City, thanks to a dam that was built in Lake Mohave. They started building it in 1942, but then construction was delayed for a few years during World War II. It took until 1953 to finish it. For half a century . . .'

At those words an icy claw seemed to wrap itself around Jason's throat, and his breath faltered.

For half a century Laurelville had been dead, only thinking it was alive. But it no longer existed. After those fifty years, Laurelville reincarnated and became known as Mount Peytha City.

'Jason?' Kayla asked. 'Is something wrong?'

'No,' Jason said, recovering. 'Half a century later,' he continued, 'they built the new town, named after, you guessed it, the highest peak in the mountain range there. At first it was just a village. But by 1980, twenty thousand people lived there; today that number is closer to forty thousand. According to information on the Internet, the city council is planning on a hundred thousand residents in another fifteen years. They hope to achieve such rapid growth by stressing tourism and leisure in their promotional campaigns. More importantly, they hope to benefit from the Laughlin casino resort, located a few miles away across the Nevada state line. That seems a sure bet.'

'Cute. Pun intended?'

'Yes, of course.' He smiled across at her.

'Go on.'

Jason cleared his throat. 'Laughlin was also named after its founder, who passed over the area in his private plane twenty years ago and thought it would be a perfect place to start a gambling casino. He started out with a small hotel, and now the town boasts eleven casinos. Laughlin is also the reason why Mount Peytha City has an airport. Most of the planes landing and departing from there are casino flights.'

'So the fortune hunters of the past have returned, in a way,' Kayla observed. 'Except that these modern-day fortune seekers are more content with a one-armed bandit than a pan scraping a river bed for gold nuggets.'

'You could put it like that,' Jason said. 'It's also one of the hottest places in the United States. In the summer the temperature soars well above a hundred degrees every day. Even in the winter it's in the sixties or seventies. That's why more and more snow birds from up north fly there in the winter.'

'It's mainly a tourist place, you said. So what's a fun thing to do around there? Watch the cactus grow?'

'You don't give up, do you?' he said, grinning. 'Actually, there are all sorts of things to do.'

'Such as?'

'Hikes in the mountains, trips to the old mines. Rodeos, water sports, that kind of thing. The scenery is supposed to be amazing, and it offers fun activities for all ages. Even for skeptical Kaylas.'

'You know, you should consider a career in advertising,' she said.

He glanced askance at her, grinning. She was finally cracking some jokes, however cynical they might be. But then again, he hadn't been the most cheerful of people during these past few days.

'I forgot to mention that you can also take a ride on an old-fashioned riverboat,' he told her. 'You know, the ones with the big wheel on the side or at the stern. Mount Peytha City is a great place to fish, and it has so many festive events I wouldn't know where to start. To many people, it's a version of paradise.'

And I'm going there to visit a graveyard.

The smile slipped from his face. Kayla noticed the transition and fell silent as they drove on. No doubt, Jason mused, she was thinking along the same lines.

It was late afternoon when they left Highway 59 and drove into Mount Peytha City. The silvery blue Colorado River, which had enhanced their view for many miles, disappeared from view. In the near distance they saw rows of stiff bushy trees and palm trees beside the road, and in the far distance the hiking, climbing and mountaineering Mecca of the Table Mountains. As they approached the town they were surrounded by buildings with gardens that appeared to be well tended and well watered. Mount Peytha was a town of white bungalows, white luxury mansions and smaller white homes on the cheaper end of the local real estate market.

'So? Do you recognize anything?' Kayla asked.

He looked around and shook his head. 'No.'

'You haven't been here before?'

'No, and I'd swear on a stack of Bibles I haven't.'

'Couldn't there be some *other* reason why you wanted to come here, apart from that inner urge you felt? Maybe because you read about the place? Or because someone may have told you about it?'

Jason shrugged. 'Sure, it's possible that I talked to someone who mentioned this town. But as far as I know, this is the first time I've ever been here.'

'And how does it affect you?'

'It doesn't affect me at all, really. Not yet, anyway.'

First on their 'to do' list was to find a motel. It didn't take long to select the Mount Peytha Inn, a seemingly standard Holiday Inn type motel situated close to the highway. They got out of the air-conditioned Chrysler, walked a few paces through a wall of blistering heat, and entered the lobby. The bored receptionist, a skinny young Hispanic man, kept glancing up at a talk show emanating from a small television set mounted high up in a corner even as he watched Jason fill out a guest registration form. He groped for a set of keys on the board behind him and assigned them room number nine. A few moments later, Jason and Kayla set down their luggage in a room that was spacious and surprisingly clean and odor-free.

'What do we do now?'

'Take a shower,' he suggested.

'I agree. But after we do, we'll still have a couple of hours of daylight left. We have to meet with that undertaker in the morning, but before then, we'll have a look at this graveyard. Were you planning to go see it this afternoon, or tomorrow before our meeting with Cleigh?'

He scratched behind an ear. 'I don't want to make all the decisions here and exclude you. What do *you* want to do?'

Kayla planted her hands on her hips. 'Coming here was your idea, Jason Evans, so don't start . . .'

She flicked a hand dismissively. 'Never mind. The last thing I want is to be at each other's throats. If you ask me, we should drive to the cemetery right away and get it over with.'

'Then that's what we'll do,' he said. 'But I'll have to ask for directions. All I have is the address. I bet that guy at the reception desk knows where it is.'

'Then I suggest you hit the shower and go ask him. I'll freshen up in the meantime.'

Jason took a quick shower and then asked the receptionist for the easiest way to St James Cemetery. He also asked for directions to Cleigh Abbeville's Funeral Home. The skinny young man frowned when Jason asked that but didn't ask questions.

Back inside their room, as he waited for Kayla to emerge from the bathroom, he began feeling nervous. Most likely it was because they were really in Mount Peytha City now and would soon be on their way to the graveyard.

What if St James turned out to be the same cemetery as in the Polaroid photographs?

He took a moment to digest that question.

If that were true, he definitely would be on the road to discovering the truth.

But do I want to know the truth?

How odd, he thought, that he should start having doubts now. He remembered Kayla's assertion that they just forget the whole thing.

But I have to go on, don't I? Is there even a way back?

Jason took the three photographs from the little black folder and reviewed them once again. They didn't tell him anything he didn't already know.

TWENTY-ONE
St James Cemetery

Kayla came out of the bathroom, her hair hanging wet across her shoulders. She was wearing a sleeveless white shirt and a knee-length brown skirt. Her Ray-Bans dangled from her hand as she followed Jason outside.

As they drove through the center of town Jason noticed pedestrians hurrying this way and that, intent on their final shopping of the day. Then they passed a long row of market stalls selling postcards, maps, photo books and knick-knacks – decks of cards, mini slot machines for children, but also lumps of fake gold and even charcoal-gray pans similar to the ones gold-diggers of an earlier era had used to fish nuggets of precious gems from local rivers.

Despite the heat of the sun diminishing a little, the full blast of the Chrysler's air-conditioner still felt good.

Up ahead a mall with multiple levels of shops and restaurants confirmed that tourism lay at the commercial heart of this desert town.

They left the shops and tourists behind as they drove out of town toward St James Cemetery, following the directions given to them by the hotel clerk. A square black sign with raised gold lettering spelled out the name of the burial site. Behind the sign was a parking lot, and behind that a row of olive trees. In between, a narrow concrete path led into the cemetery.

Jason eased the car to a stop and switched off the ignition. 'Here we are.'

'Right,' Kayla said. 'Well, no point in dilly-dallying, right? Let's go take a look.'

They got out and started walking toward the path. Behind the olive trees they spotted a wide vista of graves. The sight of them sent a shiver down Jason's spine.

Within minutes he spotted the pyramid-shaped structure, splendidly displayed in the setting sun, not fifty yards away. As if this was not evidence enough, he also recognized the same row of small trees, the same gravestones and the same tall grass depicted in the photographs.

Overcome by a feeling he could not describe, he nonetheless knew now what was giving him shivers.

I'm here because I knew. *I found it inside myself.*

At the core of it was that he hadn't needed anybody's help to find the cemetery depicted in the photos; he already had the knowledge programmed in his brain. What that meant, he could not determine. But at the moment he was too excited to give it much thought.

He strode rapidly over to the pyramid, with Kayla following close behind. When he reached it, he saw an inscription in the dark marble that read IN HONOR OF THOSE WHO HAVE GONE BEFORE US. Apparently, this was not a tomb, but a monument. Beside it were benches not visible in the photograph. Jason slowly circled the pyramid until he could no longer see the benches, and then stopped.

He was looking at the real-life version of the second photograph and was struggling to comprehend it.

Where's the gate?

He couldn't see it, and the entrance they had used to get here looked nothing like the gate in the first photograph he had received. He would worry about that later. Something else was intriguing him. 'Where's the grave?' Jason asked aloud. 'Where *is* it?'

He slid the third photograph out of the folder.

The superimposed letter M stood out on a smooth background of gray stone.

Dammit, it's a message, a cryptic key, a code.

The grave he was looking for had to be here, close by.

So close.

Jason walked farther into the cemetery. Between the bushes were row after row of headstones and crosses, some of them elaborately decorated. Stone angels, engraved flowers, a taller tomb with stately columns here and there. Kayla looked tense, like a child in the doctor's office waiting for a flu shot. Graveyards scared her – to death she had once claimed, not in humor. But she didn't say anything or complain. She just stood there, quietly watching her husband.

Walking slowly, his gaze shifting back and forth between the graves he saw and the grave profiled in the third photo. With mounting despair he wondered how he would be able to recognize the headstone. They all looked the same and they were all made of the same sandstone.

Underneath the big letter M in the photo were irregularities, lichen and a few cracks. But these signs of erosion were visible on most of the hundreds of headstones at St James Cemetery. How Jason wished the photograph had revealed a name and not just a cut-out. It didn't offer any help or clues. Without a larger picture of the grave marker, it was an impossible task to find the stone he was seeking.

Kayla joined him and they walked past a row of five seemingly identical headstones.

Jason knelt down and, against his better judgment, examined the stones to see if they had the same traces of erosion as the headstone in the photograph. In no time he sensed the futility of comparing the picture to this grave, where a man named Douglas Weber was buried. On the next one were inscribed the names of Ellen and Sonni Bolch. The next grave was the final resting place of an individual named Lynell Hansen.

Jason carefully checked grave after grave. He was not a man to quit easily; he kept after things. But this nut was too tough to crack. Still he continued on scrutinizing headstone after headstone, because he felt he needed to do *something*. This was like looking for the proverbial needle in a haystack, but he couldn't help himself.

The cemetery in the photograph may no longer be a mystery, but the grave site was, and if they couldn't find it their trip here would have been for naught.

Kayla followed him aimlessly until she decided to take off in another direction to inspect some graves on her own. She was probably questioning the point of this exercise, Jason thought to himself, and who could blame her?

Don't give up hope, his thoughts insisted. *Don't give up*.

Dusk was setting in. Soon he would be forced to give up.

As he knelt down before the grave of James Weiss, he felt a headache coming on and paused to massage his temples.

Then, suddenly, the gravestone tore open. Jets of flame broke from the ground, and inside the flames a skeleton rose up with fire in its empty, hollow sockets. A sputtering orange-yellow glow enveloped its bones.

'Come here,' the skeleton said in a harsh, grating voice. 'Come to me, Jason, come to me!'

He stared at the burning specter that seemed to be cruelly grinning at him. James Weiss, or whatever this was, leaned toward him and tried to grab him.

Jason scrambled back, closed his eyes, shook his head to drive out the demons, and then opened his eyes. The gravestone was just a stone. It hadn't cracked open; there was no fire raging from the grave, no skeleton.

'Jesus,' he mumbled. 'Jesus, what the hell was *that*?'

'What's up?' Kayla called to him from a distance.

He was trembling as if he had been shocked by a live electrical wire.

'Nothing,' he responded. 'I hope.'

Or maybe I am going out of my mind, like Noam Morain.

And if he was sound of mind, what in God's name had he just seen?

Nothing, not a thing, just a hallucination. Brought on by the severe stress you've been experiencing. Stress can make you see things that aren't there, that's all.

Could be. He prayed that was the case and that the ghosts inside his head would leave him be.

They remained in St James Cemetery until the last of the sunset glow had disappeared beneath the horizon. It had been less than two hours since he had found out with a mixture of amazement and excitement that they had come to the right place. But now he felt disappointment.

They hadn't found the grave they were searching for. And they might have walked right past it, unknowingly, without any chance of ever realizing.

'I think we should go, Kayla,' he said dejectedly. 'There is nothing more we can accomplish here.'

'I agree,' she said.

They drove back to town and ate at a steak restaurant. Kayla was first to break their silence. 'Jason, we've come this far. Don't give up now.'

He looked at her in surprise. If it had been up to her, they would not have come here in the first place. He knew how much she hated death and, consequently, graveyards. They were looking for an actual grave, perhaps even one with his name on it – if his theory about past lives possessed an inkling of truth. And now she was setting aside her misgivings to make him feel better.

'It's sweet of you to say that.' He searched her face, looking for clues. 'How are you coping?'

'Don't know,' she said in a small voice. 'It's scary, and the longer it goes on the less sense it seems to make.'

She glanced briefly at an obese man who got up from the table beside theirs. He strolled past, bade a jovial goodnight to the waitress, and padded out the door.

That same waitress brought them their steaks and wished them *bon appétit*. Jason picked up his knife and fork and started eating – and musing.

Maybe the Polaroid photographer was the only one who could tell him the location of the grave he was seeking. It had to be somewhere in St James Cemetery.

So close. And yet still so far away.

TWENTY-TWO

Chuck

The doorbell at the funeral home was answered by a lanky kid dressed in a pair of knee-high shorts and a loud shirt a few sizes too big for his frame. Jason introduced Kayla and himself and said he had an appointment with Chuck Cleigh. The boy nodded, invited them in and went to get Chuck.

Moments later a man in his fifties appeared, dressed in jeans and a dazzling white shirt.

'Good morning. I'm Chuck Cleigh,' he greeted them.

Jason offered his hand. 'I'm Jason Evans. This is my wife, Kayla. Thanks for seeing us.'

Cleigh shook hands with them both and then gestured for them to enter the parlor, a room with darkly tiled floors and walls, candelabras and candles, befitting the solemn ambience of a funeral home. From there Chuck led them to a small office through one of the side doors. In the office stood a desk and a filing cabinet. On the wall behind the desk Jason noted an abstract painting of crooked lines in yellow, red, green and black that hurt his eyes just to look at it. Cleigh offered them chairs and then sat down behind his desk.

'How may I help you?' he asked cordially.

Jason repeated what he had said before, that he was here because of his genealogical research. Last night and this morning he had thought hard about what he could ask Cleigh, but he hadn't come up with much. He could ask the man for a list of those deceased whose last names started with the letter M. But that was pointless – it would yield dozens of names, perhaps hundreds, and there was no assurance that any of those names would provide a clue to this mystery.

He had two other names he could put before Chuck: 'Mapeetaa' and 'Mawkee'. It was probably pointless, because they seemed to refer to Mount Peytha City and St James Cemetery, not to a deceased person. But he had nothing to lose.

Somewhat sheepishly he asked the funeral home director if there were any graves with either of those names inscribed on them. Chuck checked his computer and opened a few files. After scrolling through them for a few minutes, he shook his head.

'Nothing. Nothing at all, I'm afraid.'

What now? Jason wondered. He was here with Kayla, and he didn't want to get back in the car and leave. He felt he had to at least ask the man another question. And he had one. Or two, really, but they didn't matter much; neither of them was important and he only needed them for backup to avoid looking like a complete moron.

He showed Cleigh the second photograph with the marble structure. He placed it on the desk and kept his finger pressed down on it. He didn't want Cleigh to pick it up and see what was written on the back.

'This pyramid . . . what is it?'

'Ah, yes,' Chuck said, recognizing it. 'A memorial for a cemetery that used to be here, in the days of the early settlers. We're rather proud of it.'

'I see,' Jason said.

Then he showed the undertaker the first picture with the gate, a different gate from the one he and Kayla had opened the day before.

'North Gate,' Chuck commented after only a cursory glance at the photo.

Jason gave him a quizzical look.

'The northern entrance to the burial site,' Chuck explained. 'Visitors arriving from Chloride Pass often use it. It's about a quarter mile past Pete's Ranch.'

After that clarification, what passed for a conversation summarily ended. Jason stuck to his lie and said that he was 'glad to have found the right cemetery' since the details of it tallied with his research. That was important, because it gave him more to go on, he claimed. Chuck asked if there were any graves in particular he hoped to find at St James's; he might be able to assist in the effort since he had a comprehensive list of all the graves. Jason sensed that the offer was extended out of courtesy, and that the man had no real interest in helping them. Jason thanked him anyway, and said that he might take Cleigh up on his kind offer at some later time.

He and Kayla said goodbye and walked back outside. They left Chuck scratching the nape of his neck, probably wondering why these two people had driven all the way from Los Angeles to ask such vague questions. That is, if he cared at all.

Getting to North Gate involved a three-mile detour. Jason's sense of direction told him they were driving in a wide arc around the graveyard. On Chloride Pass Road they passed a wooden sign that said PETE'S RANCH and then another one a little farther on that said ST JAMES CEMETERY. Soon they reached the entrance Cleigh had mentioned.

Jason stopped the car, peered at the gate, and saw the first photograph.

Beyond the gate he saw a narrow path leading to the graves. He walked into the cemetery and discovered why they hadn't seen North Gate the day before. The second entrance was hidden among the greenery surrounding the entire graveyard.

Now what? He could walk past the graves and look at them one by one, as he had yesterday, and hope to miraculously stumble upon something, even if it was only a small, seemingly meaningless detail that he would recognize from the third photograph. But that plan was bound to fail, just as it had the day before.

Breaking the 'code' seemed to be his only hope.

Could the M be a very specific message after all?

But he had already deciphered the letter M, he reminded himself. It represented Mount Peytha City, and together the three Polaroid photos had served as signposts leading him toward this cemetery.

What if I've overlooked something?

He reviewed everything in his mind yet again. His life during the last four years had been normal, without nightmares – he had convinced himself that he had left all this misery behind him. Receiving the three photographs had convinced him that he was living an illusion. Then a door had opened inside his mind and he had remembered 'Mapeetaa', which had directed him to Mount Peytha. But here was where he appeared to have run out of road.

I must have missed a clue somewhere.

Yes, that had to be it. Whatever the photographer wanted, he wouldn't steer Jason toward this cemetery if there was no chance of finding the grave in question. So there had to be more clues hidden inside the messages.

The pictures had depicted a destination; the messages printed on the backs were directed at him personally. Literally speaking, they said that he was dead and buried in this cemetery, beneath the headstone in the last photograph.

And that headstone had a date on it: August eighteenth.

That was what he needed to search for; a date, not names.

'What are you brooding about now?' Kayla asked.

'Maybe our friend did take a picture of my grave after all,' he said casually. He shouldn't have said it – it was, in fact, the worst thing he could have said – but it had popped out of his mouth before he could help himself.

They had arrived back at the memorial.

Kayla sat down on a bench. He sat beside her and put an arm around her shoulders. She avoided his eyes.

'Here's what I don't like,' she said icily. 'In fact, there are several things I don't like. The first is that you're calling this psychopath your "friend".'

'I was being flippant. It was meant as a joke.'

'What is worse to me,' she continued, ignoring him, 'did you listen to yourself just now? Did you hear what you said? You're talking about your own grave, as though that is the most natural thing to discuss. I love you, Jason, I truly do. And I want to help you. But if you're going to start with *that*—'

'I didn't mean it like that,' he interrupted.

'Then what *did* you mean?'

'I . . .'

He wanted to explain that it had simply been a thought but, confused by her caustic response, he couldn't find the right words.

'Forget I said anything, Kayla. It was nonsense, I shouldn't have said it.'

'No, you shouldn't have,' she said, her voice rising in anger. 'And I don't want you to talk about it any more, do you hear me? Don't ever talk to me about your own death. Not ever. I don't want to hear it!'

'Kayla . . .'

She buried her face in her hands. He heard her sob and then she said, quietly, 'You . . . bad things might happen and then . . . and then I'll lose you too.'

He knew whom she was talking about and that was why she couldn't come to terms with what he was doing now.

I'm not Ralph, honey. I don't know who I am, but I'm not Ralph.

He was afraid of fire; she, in turn, was afraid of death. Her cup had slowly filled, and it had finally reached the tipping point. The last drop had been his careless, thoughtless remark.

Kayla was fearful and her fear made her angry. He had no doubt that she loved him. But no doubt he was making her life pretty damn miserable with this quest of his. Had there been an easier way to do this, he would have jumped at it. But unfortunately there was no other way.

'What do you say we go back to the motel?' he suggested.

'Yes. I want nothing more than to get the hell out of here.'

In their motel room, Kayla lay down on the bed, but Jason was too restless to join her. She hadn't said a word to him during the drive back. Kayla's mind was on Ralph, he suspected; the memories of losing him were probably replaying in her mind's eye for the thousandth time. Ralph, who had died so unexpectedly during a hike, and most likely she had been alone with his dead body for hours before help finally arrived.

'Kayla . . .' he said gently. 'What can I do for you?'

'Nothing,' she mumbled.

'Listen, I know this brings back memories—'

'No!' she cried, turning her back to him and burying her face in the pillow. 'Go away! Leave me alone!'

She was at once both angry and despondent. His heart wrenched as he sat there, staring at her shaking shoulders. He caressed her wavy black hair carefully with a finger, listening to her wretched sobs. Nothing he could say could ease her pain. Eventually he walked out of the room, exchanging the cool air-conditioned room for the oppressive oven outside. He sat on the curb, fished his sunglasses from his shirt pocket, and put them on, idly watching a Land Rover drive into the parking lot. A rotund man got out of the car, his head covered by a large black Western-style hat. With a brown briefcase tucked under his arm, the man disappeared into the reception building. In the distance, Jason could hear the muted sounds of the highway. The desiccated leaves of the palm trees, on either side of the dusty neon welcome sign for the Mount Peytha Inn, hung limply in the sizzling desert heat.

Would he sit here until she had cried herself out? He had seen her like this before; this wasn't her first crisis. Previous occasions had taught him that efforts to comfort her would do no good. Kayla Evans, formerly Sheehan, was normally a lively, cheerful woman. But if she were having problems, it was best to steer clear.

He had sometimes wondered whether Kayla had loved Ralph more than him. He didn't think so – he didn't *want* to believe it – but he knew he would never have married her if Ralph Grainger had lived.

The source of Kayla's fear was obvious, but the seed of his pyrophobia was still an enigma. Convinced he needed to dig deeper into his psyche, Jason knew that he would soon go back to Mark Hall for another hypnosis session – or two, or three, or however many it took.

But now he was here, in Mount Peytha City. Mark's couch was three hundred miles away.

What in God's name has this photographer done to me? I'm walking around thinking I had a previous life that may have ended

in a fire on August eighteenth. I get this urge to go to Mount Peytha
City and find St James Cemetery. Is this where I was buried?

In a previous life he would have had a different name. Maybe a
name starting with an M.

All this was guesswork, of course. Suddenly he realized he had
something more substantive to delve into. Which individuals buried
in the Mount Peytha cemetery had died on August eighteenth?

That's what he should have asked Chuck. How could he have
been so stupid that he had never thought of this before? On the
other hand, there was a simple explanation. Being very much alive,
searching for your own grave was not something you did as a matter
of course, even though this obsession had controlled his life for the
past two weeks.

Quickly he made up his mind.

I'm going to ask Chuck. Right now.

Twenty minutes later the beanpole young man at the funeral home
answered the door. Jason wondered what the boy's name was and
whether he was the son that Chuck was training to some day take
over the business.

The young man led him to Chuck's office, who glanced up from
a stack of paperwork, his surprise clearly registered on his face.

'I was hoping I might ask you one more question,' Jason said
before Chuck could object.

'Go ahead.'

'It relates to my research into my family tree. I've gone over it
and I think that the person involved may have died on August
eighteenth. Mr Cleigh, would you mind checking that for me?'

Chuck frowned.

'It's not as easy as that. I would have to review all of the names
one by one. Have you any idea how many thousands of graves we
have here? It would take hours.'

'I understand that,' Jason said quickly. 'I would be willing to go
over the lists myself. I do not want to inconvenience you.'

Chuck shook his head. 'I can't give you access to our files.
Company policy.'

'Oh,' Jason said, dismayed.

Reluctantly, Chuck continued, 'Tim, my son, has some spare
time. I'll have him work on it. He needs to become more familiar

with the files in any event. If you leave your phone number, we'll call you back.'

Now Jason knew the name of the boy who had opened the door for him.

'Thank you,' he said softly. 'I would of course expect to pay Tim for his time.'

Chuck nodded and folded his hands. 'That's it?'

Yes, that was it. Unless . . .

The most morbid thought of all kept gnawing at him, like a crushing headache that refused to go away no matter how many aspirin he swallowed.

'It may be,' he started, 'that the deceased is a namesake of mine. Mr Cleigh, just one more question: *is* there a grave with the name Jason Evans on it?'

Chuck sighed and invested a few minutes peering intently at his computer screen. Jason, on the other side of the desk, felt an urge to get up and peek over the man's shoulder. But he held himself in check and remained seated.

'We have five by that name,' Cleigh said.

'*Five?*'

Chuck shook his head. 'Five people named "Evans". Not one of them is named Jason. The first one is Zack, died March sixth, 1988. Then there's Greg, June twelfth, '76. Elizabeth, died November twenty-eighth, '97. Then a Sam, first of July 1970. And finally Jeff Evans . . . date of death December twenty-fifth, 2005. Are any of them related to you?'

'No,' Jason said.

Of *course* there was no Jason Evans buried here. If there had been, it would only have been a coincidence.

He rose. 'I'll wait for your phone call, then. Again, I'm very grateful that Tim can take the time to do this research for me.'

'We aim to please,' Chuck said primly.

TWENTY-THREE
Funeral

Kayla was sitting on the short white wall beside the motel sign, in the shade of a date palm tree. She watched as he parked his car and walked up to her. When he kissed her on the lips, she responded, signaling to him that her anger had cooled.

'How are you feeling?' he asked her tenderly.

'Better,' she said less than enthusiastically.

'I should have kept my mouth shut at the cemetery.'

But I did go over to the funeral home to ask Chuck Cleigh about a grave with my name on it.

'What have you been up to?' she asked.

'Just walking around a bit,' he said evasively. 'Trying to sort things out. I did ask Chuck to do some digging for me. So we'll have to wait and see now.'

He was becoming increasingly concerned about the distance between him and Kayla. Neither of them said anything about it; they didn't have to. He could feel the gap widening and deepening, and it sickened him.

It was entirely his fault. He was dragging her along on a quest she detested and wanted no part of. Just a couple of weeks ago they had been overjoyed about their decision to start a family. But since then, all that he had been thinking about was death and misery. He had talked her into coming with him on this trip, and she was too loyal and loving a wife to refuse him.

You're a jerk, you know that? She deserves better.

Still, what else could he have done? Ignore all this? What good would that do? For them to rediscover the joy they once shared, he needed to solve this mystery. And he felt he had to solve it before August eighteenth, a day that was fast approaching.

At seven they went to The Wagon, a real-life covered wagon turned into a bar in which bottles of whiskey, vodka and other spirits held court in the center of the restaurant. Around it, in a circle, were dining tables.

Jason's gaze traveled around the room. A heavyset man with a felt hat sitting at the table in front of theirs was visibly enjoying a juicy steak. His knife and fork tingled rhythmically against his plate. He was eating noisily and had eyes only for his dinner. At the table beside his, a waitress served glasses of ice-cold beer to two men who could be father and son. They were laughing. The older man smacked the younger on his back with a hand covered with what looked to be calluses formed by decades of hard work on the range.

The three men, seated side by side in a row, had each found their own way through life. They seemed content. Until recently, Jason had been more than content. He had what he believed was the perfect life. Now everything had been turned upside-down. He prayed it was only temporary.

'Jason?' Kayla said. 'What about Chuck? Has he come up with anything?'

'Chuck hasn't called back yet,' he answered forthrightly. 'Apparently his son didn't have so much time on his hands that he could check the list right away. Maybe we should go back to the cemetery tomorrow and start looking for graves with August eighteenth on them. Who knows, we might get lucky. What else can we do?'

His voice held little hope. Nor did his heart.

'And if that leads nowhere?'

Kayla's words held an uncharacteristic coldness, a reminder of Carla and Tracy that made him blink. Trace had been an alcoholic, and all Carla was concerned about was herself. Now he, Jason, was only thinking of himself, working on a mystery that had morphed into an addiction.

Jason reached out and placed the palm of his hand against the softness of her cheek. 'If we can't find it, and if Chuck can't help us,' he said, 'we're going home. And then I'm going to forget the whole thing.'

Did he believe that? Did she?

That night proved to be a restless one. Sleep came easily to neither of them. They still had their loving bond, but fear was gnawing away at it. His search was increasing hurtful to her. She supported him because she loved him. But how much longer could she offer her support?

Time was growing short. More keenly than before, he feared he might lose her over this.

That he could not bear to even *think* about.

Next morning they went out for a cup of coffee before paying another visit to St James Cemetery. As they walked toward the town center, Patrick Voight called Kayla on her cell phone. He wanted to know whether she would be back for work tomorrow. On Monday she had told him she would probably be gone for three days, maybe four, and Patrick hadn't heard from her. Kayla threw an inquisitive glance at Jason. What she desperately wanted was for him to say: *OK, this is it, we're going home and we'll let the police handle it from here on.*

'Just a little while longer,' he whispered.

'Patrick?' Kayla said, keeping her eyes on Jason. 'We're still in Arizona. The soonest we'll be able to leave is tomorrow. I'll be back at work on Monday.'

Voight complained that she was leaving him in the lurch by staying away this long a week before she was due to leave for vacation. Kayla apologized and told him she understood, but unfortunately she had no choice in the matter.

After she hung up, Jason grabbed his cell phone. He had remembered an appointment he had made with Mark for tomorrow. He had to cancel, and he would do so in a minute. But first he had to make a less pleasant phone call to his own boss. Brian had already been upset because he had gone out of town on such short notice, and he would be angrier still when he heard that the head of the Tommy Jones team wouldn't be back in the office until Monday – even though Jason had told him that would likely be the case. Before speaking to Brian, he spoke to Tony, Donald and Carol. Then he spoke to Brian, who told him straight out that he was expecting Jason to show up for work as soon as possible, before he dropped the dreaded and hated words 'Tommy Jones'. Jason told him that something had come up, he realized it was a terrible inconvenience, but he would return to Los Angeles this weekend and be back at work at Tanner & Preston on Monday.

'Jason, you're making me very unhappy,' Brian protested. Today he sounded as unhappy as when he'd griped about his wife Louise backing out on their planned trip to Las Vegas. That had been one day after George, the mailman at Tanner & Preston, had handed Jason the first Polaroid photograph, the first in a series of three that had turned his life into chaos and that now prevented him from fulfilling his contractual obligation to the Automobile King.

Brian, if only you knew what a macabre world I'm living in, Jason thought bitterly.

'I'll work evenings next week,' Jason promised. 'We'll get the job done.'

'Jesus, Jason, what the hell are you up to out there?'

Trying to find myself, Jason thought, and then had to bite his hand to keep himself from laughing out loud.

'I'll tell you about it later.'

Brian hung up on him without another word.

'What's next, Jason?' Kayla asked.

They were approaching a Starbucks. 'Coffee, that's what's next.'

Jason forgot to cancel his appointment with Mark.

They drank their coffee watching people passing by outside. It was ten thirty.

'Do you think that maybe he lives here?' Jason mused.

'Who?' Kayla asked.

'The photographer. If this city is the focus of this mystery, he is likely someone who knows a lot about Mount Peytha. Could be he lives here.'

Kayla drew a lock of hair from her eyes and tucked it behind her ear. 'Sure,' she chuckled, not in humor. 'Maybe he's watching us, maybe even stalking us. Hey, who knows, maybe it's that slacker of a motel receptionist. Or some guy we met in the street.'

'OK,' he sighed. 'Point taken. It could be anyone, or it could be no one.'

'Since we don't know what we're looking for,' she concluded, 'there's no chance of finding it.'

'That's deep,' he said. 'Unfortunately, you happen to be right.'

He studied grave after grave, walking up one lane and down another. The only clue he was seeking was the date the deceased had passed on to the afterlife. After sweating in the searing sun for ninety minutes, he had not found a single grave inscribed with the date August eighteenth. But there had to be a few, at least. As Chuck had said, there were thousands of graves here, and there were only 365 days in a year. Statistically, there *had* to be multiple grave sites bearing that date.

The heat of the day intensified and the sunlight became ever more blinding, perhaps preventing him from seeing something horrible, such as someone hiding behind a gravestone. Possibly the photographer.

Kayla was first to come across something. 'Jason!' she suddenly called from a distance, gesturing to him with both arms. He ran over to her.

He looked at what she was pointing at: the grave of a man named Donald Luke. The clear lettering and numbers indicated that he was born on March twelfth, 1931 and died on August eighteenth, 2004.

Jason crouched down. He felt no excitement. The name Donald Luke had no M in it. Nothing in Jason's psyche reacted to the name or the grave, and besides, it was much too clean, too untouched by time, to have any similarities with the headstone in the photograph. When he glanced up at Kayla, he noticed from the corner of his eye that a procession of people had gathered about fifty yards down the lane. He had not noticed them before.

'This can't be it, Kayla. Look, the . . .'

He fell silent as again his gaze was riveted on where he had seen people in the distance.

Except, no one was there now. Where a moment ago had stood a knot of men and women was now an open, empty space.

'This stone is much too new and undamaged,' he said absently, 'compared with the photograph.' His eyes remained transfixed on where he had seen the people gathered.

Kayla had not noticed them; otherwise she would have said something.

He stood up. 'Let's keep going.'

She mumbled something incoherent, shrugged, and continued walking.

Half walking, half running, he crossed the fifty yards to the area where the small crowd had convened. He wondered what sort of vision he had seen. Around him, another ten or twenty gravestones jutted up from the ground. He wandered around searching for . . . what?

Then he noticed a gravestone that was a little bigger than the other ones, and it had 'ears' – round shapes with notches at the corners. He scrutinized the names on the stone and the date of death. As he did so, he felt someone watching him.

He turned on his heel, but saw no one.

Then it dawned on him what had been wrong with the procession of people, other than the fact that they had disappeared so suddenly. They had looked different – and it was their clothes that made them look different. Jason didn't know much about fashion, but he did know that the wide-brimmed hats and the flared pants the men had worn were from a different era, as were the short dresses worn by the women. Their clothing had been *old-fashioned*, at least to the eyes of his modern generation.

His heart pounding, he turned back toward the grave marker and reread the names inscribed beneath the elegantly chiseled and moss-covered flowers on both the ears.

CHAWKINS
ROBERT J.
4 JUNE 1937–18 AUGUST 1977

AMANDA Z.
12 FEBRUARY 1943–18 AUGUST 1977

MIKE W.
29 JULY 1977–18 AUGUST 1977

TWENTY-FOUR
Separation

That date, August eighteenth, took his breath away. That name, Mike, grabbed him by the throat. And what followed fell with the force of a sledgehammer.

He was perspiring and could smell his own body odor. Kayla was walking toward him with a frown on her face, apparent even from this distance.

'What's the matter, Jason?' she asked when she reached him.

When he did not respond, she said, 'You look pale. Are you going to be sick?'

What's happening to me? he wanted to scream, but the words were clogged in his throat.

He crouched down and compared the stone with the Polaroid photograph. The similarities were obvious and easy to spot. The mossy layer, the cracks, the irregularities. This was the headstone he had been searching for. Absolutely no doubt about it.

'Mike is Mawkee. *Mikey,*' he said hoarsely. 'He was a baby, only a few weeks old when he died on August eighteenth. The same date as the other two, Robert and Amanda. His parents, I think. They all died on the same day.'

Kayla knelt beside him, but said nothing.

'I saw people,' he whispered. 'Funeral guests. I can still sense *something* here.'

She gave him a skeptical glance. 'What on earth are you talking about?'

His mouth opened, then closed, once, twice, like a dying fish on the bottom of a boat. He shook his head. 'I'll explain, but you won't believe me. There were people here. Maybe twenty, maybe more. They were all wearing clothes of an earlier era. I saw them, just for a moment. And then they were gone. Only, I think they're not entirely gone, because there's still something that's not entirely right. Aren't you cold?'

He hugged himself, shivering. Despite the intense desert heat he was trembling from the cold. Kayla was staring at him in utter stupefaction.

'It's boiling hot, Jason.'

'No,' he said. 'No, it's not. It's freezing cold.'

He clenched his teeth.

'Come with me,' she said, taking his arm. 'We're leaving.'

'How can we leave now?' Jason growled. 'We've found what we've been looking for. This is it. It's about Mike W. Chawkins.' He pointed at the gravestone. 'He's dead, he no longer exists. This is about *him!*'

'You're scaring me,' Kayla said quietly. 'Come along now.'

She put a hand on his shoulder, but he brushed it off and remained where he was, crouched down, rubbing his hands for warmth.

'Just look!' he said angrily. 'Look at the photograph and then look at the gravestone. They're one and the same. Even you should be able to see that.'

She rose and took a step backwards.

'What's *wrong* with you?' she almost spat.

'*I* am Mawkee, Kayla! Don't you get it? This is my grave. I found it! The people I just saw were the people who came to my funeral. My own funeral procession.'

He made a sound that could have been laughter, but came out more as a sob.

Kayla took another step back.

'I really want to leave this place,' she said softly but resolutely.

He shook his head again and sobbed. He could not stop himself. It seemed he couldn't stop *anything* any more; he was losing his grip on reality, as if he was drunk or on hallucinating drugs.

'Jason? Did *you* take those Polaroid pictures?'

He froze. Suddenly his sobbing stopped, along with his shivers. Slowly he turned toward her.

'*What?*'

She stood there as if she were made of stone. She had her arms crossed over her chest, standing there between the gravestones. Her gaze was crushing.

'You have two Polaroid cameras at home. You're good with that kind of equipment.'

'Have you lost your mind?' he whispered hoarsely.

'How odd you ask that. I was just wondering the same thing about you.'

His anger rose like a rumbling volcano spewing from the depths of the earth.

'I think you should go back to Mark,' she stated emphatically. 'You're right. Something is *not* right. Maybe something is not right with *you*. Look, I've been supportive of you from the get-go. But then you start talking about a creature of fire. You have visions, or something. You see things that aren't there. You even believe you're dead. You think this is your grave. Please tell me what in the name of God I am supposed to make of all that?'

'And so you assume that I've set the whole thing up myself.'

He no longer felt like a raging drunk. He was stone-cold sober, and he could not believe what he was hearing.

'Ralph said he would die young,' she plowed on, oblivious to roadblocks or warning signs. 'Where did that come from? How had the thought entered his mind? I'll never know. And that will always bother me. Maybe he was making himself believe it. Maybe he knew about his heart valve. Maybe someone else had told him he would die young – God, or a twisted fortune teller, or someone who hated him. It doesn't matter. The point is, *he believed it.* You believe you're dead or will die soon. It's the same wretched thing all over again, only this time there are photographs involved. Maybe you want to believe this so badly that you set the whole thing up yourself. What do I know? But whatever it is, I want nothing more to do with it. I'm done.'

She made an axe-cutting gesture with her arm, and then she broke. Tears welled up in her eyes and she buried her face in her hands. She turned around and started walking away, quickly breaking into a run. He stared after her, stunned, standing on the green grass growing on top of his own grave.

It felt as if Mike W. Chawkins were watching him to see what he would do next.

By next morning they still had hardly spoken to each other.

Despite the desert heat Kayla had walked all the way from St James Cemetery back to Mount Peytha Inn. Inside the room, she had turned on the air conditioner full blast and sat down in one of two chairs. He had returned around sunset, while the blazing orb of a yellow sun was dipping behind the mountains. He had calmed down, and so had she.

But an icy silence remained very much in evidence. Instead of going out to dinner, they had remained in their motel room throughout the night. The next morning, nothing had changed. While she was in the shower, she decided to return to Los Angeles, no matter what. And she told him exactly that, when she stepped out of shower and into the bedroom and stood before him, naked.

'I'm going home. Are you coming?'

Slowly he shook his head.

Streaming droplets were sliding down her body. 'Please, Jason,' she said, 'let's go see Mark. He'll know what to do.'

He looked at her, his eyes puffy from lack of sleep. 'I can't leave now, Kayla. Please try to understand. I've found my grave. Now I have to move on from there.'

Kayla clenched her fists. She *had* to scream, and scream she did. 'I've had enough,' she cried hoarsely. *'Enough! Do you read me?'*

A fresh wave of tears assailed her. 'I really *am* leaving!' she heard herself cry in no uncertain terms.

He groaned. 'Kayla . . .'

She squeezed her eyes shut and clenched her fists, her fingernails biting into the palms of her hands.

Our marriage is destroyed. You, Jason, have wrecked it.

She really believed it. Suddenly her love for Jason died; gone in a sigh, just as it had with Ralph. In its place came anger, rolling dangerously back and forth through her mind.

I had to let go of Ralph, and you need to let go of this. Or else.

In her mind's eye, she saw Ralph's body lying motionless beside her in the tent. Far from the nearest hospital, much too far away to save him. As she held his cold, lifeless hand, she kissed him one last time. And then she had wept long and hard. For the death of love, and for the death of peace in her life.

A fog settled inside her head as she got dressed and packed her weekend bag.

'I'm taking the Chrysler,' she told him as a matter of fact. It was as though she was going to the store to buy groceries. 'After all, it's my car. You have your credit card. Will you fly home?'

'I'll get home somehow,' he said. 'But you're not serious, are you? You're not really going to leave me here?'

'I'm doing this for you, and for us,' she said, her tone of voice inviting no debate. 'There is nothing left for me here. You're better off without me.'

It was ten fifteen; the day was still young. Outside, a desert storm had erupted. Clouds of dust were pirouetting. Palm fronds bowed before the wind, and tumbleweeds rolled across the sandy tarmac of the parking lot. Now and then the sun, fierce as ever on the torrid threshold between July and August, was hidden by the thick, soaring dust.

He desperately wanted to discuss her decision, but since her mind was apparently made up, there was no point. She was in no mood to change her mind. Jason knew how headstrong she could be. Conversely, she knew the same about him.

She picked up her car keys and bag. 'I'm off.'

He nodded. 'I'm sorry I yelled at you in the cemetery yesterday, Kayla. I was not myself. I haven't been since this damn thing started.'

'Are you coming?'

It was the third time she asked. The final time.

'I have to look into these Chawkins people. Who were they? How did they die?'

'So you're staying here,' she sighed.

'Now that I have a lead, I don't see how I have any other choice,' he said. 'And I want to find out what's going on with me. Where did those hallucinations come from? If I don't find the answer to these questions, Kayla, I will be no good to myself – let alone to you. So you see, my staying is for us both.'

'You could ask Mark about this.'

He looked down at his feet. 'I will. I promise you I will. Later. I'm here at the source now. And I'm telling you, there is a photographer who needs to be exposed before August eighteenth. I have to make sure that nothing terrible happens on that day.'

She nodded. 'Have it your way. I'm leaving.'

She crossed to the door.

'Kayla.'

She turned around.

'Please be careful. I'd rather not have you home alone. You never know. Go stay at Simone's house.'

'We'll see,' she said. 'Will you be careful, too? I don't mind telling you that I'm not at all comfortable leaving you here.'

He smiled. 'I'm a big boy. I can take care of myself.'

Kayla considered giving him a kiss goodbye, but decided against it. She opened the door and stepped outside into the gray, biting sandstorm. She leaned into the wind and walked toward the Chrysler.

She got in, started the engine, and backed out of the parking space, looking at him the entire time. He had stepped outside, and was standing by the short wall in front of the motel.

Kayla turned on to the road and kept looking at Jason in the rear-view mirror until she could no longer see him.

Only then did she wipe her tears away.

TWENTY-FIVE
The Chawkins Tragedy

As he watched Kayla's car disappear into clouds of dust, Jason leaned hard against the wall of the motel, afraid to take a step forward. He felt as if, at any moment, a trapdoor might open up before him and he would tumble into the depths.

Kayla had left him. She had really gone.

You've lost her forever, an inner voice reproached him.

But what he had told her was true. Because he had come this far, he had no choice but to continue. And he knew where he would go first, just as soon as he was able to collect his thoughts and emotions.

'Could you tell me a bit more about the Chawkins family?' he asked an hour later. It was Friday morning the thirty-first of July, and he was back in Chuck Cleigh's nicely appointed office. He had told the man that the Chawkins' grave intrigued him because of how it tied to his genealogical research.

Chuck sighed heavily. 'Listen, Jason, I'm really sorry we haven't called you yet. I don't have time for this today. If all three of those people died on the same day, as you say, then there must have been special circumstances. But don't ask me to delve into that for you. It's not what I do.'

The owner of the Cleigh Abbeville Funeral Home, dressed in faded jeans, sat behind the desk, drumming his fingers on the table. Jason knew that the man wanted him gone and that he could not – or would not – tell him anything.

'Is there anyone else I could talk to?' Jason asked. His voice sounded distressed, even to him.

Chuck scraped his chair back.

'This is very important to me, Mr Cleigh,' Jason added, moving his chair in. 'You have no idea *how* important.'

Chuck said nothing for several moments. He cast a puzzled look at Jason, his grimace a clear signal that Jason's welcome in his office was rapidly running out.

'You could try the newspaper,' he said eventually. 'The *Mohave Herald*. Or, better still, talk to Freddy Padilla. He's a retired reporter for the *Herald* and currently the manager of the city archives. I know him well. If anyone can help you, he can. He knows everything there is to know about Mount Peytha City. The man is a walking encyclopedia.'

'Do you have the address for this city archive?' Jason asked.

'Yes, I do,' Chuck Cleigh allowed.

In a corner of the city archives, Freddy Padilla sat behind a modest wooden desk with a green banker's lamp perched on it. At least, Jason assumed it was Freddy Padilla. He guessed the man to be in his mid-sixties, judging by his white beard and his long hair curling up at the back of his neck. He had a bulging stomach, the natural consequence of beer and gluttony, and the red-and-white checkered shirt he sported stretched across it like table linen.

Jason walked up to him. 'Good afternoon,' he said in greeting. 'My name is Jason Evans. Are you Mr Padilla?'

A flash of bright blue eyes gazed at him for a moment. 'Yes, I am.'

'Could I ask you something?'

'Sure,' Padilla said jovially. 'Have a seat. What's on your mind?'

Jason sat down and brushed a hand through his hair. 'I'm conducting an investigation. Chuck Cleigh of Cleigh Abbeville's Funeral Home advised me to contact you.'

'Ah, yes. Chuck!' Freddy exclaimed. 'Please continue.'

'I need some information,' Jason said, adding, 'I'm told you might have that information and if so, I would of course be happy to pay you for your time.'

'Money? Means nothing to me,' Padilla said with a harsh laugh. 'I'm the exception in this country of money-grubbers. That's why I've always been poor.'

'Yes,' Jason said, because he didn't know what else to say.

As on a mission, Padilla added, 'It's a shame the casino palace in Laughlin keeps expanding. Even here the money-grubbing is getting worse. It's a blemish on our beautiful Mount Peytha City. But unfortunately I can't change the world by myself.'

'I guess not,' Jason dead-panned.

'Some people walk around with dollar signs in their eyes, but not me,' Freddy continued. Then: 'But enough of that. What do you want to know?'

'Mr Padilla,' Jason launched in, 'I hope this is not going to be too complicated . . .'

'Please call me Freddy.'

'OK, Freddy. Here's the thing . . .'

Freddy plucked at his beard, nodding to Jason to get to the point.

'There's a grave in St James Cemetery that interests me.'

'Really. Whose grave is it?'

'It's the grave for the Chawkins family: for Robert and Amanda and their son Mike. I'd like to know a bit more about this family.'

'Why?' Freddy wanted to know.

'It has something to do with genealogy.'

Freddy shrugged.

'I'll look into it. Give me an hour.'

Jason waited outside until the hour was up. He thought of Kayla and decided to call her. She picked up, but it was an awkward conversation. He repeated what by now seemed almost like a mantra, that in this circumstance he could not be an ostrich, sticking his head in the sand and hoping that evil would leave him alone. Some lunatic had sent him three photos with inscriptions, and perhaps had even caused their so-called accident in the car. Fate had led him here, to this town, and he couldn't leave until he understood why. What would happen, he wondered out loud to her, on August eighteenth? He repeated that he wanted her to stay at Simone's house until he got home. Kayla responded by repeating *her* mantra: that he was imagining things and he should seek help from Mark.

He hung up with nothing resolved and was soon back at Freddy's desk.

'I actually remember this incident,' the former reporter informed him. 'I wrote about it for the paper, so I did a quick read through my own stories. I didn't think of it straight away, since it happened so long ago.'

'I'm very curious what you found out,' Jason said, struggling to maintain his composure.

Freddy gazed past him.

'It was a terrible accident. A trucker pushed them off the road. The driver was drunk or out of his mind, or both. With that enormous rig of his, he rammed into the Chawkins' car from behind, causing it to somersault and explode in a raging inferno. Those poor people died horrible deaths. And the trucker? He drove on – a hit-and-run driver – although he was caught eventually. His name was Silverstein. Steve Silverstein.'

Jason's mouth went bone dry. In his mind's eye he saw the headlights from behind that had blinded him. His body twitched with the memory of the crash that had ensued.

'Go on,' he said hoarsely.

'As I said, Robert, Amanda and Mikey died horrible deaths. It happened on State Highway 98, just outside Sacramento Wash, five miles from Mount Peytha City. Robert, the father, was active in the life of the community, as was Amanda. They lived at Mount Peytha Ranch, which Robert had built himself. He had made a name as a horseman and horse breeder. And the truck driver? I checked him out as well. He swore he hadn't seen the car roll over and catch on fire. He heard about it later. When he had sobered up and realized what he had done, he was devastated and filled with remorse. Or so he claimed.'

Freddy's phone rang and he picked up the receiver. 'Beth! Can I call you back? I'm in the middle of something. Yeah, thanks.'

He put the receiver back in its cradle. 'I found some other details in my files. A report from Tom Daunt, the firefighter who was first to arrive on the scene and remove the bodies from the car. He said there was nothing the emergency services could have done. And the pathologist, James Felch, said that identifying the bodies had been one of the toughest jobs in his long career. A baby was a victim, and that had affected him deeply.'

Freddy sighed heavily. 'Silverstein was convicted and sent up the river for thirty years. The ranch was sold to a friend of Robert's, a man named Joe Bresnahan. Joe still lives there now.'

Another story that Jason had found on the Internet, just last Sunday, crossed his mind. It was about a sixty-year-old Russian woman named Anya who had been experiencing the same nightmare for years. In her dreams she ran past houses and across rooftops fleeing from enemies dressed in Nazi-style uniforms. Sometimes she heard strange screams. They were unbearable, demon-like, as

Anya had described them. When she heard these screams, she would clap her hands over her ears to block out the horrible sound. On one day, during a yoga class, she had a horrifying vision. A mass grave had appeared in her mind's eye and she heard people screaming.

When those sudden, terrifying images disappeared, she started to believe in reincarnation. *It felt so intimate. As if a fountain of sorrow had sprouted from inside me. The vision was related to my own past*, Anya had said in her story.

She went into regression and returned to a past life. She ended up inside one of Joseph Stalin's prison camps, a starving and haggard woman in her late twenties. Anya remembered incidents of torture and sexual abuse, and ultimately her death. During her regression she had seen how sickness and exhaustion had finally killed her inside a small, dark room void of any light. When she relived the horror of that life, she understood why in her present life she sometimes suffered panic attacks in the dark.

Dying inside Stalin's camp had ended the pain. After that, everything had been bright and white and peaceful. She had the feeling she had 'been asleep for a little while', and she had been reborn as Anya only a few weeks after her demise in the death camp.

After her regression therapy she became aware of her previous life, and also of the people who had been her friends and relatives in her other existence. She had looked them up, but of course these people from 'before' hadn't recognized her. *I wanted to shout at them that it was* me. *I'd been dead for a little while, but now I was back*, Anya reported in her story. Finally, however, she had come to the realization that she had to let go of 'before' and find her own way in life 'now'.

Was this what Jason was experiencing? Could it be that a previous life was at the root of his anxieties? He had been born on September second, 1977, as Jason Evans. But had he been Mikey Chawkins before that?

Jason remembered another strange but apparently true story. It concerned a young Lebanese boy who had memories of a previous incarnation. One day the child was walking outside in his birthplace and met a man he had never seen before. But the boy walked straight up to him and called him his neighbor.

And he kept talking about an accident in which a truck had run over a man, severing both his legs. In addition, the boy kept pestering his parents that he wanted to visit a nearby village, even though he could not explain why he wanted to go there.

The boy's parents did some research and found out that the man their son had called 'neighbor' lived in this nearby village. They also discovered that someone in that same village had lost both legs in an accident involving a truck and had died shortly thereafter. The man the boy had addressed as neighbor had actually been the victim's neighbor.

There were other similarities. As it turned out, the boy could tell exactly what the victim had said just before he died. Also remarkable were the many characteristics that the child and the man who had died had in common: the man had been an avid hunter; the boy had an intense interest in everything to do with hunting. And the deceased had been fluent in French; the boy's command of the language was exceptional for his age.

Researchers had no explanation for this case other than reincarnation. After the man's death, his essence and energy had lived on in spirit form until recalled to Earth to live in physical form.

So the boy had become a new person with new possibilities, but inside his mind he would forever remain connected to the man who had died in the accident.

Could Jason be carrying inside of him the fears and memories of little Mike W. Chawkins?

It was a scenario that billions of people on Earth who believe in reincarnation would deem more than a possibility. For him, no matter how down-to-earth he had assumed himself to be before being plagued by hallucinations and visions, the same thing applied.

But what still made no sense to him was the role of the photographer. Whoever that person was, he seemed to be aware of Jason's previous existence – and that was the Achilles' heel in this entire theory. The photographer also had to know about the Chawkins' accident, because Jason and Kayla had experienced a similar chain of events as had that unfortunate family. So the crash on Monte Avenue between Cornell and Fernhill *had* been deliberate, although Jason doubted whether the police would see it that way. No, they would not take this bridge to a previous life seriously. Which meant that he was still on his own, that he needed to continue this investigation on his own.

Now he knew what his next step would be.

He thanked Padilla and, once outside, attended to some practical business. He needed a car. He had taken a cab to Chuck's, and he had covered the three miles to the city archives on foot. But Mount Peytha Ranch was outside of town, Freddy had informed him, and that was too far to walk.

When, a short time later, he was behind the wheel of a rented GMC Yukon, Jason drove off for his third visit of the day.

The stately farm located on Bullhead Road featured a long dirt road leading up to it. Behind it, on the distant horizon, Jason noted a scenic landscape dominated by mountains. A sign to the left of the dirt road read: MOUNT PEYTHA RANCH. Next to the sign was a mailbox, and beside that was an old fence with a gate closed across the road.

Jason put the car in neutral, got out and walked up to the gate. It was ornately decorated, and the bars had been cut out in the middle in the shape of an oval. At the center of the oval a letter had been welded to the iron.

It was the letter M.

The same elegant, curly M as depicted in the third Polaroid photograph.

TWENTY-SIX

'M'

Joe Bresnahan sported a sagging beer belly and paper-white hair. He was as hospitable as he was loquacious, and he treated his visitor like an old friend. He never asked why Jason had such an interest in Robert, Amanda and Mikey Chawkins – which suited Jason just fine. He was content to listen while Joe talked.

After his initial gut reaction to seeing the M in the gate outside, Jason had taken a bold step. He had come to Mount Peytha Ranch to uncover the secret of the grave, and the mystery of the letter M played a key role in that investigation. He felt sure the Bresnahans knew the salient facts.

The gate had been unlocked and he had walked across the dirt road toward the farmhouse. Next to one of the twin adjoining sheds was a tidy vegetable garden set beneath a row of small Joshua trees. From what Jason could discern, a wide assortment of vegetables grew in the garden: tomatoes, Brussels sprouts, peppers, radishes and onions.

When he rang the doorbell, Joe Bresnahan had answered it. After a few preliminaries, Joe confessed that he was alone at the moment. His son was out working, and his wife had gone over to a friend's house for a tea party. As the conversation progressed, Joe explained that he had retired years ago, and as long as his son did not kick him out and put him in an old folks' home, he would stay put. He loved it here, he said. Joe chatted cheerfully on and told Jason that he had known the Chawkins family quite well. In fact, he and Robert had grown up together in this backwater town, before Mount Peytha was incorporated as a city. He had considered long and hard whether or not he should buy this farm. But Robert's family had insisted, and in the end he had found he couldn't resist. He loved it here, he informed Jason again. Robert had been a fine man, Joe said, the salt of the earth. He was a horse trader and everyone in town knew that Chawkins had the best stock in town. The man had a gift for handling the animals, Joe said.

His wife Amanda had been a beautiful woman, as lovely on the inside as the outside. She was always friendly, always smiling. The two had been highly valued in Mount Peytha City because they had always contributed so much for the community. Always the first to volunteer for charity work.

Jason let him continue on his happy passage down memory lane for a while before asking the question he was there to ask. 'Mr Bresnahan, the gate outside has a letter "M" embedded in it. Does that letter stand for Mikey?'

Joe waved his flabby arms. 'Oh, yes! When Robert became a father, he was so happy he was living on cloud nine. He wanted the whole world to share his joy. He forged that letter and welded it into the gate himself. He was so happy!'

'Not long after that, the accident happened,' Jason observed. 'You probably attended the funeral.'

Joe Bresnahan nodded. 'The place was packed, as you can imagine. It was a sad, sad affair, but impressive at the same time because it embraced nearly everyone in Mount Peytha City. Even people who hadn't really known Robert and his family sat there, crying. I'm telling you, there wasn't a dry eye in the place.'

Jason thought of his vision in the cemetery. He had *seen* the funeral procession.

Or had it been a hallucination after all, a sign that he was losing his mind? But somehow it didn't feel like that any more.

'Mr Bresnahan—' Jason began, another question bubbling to the tip of his tongue. But Joe cut him off.

'I have some photographs of the funeral somewhere, if you'd like to see them.'

Jason's jaw dropped.

'The Chawkins' funeral?'

Joe nodded.

'You have *photographs*?'

Again, Joe nodded.

'Yes, I'd most definitely like to see them,' Jason said eagerly.

'All right. If you'll wait here, I'll go get them.' Joe Bresnahan hoisted his considerable frame up from his easy chair, shuffled out of the room and walked up a flight of stairs.

Jason remained seated, the tension becoming unbearable. Would he soon be faced with images from his vision? Would the same people be in the photographs, dressed in their old-fashioned garb? He did not need to wait long to find out. Joe came stumbling down the stairs with a stack of yellowed black and white photos in his hands.

'Here they are. A newspaper photographer took these. Like I said, Robert's death was big news in these parts.'

Jason took the photographs from him. After a brief flick-through, he found nothing of value. The photographs had not been taken at St James Cemetery, but outside of a church, presumably the place where the memorial service had been held. A procession of people was leaving the church. All five photographs had been taken at approximately the same time. The photographer had clicked away, sent the photos to the newspaper, and had probably let the editor pick one. Somehow, Joe had ended up owning the entire set.

The only thing Jason recognized in the photos was the clothes worn by the mourners. He had recently seen jackets, ties, hats and dresses just like these. But everything else . . .

Something caught his eye. No, it could not be. It was impossible. He lifted the picture and stared at it. Moved it closer to his eyes.

Impossible or not, he was *there*.

Jason put the picture aside, his heart skipping a beat. He picked up another one of the black and white images – yes, there he was again. And in the next picture, and the next.

Of course; if all of the photographs had been taken at around the same time, he *had* to be in them all.

'One is missing. Now where did that one go?' he heard Joe Bresnahan mumble to himself.

Jason looked up. 'That's OK, Mr Bresnahan. I've seen enough. You have no idea how grateful I am.'

Yes, he was grateful.

And shocked out of his mind.

TWENTY-SEVEN
The Man in Black

Kayla arrived home early Friday evening, sad and depressed. Jason had called her one time. She had been angry when she spoke to him, but she no longer felt mad. When would she hear from him again?

Restless, she roamed around Canyon View, turned on the electric kettle, and made herself a cup of tea, taking it with her into the study. Leaning against the window sill, one hand holding the mug of tea, she leafed through the album containing his childhood pictures that he had left out on his desk. Little Jason on the baseball field. A somewhat older Jason during his high school years. Jason with a few friends she vaguely recognized but whose names she couldn't remember. Jason as a boy again, standing between Donna and Edward.

Kayla had seen these pictures before. Photographs from the first years of his life. The one on the cover page was the first one ever taken of him. He had been photographed together with his parents, and underneath it his mother had added his birth certificate. Another photo depicted Jason as a baby being bottle-fed; still another featured a smiling infant crawling around on all fours. And so it continued. She went back to the first picture in the album. Donna was in bed, and Jason's father sat in a chair at her bedside and held their little boy in the crook of his arm, proudly showing him off to the world. Both parents were beaming into the camera lens. Donna's handwritten title with the photo was: WELCOME, MY DEAR JASON.

Then Kayla looked at the birth certificate. At the top of the sheet it said STATE OF CALIFORNIA, and underneath CERTIFICATION OF VITAL RECORD. A list of numbers followed, the name of the newborn, JASON, and the date of his birth: SEPTEMBER 2, 1977. The names of his parents had been penned in by his mother and father.

Kayla closed the album, wondering what was going through Jason's mind at this moment. Could it really be that he thought his previous incarnation was somehow reaching out to him?

She did not like being alone, so she called Simone. When Kayla asked her friend if she could stay with them, Simone said it would be no problem at all.

In Simone and her husband Cliff's living room, Kayla waited for his phone call – in vain. She told them that Jason was out of town. She did not mention that they had had a fight, nor did she divulge what he was doing in Arizona. Simone was convinced there was more to this story than met the eye and probed a little deeper. Kayla answered all her questions, but she barely heard herself talking. She could not concentrate. She kept glancing at her silent telephone.

At ten thirty she was in bed in the guest room, and that was the start of the second worst night of her life. The worst had been the night Ralph died.

The next morning, Saturday, August first, she went out for a walk because she had nothing better to do. She didn't call Jason; her pride was holding her back. For the entire day she was a nervous wreck, feeling as though she were walking a tightrope over an abyss, and her doubts and anxieties kept trying to push her off.

Had she done the right thing?

Had *she* abandoned *him*?

She kept her cell phone within easy reach at all times, but he didn't call. She *could* call him herself. She repeatedly considered doing that, but each time she held herself in check. God, she *hated* her pride.

How could she have left him there on his own? But then she thought of how stubborn *he* had been. He had let her down just as badly, if not worse.

It doesn't matter. This wasn't necessary. There is no need for us to be apart now. We could have prevented it. Together we could have prevented it.

Then Jason did call, around eight o'clock that evening. He said he was no longer in Mount Peytha. He had driven to Las Vegas that morning and had taken an afternoon flight to San Francisco. He would tell her all about it later.

She was too stunned to question him. He asked how she was doing. She said she felt like crap and he said he was sorry. She ended the conversation quickly, her way of saying 'come home', but after she had hung up, she thought of all the other things she had wanted to say and hadn't.

Late that night she was in her own bed. She was determined to wait for Jason at home. He had told her that their house might not be safe, but even if the secret photographer were watching Canyon View, she no longer cared. What else could he destroy that he hadn't already?

Her mind kept on churning, but finally she fell asleep.

When she awoke during the night, she saw a towering figure in a black robe at the foot of her bed. His face was hidden by a black hood, and his bony, skeletal hand held a razor-sharp scythe.

She screamed, fumbled for the light switch, and flicked it on. In the light her enemy, the Grim Reaper, had disappeared.

For the rest of the night she sat up in bed, fully awake.

A new day dawned and the phone rang. It turned out to be Simone, worried that Kayla had not been feeling herself on Friday. Kayla told her friend she had spoken with Jason and Simone proposed having lunch together. She was a wonderful friend, very sympathetic, and Kayla readily accepted.

'Great!' Simone enthused. 'Where do we meet?'

'How about the Milano? Isn't that one of your favorite places in Mulligan Square?'

Kayla was well aware that Simone liked the small, cozy Italian restaurant. They served fresh food and its location was on a pretty square between Hollywood Boulevard and the Loews Hotel. It was quite a drive for them both, but in their opinion, well worth it.

'What a wonderful idea!' Simone said.

After the phone call, Kayla made herself another promise.

This silence on the telephone had gone on long enough. Today she would call Jason and talk things over. She couldn't take it any more. She wanted to find out what had been happening. If only things had gone well, if only he weren't in trouble, if only . . .

If only he's coming back.

That was her most devout prayer.

Kayla found a parking spot for her Chrysler and followed the Walk of Fame toward Mulligan Square. The sun felt hot on the back of her neck. She adjusted her Ray-Bans and glanced in passing at the street show in front of Mann's Chinese Theater. Today featured a performance by a man in Spiderman garb. Beside him stood Darth Vader accompanied by Star Wars soldiers in white uniforms. A group of tourists clicked away with their cameras.

She passed the statue of Charlie Chaplin, looking back at her from beneath his bowler hat with his famous grin, and thought: *Life was simpler in your day. Had the Polaroid camera even been invented yet?*

As Kayla ascended the steps to Mulligan Square, music blared from across the square. She had to think a moment before she recognized the singer. Sheryl Crow. She passed an ice cream vendor and yet another stall selling hotdogs. From there she crossed beneath an arcade and walked up some stone steps toward the Milano. Once inside she scanned the tables. Simone hadn't arrived yet. She found a table, ordered a glass of wine, and waited.

Simone bounced up the steps fifteen minutes later, beaming. Kayla rose, they hugged, and soon were chatting away as close friends are wont to do. Simone's chatter and buoyancy cheered Kayla up. She could put her troubles on the back burner and lose track of time.

But questions continued to nag at her. What was going to happen after this afternoon? What was Jason doing in San Francisco? More importantly, how much damage had their relationship sustained, and could that damage be repaired?

Later. Not now. Right now I'm here with Simone.

A waitress brought Simone's pasta dish and Kayla's Mediterranean salad. They touched glasses.

'How's Cliff doing?' Kayla asked as she dug into her salad. 'I hardly talked to him while I was staying at your place. Or to you, for that matter.'

'Oh, Cliff is doing fine,' Simone said. 'Latest news, hot from the press: he's been promoted *again*. He's a senior salesman now.'

'Congratulations.'

'There's a downside, though. It means he'll be away from home even more than before.'

Cliff worked at AT&T and put in long hours, Kayla knew. She also knew that Simone wouldn't mind Cliff taking on a less demanding job, one that would allow him to spend more time at home. But Cliff loved his job and was ambitious. More so than Jason, Kayla speculated, although he had often wondered out loud what it would be like to be his own boss and manage his own business. She had advised against it, worried about long nights, back-breaking work and poverty. The latter she could live with, maybe, because money wasn't nearly as important to her as her marriage. But if some day he decided to take the plunge, well, she would be there for him.

She would cross that bridge if and when she came to it.

Although Simone had never taken another job after waitressing at The Duchess, she did volunteer three mornings and two nights a week at a telephone helpline for abused or battered children.

Children. It crossed her mind that she hadn't told Simone about Jason's and her decision to try and have children. Should she mention it? No, she decided. Simone and Cliff had been trying for a long time to have children themselves. The latest medical exams had suggested that the problem lay with Cliff and not Simone. He had a low sperm count, Simone had confided to her recently.

But the crisis in her own marriage was really why she refrained from broaching the subject. It was as if a black cloud had descended on her, and it was one that Simone noticed.

'What wrong, Kayla?' she asked her friend with concern. 'You seem distracted.'

Kayla managed a smile. 'Oh, just some small issues. But I'll iron them out.'

'Is something wrong between you and Jason?'

Kayla had said nothing to her, but Simone's intuition had pieced together the puzzle while Kayla was staying at her house. And now she had asked the question that she had been dying to ask.

'Some other time, Simone, please,' Kayla begged off.

'You can trust me. I'm your best friend.'

'I know. I know that all too well. But I'm not done with this. I have to find out for myself how this will end and then I have to deal with whatever it is I find. If you understand what I'm talking about.'

'Of course. I understand. Mum's the word.'

Simone didn't mention it again, as was her nature. She could be patient, no matter how curious she might be.

They enjoyed a delightful lunch that ended with a cup of tea, after which they paid the check and left the restaurant. The two women didn't hurry when they walked back toward Hollywood Boulevard and past the shops on Mulligan Square. Simone talked about a trip to New York she and Cliff would be taking the following week to visit his family. She was looking forward to it, she said, although she wasn't as thrilled about the stifling August humidity in the Big Apple. She chatted at length about Maura and Claudia, Cliff's cousins, with whom she got along and was looking forward to seeing. Claudia had been dieting and had lost forty pounds, apparently, and Simone wanted to see the result with her own eyes.

Kayla paused to peer into the window of a souvenir shop. A necklace made of silver, prettily decorated, had caught her eye. It was delicate, shaped like a flower, and it had much to commend it.

But the necklace also touched her on a deeper level, and seemed to cast a spell on her. Suddenly she felt a wave of fatigue wash over her. Surely, she thought, it could not be from the two glasses of wine she had consumed at the restaurant. It had to be caused by the strain she'd been under lately. It had exhausted her; she needed some rest, some quiet in her life. When would that blessed feeling of peace and contentment finally return?

She returned home late in the afternoon. Her cell phone had remained silent that entire day, but as she sat down on the couch it started playing her ringtone. It was Jason. He asked her how she was doing. She said she missed him and asked when he was coming home from San Francisco.

'We have to talk about things. I *want* to talk about things.'

'Me, too,' he said with a sigh. 'Me too, Kayla.'

'What are you doing out there?'

'I'm looking for something,' he said. 'But it's not going so well. I'm stuck.'

'What are you looking for?'

'I'll tell you later. I think I can wrap it up here pretty soon. After that, I don't know.'

His voice had an edge of desperation in it, she got the distinct impression that he *was* desperate. She didn't ask him what the trouble was. She didn't care. For her, there was only one thing that mattered.

'Promise me you'll be back soon?'

'I promise,' he said quietly.

The hours crawled by. She clicked through a number of channels on television without paying much attention to anything that was on.

At ten o'clock, he called again and sounded radically different. He was excited, enthusiastic, as though possessed by something. Even his voice sounded different. His words came out in staccato fashion like rounds from a machine gun, but nothing stuck in her head. She did hear that he wanted her to return to Simone's house. He didn't want her to be home alone. He had discovered something, was on to someone, and he would take the six o'clock flight from SFO back to LAX the next morning.

Then he hung up, and she sat gazing mutedly at her phone. It was much too late to call Simone and ask her if she could spend the night at her house. And besides, she didn't feel like going over there. So she decided to stay at Canyon View.

Although that night was free of the Grim Reaper, Kayla dreamed of being inside the tent with Ralph. Only this time it wasn't Ralph beside her; it was Jason. He screamed – he was on fire. Flames leapt furiously around his face, his arms, his entire body. His skin was bleeding and blackening. He shrieked in horror.

He turned and threw himself at her in his panic, and she felt him, *really* felt him. She started awake to feel a hand pressing down on her mouth.

A figure draped in ebony black clothing towered over her. A man of flesh and blood. He was inside her bedroom and his hand was at her mouth, making it hard for her to breathe. He was large, wide-shouldered and strong as iron. In a flash he removed his hand and struck her a searing whiplash across the face. Kayla screamed.

Another slap. And another . . . And another. He did not stop. He seemed possessed. She tasted her own blood. Her cries of pain grew louder.

On the bed stand, within reach, her cell phone played its ringtone. But she could not reach it. Now the man in black was holding a knife in his fist. The weapon glittered in the moonlight shimmering in through the window. Her screams faltered.

The man stabbed her with the knife, plunging it deep into her stomach.

Pain exploded. He was killing her.

Roughly, he turned her over on to her stomach.

One hand slipped beneath her panties and squeezed her buttocks. With his other hand, he drove the steel blade deep into her back.

The stabbing pain undid her and she blacked out.

TWENTY-EIGHT
San Francisco

After saying goodbye to Joe Bresnahan at his ranch, Jason made arrangements for his next trip. In Frank's Cafe on Palm Square, he used the Internet to buy a plane ticket from Las Vegas to San Francisco, paid an extra fee to drive the Yukon one way to Vegas, and left Mount Peytha City at the break of dawn the next morning.

Two and a half hours later he arrived in Las Vegas. The glitter and glam of the gambling capital of the United States remained oblivious to him; he didn't want to risk missing his 2:40 p.m. flight to San Francisco.

Ninety minutes later Jason was renting another car at San Francisco International Airport. He left the airport in a Ford sedan and soon arrived in the suburb of San Francisco that was his destination. Jason steered the sedan toward a detached bungalow and parked in the driveway. He got out, surveyed the area, and then walked past nicely tended flower beds to the front stoop protruding from the front of the nondescript off-white house.

As Jason approached the front door of the bungalow, a balding, fifty-year-old man opened it and stepped outside. He was wearing a baggy Hawaiian shirt that did more to emphasize his prominent stomach than to hide it, and a pair of khaki shorts and sandals. His name, Jason knew, was Phil Wallace.

During Chris's funeral Jason had briefly spoken with the man who had been his uncle's next-door neighbor for three decades. As it turned out, Jason's telephone conversation with him last evening from the Mount Peytha Inn had been about as brief as their conversation at the funeral.

'Good evening, Jason,' Phil said. 'I saw you drive up.'

Jason walked up to him and shook his hand. 'Hello, Phil.'

'Did you have a good trip?'

'It was an uneventful one.'

Phil nodded. 'The best kind. Do you want to come in? Can I offer you something?'

He gestured with his arm to the open front door of his bungalow.

'Thanks,' Jason said. 'Could I come back tomorrow? I'd like to stop at that motel you suggested, and I'm meeting Hugo Shaver tonight. He couldn't make time for me tomorrow or the day after.'

'So you got hold of him, did you? The number I gave you must have been the right one.'

'It was. And the one for Felipe as well. I'm meeting him tomorrow. I just wanted to stop by to tell you I'm here and to thank you.'

Phil dismissed that with a wave of his hand, as if he was chasing away a fly. 'Take your time. I'll be here tomorrow after work, around five. Would that work for you?'

'Completely.'

Jason thought a moment, then: 'Maybe I could ask you something, now that I'm here. Did Chris ever mention business he did in Mount Peytha City?'

Phil frowned. 'Mount Peytha City? Isn't that in Utah somewhere?'

'No. Arizona.'

'Arizona, yeah, you're right. What about it?'

Jason sighed. 'I was hoping you could tell me. Did Chris ever mention that town to you?'

Phil shook his head. 'No, it doesn't ring a bell. What's this about?'

'I'll tell you tomorrow,' Jason said, reluctant to delve back into the entire story. 'One more thing, if you don't mind. Does the name Chawkins mean anything to you?'

Phil pondered that and then shook his head. 'Sorry, no. Should it mean something to me?'

'Honestly, I don't know,' Jason confessed.

This was not going well. Kayla had left him, and now Jason had traveled from the Great Southwest to northern California, so far for naught.

Perhaps he would have better luck with Hugo and Felipe Garcia, his uncle's best friends.

Jason said goodbye to Phil, drove to the Surf Hill Motel, and after checking in to his room, called Kayla. It was a short conversation. But at least she was talking to him.

For now.

By late afternoon on the next day, Jason's initial feeling of disappointment had yielded to desperation. His investigation into secrets his Uncle Chris may have kept hidden were leading nowhere. Hugo hadn't been able to supply any information about Mount Peytha City or the Chawkins family, and neither had Felipe. However, both sixty-year-olds, one of them lean and gray, the other with chestnut skin and still blessed with surprisingly thick dark hair, had reminisced endlessly about the past – remembrances that Jason had no wish to hear.

These trips down memory lane were mostly about his uncle's avid prize collection. Chris had been exuberant about any type of medal, certificate, coupon or monetary prize – no matter how small. One of the last times Jason had seen his uncle in such a state of euphoria was during his father's previous birthday party, after he had won yet another fishing trophy. Jason had promised Chris that he would visit him soon, but that never happened. San Francisco, where his uncle lived, was not around the corner from Los Angeles and there had always been more pressing matters – or so it had seemed at the time. Of course, his excuses to keep postponing a trip to San

Francisco had been no more than that: excuses. Jason would surely have gone had he known how seriously ill his uncle was. But as elaborate as Chris had always been about his harvest of prizes, he had been equally reticent about the dark side of his mind.

What had driven the man to hang himself? Hugo and Felipe could not enlighten Jason. Yes, they had noticed that Chris had been feverish and had lost some weight, but they had never made the connection to cancer. Jason would have thought it impossible to keep something like that a secret. But his eccentric, inimitable uncle had somehow managed to do it.

The only option he had left was to talk to Phil. After that he would return home and try to mend fences with Kayla.

Jason sat inside his car in the driveway in front of Chris's bungalow and stared at his bleak, red-stained eyes in the rear-view mirror.

He heard his mobile ringtone. It was *The Car Song*, by some band he had forgotten about. The song hurt his ears. He had downloaded it at a creative low point during the Tommy Jones campaign, and he hadn't bothered to erase it.

He answered. 'Jason Evans.'

'Brian here.'

Jason slapped his forehead. Damn it! He had completely forgotten to call his boss. And tomorrow was Monday, the day he had promised to be back in his office.

He decided to not beat around the bush.

'I'm sorry, Brian, but I'm not coming in tomorrow,' he said, closing his eyes in anticipation of Brian's tirade. He got one. An earful. Brian demanded to know if Jason had completely lost his marbles. He couldn't do this to his co-workers, Brian fairly shouted; it was *simply not done*, because so much was riding on the Jones campaign. Finally Brian paused in his tirade long enough to ask Jason exactly when he *would* be coming back to work.

Jason had not asked himself that question and thus had no definitive answer.

I think I need a vacation, Brian. No worries for a while, that would suit me just fine. You can stick your campaign up your ass, and while you're at it, shove Tommy Jones up there too.

'I'll call you tomorrow,' he said tonelessly. 'By then I should know more about what's going to happen here.'

'Shit! What are you doing out there? Are you still in the desert?'

'I'll talk to you tomorrow, Brian,' he said, and then pressed the end button.

He suppressed the urge to smack something, hard, and then remembered that he had not spoken to Kayla since last night. Reluctantly, he punched in her number. His voice was soft, broken. She wanted to talk, make up. It was encouraging. If she were willing to offer him another chance, he would seize it like a lifeline thrown to a drowning man.

Maybe, he reproached himself, he should have realized this long before now.

Inside his tastefully decorated living room, replete with antiques in subdued shades, Phil put an ice-cold bottle of Budweiser in front of Jason. Phil's wife Joyce came in to greet him and then returned to the kitchen, where she was fixing dinner. The countertop was full of pots and pans, Jason noticed. Phil followed his gaze, smiling.

'Joyce doesn't mind cooking, and you won't hear me complaining,' he commented with a smile, patting his ample girth. 'I get to eat better than in a restaurant. By the way, may we assume you'll be joining us for dinner tonight?'

Since Jason had no other plans, he gracefully accepted.

'How did it go with Hugo?' Phil asked, leaning back in his chair and taking a swig of beer.

'It was nice talking to him,' Jason answered. The fact that nothing had come from it did not detract from the pleasantness of the conversation.

'Have you met any of Chris's other mates? Did you see Felipe?'

'Yes, but no one else.'

'How long will you be in San Francisco?'

Jason shrugged. 'I'm not exactly sure.'

Phil leaned forward expectantly. 'OK, Jason, why don't you come clean with me? Why did you come here?'

Jason gave him a tired smile and took a sip of beer. 'As I told you yesterday, it's a long story,' he said as he placed the bottle gently back on the side table.

Phil studied him pensively. It was quiet for a moment, except for small sounds emanating from the kitchen where Joyce was orchestrating dinner.

'I assumed you came here because you don't believe it either,' Phil said bluntly.

Jason frowned. 'Don't believe what?'

'His suicide, of course,' Phil exclaimed.

Jason blinked. 'I don't follow.'

Phil sighed. 'I'm convinced. So is Joyce. Unfortunately, no one else is.'

Now Jason leaned forward. 'Could you be more specific?'

Phil shrugged. 'Not much to relate, really. Except that Chris never gave me the impression that he was planning to commit suicide. Granted, you could say the same thing for a lot of people who subsequently end things that way. It's like my mother once said: "you can look at people's faces, but not inside their minds." But I was with Chris on the night he died. I talked to him, even. Maybe I was the last one to talk to him. Because a few hours later he was dangling from a noose in his attic.'

'I never heard anything about that during the funeral. What did he say to you?'

Phil grimaced, sorrow written indelibly upon his face. 'See, that's the thing. We were supposed to go bowling two days later. He was looking forward to it, and so was I. He was laughing, determined to win – he was very clear on that. Chris *always* wanted to win. Except we never went. If he was planning to kill himself when we set the date, that would mean he'd have to be one hell of a good actor. But he wasn't that great an actor, and he wasn't acting either. Certainly not that night. I swear to you, Chris was sincere. I knew him as well as anyone on this planet. Better than anyone, in fact. He was sincere that night. Trust me on that.'

Phil fell silent as Jason sat staring at his feet.

He looked up. 'So what are you saying?'

'That your uncle didn't commit suicide,' Phil responded without pause.

A surreal feeling, as if he were having another hallucination, swept across Jason. 'Then what *do* you think happened?'

Phil's expression was etched in stone. 'It leaves only one conclusion, doesn't it?'

Jason nodded; his voice turned hoarse. 'That he didn't die voluntarily. That he was murdered.'

Phil's silence confirmed it.

'Do you have any evidence?'

Phil drank deeply from his bottle of beer. 'Well, I've discussed it with people in the neighborhood, of course. But no, I don't have evidence, and neither does anyone else. However, Burt Carlsen across the street will tell you that on the night Chris supposedly killed himself, he saw a man standing outside his house. He was on the sidewalk, staring at the house.'

Joyce poked her head around the kitchen door. 'I'm setting the table. Are you coming?'

Phil glanced across his shoulder. 'Coming, dear.'

She disappeared back into the kitchen.

'And what else?' Jason asked softly.

Phil cast him a pensive look. 'Burt happened to see it from his window, but he didn't stay and watch. Later, the man was gone.'

'So there's no evidence,' Jason said.

'Objectively, I have to agree with you,' Phil said. 'There is no evidence. I haven't been able to convince the police, either. You know what they say.'

Jason did know. The brief police inquiry had concluded that his uncle had likely gone mad from the emotional and physical pain of his cancer. They assumed he had taken a fall, because there had been injuries to his face, but he could have done that to himself. He had written a suicide note and had gone upstairs to end it all.

'And this man on the sidewalk. What did he look like?'

Phil shrugged. 'It was dark. Burt said he was built like an outhouse, someone you wouldn't want to mess with. He was dressed in black from head to foot.'

Jason considered it. This probably meant nothing, and Phil was rolling along with a paranoid theory. Maybe even an obsession. Jason knew all about obsessions.

On the other hand, he wanted to snoop around inside his uncle's house. He was here now, and during the funeral he had been mainly concerned with Kayla. All of his attention had been focused on helping her through their loss as much as he could, and that had gone surprisingly well.

'Phil, do you still have a key to Chris's house?'

'Yes. Until it's put up for sale, I'm keeping an eye on the place. Joyce goes in there from time to time to clean a little. The family has not asked her to do, mind you, and she doesn't get paid for it. But she does it anyway because she wants to.'

'Would you mind if I had a look around in there?'

'Why would I mind?' Phil said. 'Are you looking for anything in particular?'

'I'm not sure. At least it'll give me an opportunity to formally say goodbye to Uncle Chris.'

Phil stood up. 'Fine with me. We'll go over there later. Let's grab some dinner first, otherwise Joyce will be on us like white on rice.'

Jason followed Phil to the table in the kitchen. Joyce had gone all out, serving a virtual feast from soup to nuts.

Even so, Jason did not enjoy his dinner. He had no appetite. And he kept peering anxiously at the burning candle Joyce had set on the table. He would feel rude asking her to snuff it out, so he didn't.

Chris's house was meaningful to Jason. He had experienced the emotion of it three months ago, during the funeral ceremony, and he felt it again now. Except all was quiet this evening. The last time the small home had been full of people, almost his entire family had shown up. Aunt Ethel had been in tears. For once, Uncle Hank had refrained from asking whether Tanner & Preston was in the market for a big-time client. Aunt Hilary had left her journal of medical complaints at home. The atmosphere had been as black as night. Jason had kept his arm around Kayla constantly, helping her to get through it all.

Chris's friends had also attended. Hugo, Felipe, Phil and a few others; someone named Reggie Griffin and two other men whose names had slipped from Jason's memory. He had spoken briefly with most of them. All in all Chris had had few friends and had pretty much kept his own counsel. Only a new game or contest could fire up his juices. At the funeral there had been a lot of reminiscing about that. The time he lost playing cards, for example, causing what seemed like a short circuit inside his brain, manifested when he butted his head against a wall. And then there was another time he had disagreed with the judges during a contest he hadn't participated in. He had been furious nonetheless, and had even threatened to sue them.

These stories were told with the sole purpose of trying to find an explanation for what Chris had done. The conclusion Jason had reached was that his eccentric uncle had been unable to face losing. He would never be able to beat the cancer ravaging his body. It was inevitable that he would lose this one round, which was perhaps why he had decided to quit before the game was over.

He was not acting, not that night.

Jason turned to Phil, who was standing beside him in the middle of Chris's living room. The furniture was still in place, arranged just as it had been. As were the three shelves with trophies, certificates and scrap books adorned with press articles and photos. No one had dared take or move any of them. His pictures were still on the walls. Only his personal documents had been removed. Jason had the sense that if Chris walked into the room at that moment, Jason would not be the least surprised.

'When's the place going up for sale?' Phil asked.

'The family is still considering what to do with it,' Jason responded. 'They haven't decided yet.'

Phil nodded. 'It's going to be tricky to sell it. It will have to go to someone who falls in love with the place instantly. But that's unlikely. People are bound to find out what happened here.'

Jason ignored that. 'Let's go up and have a look at the attic.'

Phil led the way up the stairs. The attic, with an angled roof on both sides, had been Chris's hobby room. Daylight entered through a skylight. Across the entire length of the ceiling was the massive support beam from which he had hanged himself. Phil looked up, and Jason followed his gaze. Neither of them said anything. There was nothing to say.

Phil looked down at his feet and sighed.

She's gone over to Ralph, you know.

Jason glanced at Phil. 'What did you say?'

Phil arched his eyebrows. 'I didn't say anything.'

Jason listened intently as his gaze settled on the massive beam.

Had he been hearing his inner voice again? Or was it Chris's voice?

Suddenly the air felt as if someone had turned on an air conditioner. Goosebumps broke out on his arms.

Jason wanted out of there. He turned on his heel and walked toward and down the stairs to the living room. Phil followed after him.

'What's up?' he asked, concerned, when they reached the bottom.

'You acted funny up there. And from what I can see, you're not doing all that well down here.'

Jason was breathing as though he had been running.

I'm losing it, Phil. Just like Kayla said. Go ahead, tell me the same thing.

'I think I need to sit down for a moment.'

He sank on to the brown sofa, where no one had sat for weeks.

So here he was, in the bungalow where he had been born and where Chris Campbell had died. Chris had been in Mount Peytha City in 1977. Jason knew because he had recognized his uncle in the old black and white photographs Joe Bresnahan had shown him. He had participated in the funeral procession transporting the bodily remains of Robert, Amanda and Mikey Chawkins to their final resting place.

Jason was pretty sure that he remembered Chris mentioning Mount Peytha to him at some point, words that he had garbled as 'Mapeetaa' in his old drawing. But Jason was also sure that Chris had never said he'd been at the Chawkins' funeral.

It was another clue to a morbid puzzle.

What was Chris doing there?

The answer to that question was the key.

Earlier in the day Jason had called his father to ask this question, but Edward had not been able to enlighten Jason. They had a big family, and there were aunts and uncles who had known Chris well. On impulse, he had made two additional calls. The first was to his Aunt Ethel, and the second to Aunt Stephanie. Both calls had consumed forty-five minutes and had yielded nothing. After Aunt Stephanie's emotional outburst, he had felt disinclined to call other relatives.

'Phil, would you mind giving me some time alone?'

Phil seemed primed to ask a question, but then simply nodded.

'Will you come back over later, Jason?'

'Sure.'

'Just pull the door shut when you leave,' Phil said on his way out. 'I'll lock it after you leave.'

Alone now, Jason stretched out on the sofa. The house breathed an unnatural stillness. Ghosts from the past became tangible. From nowhere, a rhyme entered his mind; one that Chris had taught him when he was a little boy.

In the back of my father's yard, there's a vegetable tree. Here a tree, there a tree, every tree a branch. Here a branch, there a branch, every branch a nest. Every nest an egg. Here an egg, there an egg, every egg a black spot on the hole. Do you know what this is?

Chris had been fond of riddles. This riddle didn't mean anything. But still . . . a vegetable tree. He remembered Joe Bresnahan's vegetable garden beneath the Joshua trees. A black spot. Something that had burned: a scorched place? And a hole: could that be another word for a grave? An egg from a nest? A child that did what it wanted, that wouldn't stay dead? Now *that* was a morbid leap, he chided himself.

On an impulse Jason turned his head to the left.

Underneath the china cabinet, right in front of him, was something on the floor. A stone? He could barely see it, had only noticed it because he was stretched out on the sofa and his gaze had happened to fall on it.

Something inside of him told him this was important. He rose, knelt down in front of the cupboard, and reached under the cabinet, trying to locate the object. No luck. He lay down to increase his reach. When his fingers finally closed around it, he dragged it out and peered down at it.

It was a ring. A silver ring. Small and delicate, with a Celtic cross on it.

He knew whose ring this was.

And he remembered something else.

Jason closed the door behind him and walked back to Phil's house. He didn't linger; he had other preparations to make. He wanted to get back to Los Angeles as soon as possible. The 10.37 p.m. flight for tonight, the last flight out, was no longer an option; he would have to take the 6:00 commuter flight tomorrow morning. He was restless, agitated, confused. He called Kayla.

While talking to her, he remembered the eerie voice in Chris's attic and that made him even more worried about her. He insisted that she not stay at home alone, but instead spend the night at Simone's. He would come back home tomorrow on the first flight out from San Francisco. He was on to someone and it was more than a theory. He needed to go see this person, and then, he expected, things to become crystal clear.

TWENTY-NINE
Abduction

Jason awoke from a light slumber and glanced yet again at the digital clock at his bedside: 1:55 in the morning. Tossing aside the sheet, he got up, took a shower, got dressed, and tiptoed through the silent hallways of the Surf Hill motel. He left a note for the night clerk and sufficient money to pay his bill. At a quarter to three, he slipped inside his Ford and left the parking lot; moments later he was swallowed up in the night-time traffic of San Francisco.

Jason's head throbbed, his eyes were bloodshot, and he was exhausted beyond measure.

But he was on his way home.

Although he didn't understand why, he called Kayla from the car. It was the middle of the night; if she had her cell phone turned on, the ring tone should have woken her. He had no clue why he felt so compelled to call her. It was as if his inner voice was ordering him to and he could not ignore it. Nor could he understand why she didn't answer.

I'm too late, he thought. Another cause for anxiety, but it made no sense. A few more hours and he'd be home. Then they would talk things through and make a fresh start. After he made one final trip, of course.

This was not over. Not yet. Not by a long shot.

But now his worries were focused not on him, but on Kayla.

You've lost her, the malevolent little voice inside his head whispered.

Behind the wheel, driving through the night-time streets of San Francisco, he felt a chill snake through his body, the likes of which he had never known. He thought of Canyon View and the small and cozy living room, which would be much too spacious without her. Everything in that room *was* Kayla. The oriental vase she had bought at some obscure little shop in Los Angeles. He thought it was hideous and kitschy, but she had been overjoyed when she brought it home, happy as a child. *Look, Jason, don't you just love this?* The antique kitchenware cabinet she had bought for a song and had fixed up herself, spending weeks scraping off old paint, sanding it, re-coating it. The elegant tan flower basket on the glass coffee table in front of the sofa. Now that *was* lovely.

'No,' he mumbled. 'I'm not too late. I can't be.'

At a quarter to four, he was in the terminal waiting area, the first passenger on deck for United Express 3126 that didn't leave for another two hours. He tried again to phone her. Her cell phone rang; she had not turned it off. But she did not pick up. He tried the land phone in Canyon View. Again, no answer.

A sickening anxiety assailed Jason's gut. He was becoming increasingly convinced that something bad had happened. Something irreversible.

Waiting until six o'clock was tantamount to torture, and the flight itself seemed even longer. Still, it was only 7:30 on a sunny morning when his plane touched down at LAX. As soon as he was allowed to, he turned on his cell phone and saw that three messages had come in while he was in flight.

Kayla, he thought, as his spirits rose.

He listened to the messages in the tunnel between the plane and the terminal building. The first voicemail was not from Kayla, but from Simone.

'Jason!' her recorded voice said, in a panic.

Shit, he thought, *something is very wrong*.

But it was worse than anything he could have imagined.

Jason slammed the door of the airport taxi and burst into Pacific Valley Hospital. He wanted to see his wife *now* and he brushed aside everyone in his path until a tall, well-built doctor in a white coat stopped him and struggled with the help of two male physician assistants to calm him down. Although Jason was in no mood to cooperate, he did not resist. Instead, he felt suddenly deflated. As the doctor talked to him in as soothing a voice as possible, Jason gathered through the fog that Kayla was in surgery and that there was nothing definitive to report yet. She was in good hands, the doctor assured him. Jason had to be patient.

'Will she live?' he heard himself ask. 'Can you at least tell me *that*?'

The doctor didn't answer and made him suffer through the worst of it: the wait. Sitting and *waiting*.

A physician assistant guided Jason into a stark room where five people he knew were seated. The first to acknowledge him was his father. Edward Evans wrapped his arms around his son, patted him on the back and whispered, 'My God, son. My God.'

Next to him were Daniel and Tonya Sheehan. Jason barely recognized Daniel, who sat there passively with none of the joyful successful businessman appearance that normally consumed his character. Daniel Sheehan had always reminded Jason of Blake Carrington from *Dynasty*, the soap series he had watched with his parents when he was a child. Daniel had the same distinguished gray hair and powerful eyes that radiated authority.

But today that self-assurance was gone, and what Jason saw instead was a distraught old man. Much like his wife Tonya, normally a stylish and smiling woman who this morning looked utterly defeated.

Simone and Cliff were also there. Cliff was pale, shocked, silent, his hand clasped around Simone's. Simone's eyes were red and puffy. The moment she saw Jason, she broke out in sobs.

'Jason . . .' she choked.

Cliff stood, seemingly considering whether to hug Jason or shake his hand. In the end he did neither and sank back on to his chair.

'What happened? Who can tell me more?' Jason asked the five of them. It was a plea, not a demand.

'Jason, I . . . I can't . . .' Simone stammered when everyone else in the room looked at the floor and remained silent.

'Yes you can, Simone. Tell me.'

He needed to hear it. He needed to hear *something*. If no one spoke, he could only conclude that she had already passed away.

'She was attacked last night,' Simone managed between sobs. 'There is no trace of the suspect. She was stabbed with a knife, several times.'

Jason already knew this. But still his heart wrenched.

'The man left her for dead, but she was able to call nine one one. She was conscious for a few moments in the ambulance. She said the attacker was a large man, dressed in black. That's all she said, and that's all anyone knows for now.'

Phil's words came back to him like flaming arrows.

Built like an outhouse. He was wearing black.

Simone faltered again. Cliff pulled her close and she buried her face against his chest. Jason wondered whether he would have anyone left to console after today. If Kayla died . . .

No, it hasn't come to that yet, he fought to believe. *She's still alive, hold on to that!*

It was hard. What he had feared most in the darkest recesses of his mind had now happened. It was inexplicable, but that didn't make it any less true.

He stared at the gray floor, swiping at stinging tears in his eyes, desperately trying to stem the flow. Nobody would blame him for crying, but what good would it do? It wouldn't help her, or him. He had to keep his mind clear.

The six of them waited. And waited . . .

Through the window Jason saw the sun on its upward arc. He felt, nevertheless, that it had gone completely dark. Wandering around in darkness – henceforth, that would be his fate.

At eleven thirty the door to the waiting room opened. Curls of smoke wafted in past the door frame. Jason felt searing heat, just before flames leapt into the room, like the tongues of fiery dragons from the underworld. Jason stared at them in horror, then at the others in the room with him. Incredibly, they hadn't noticed anything.

From the center of the fire, Kayla appeared. It was her, no doubt, a body in flames from head to toe. She was grinning horribly, like a witch. Her hands, claws now, stabbed at him.

You left me, and now I'm dead. You abandoned me. But I won't be going alone. I'm taking you with me!

He squeezed his eyes shut.

This isn't happening, this is impossible, he thought, horrified.

He waited a few seconds. When he opened his eyes, the doctor stood in the doorway. The fire was gone. Everything was gone, except for the man in the white coat standing in the doorway.

The man looked at him with a grave expression.

Jason's heart sank.

You left me, and now I'm dead.

Now I'm dead.

The doctor had some bad news for them.

Three hours later, Jason shuffled red-eyed along the hospital corridors. He could not stop sobbing. A burly male nurse stared at him with compassion, and then quickly averted his gaze. Jason needed to be alone for a while, alone with his sorrow. He found himself outside the hospital's chapel and went inside.

Sitting in front of a small altar decorated with a bronze statue of Jesus, on a scuffed, saddle-brown bench with its paint peeling, *The Car Song* cut through the serene silence. He listened to it for a few moments, then pulled his cell phone from his pocket. He chose to ignore the call and turned the phone off. He closed his eyes and prayed. For Kayla.

He heard the door open behind him. Someone entered. It was the burly male nurse who had avoided his gaze. What was the man coming to tell him?

When he came close, Jason thought he recognized him.

Although it was not far off in his memories, it was too far to spring to mind immediately. But when the man grinned, it came back to him; not because of the grin, but because of the chipped tooth among his yellow teeth. Suddenly Jason remembered, like a recollection of a spoiled dinner he'd had the day before.

That tooth. It went with the sour brown eyes of—

He jumped up as if he had been stung by a deadly insect.

'My God,' he whispered. '*You!*'

The male nurse grabbed his arm. His grin had disappeared.

'Hello, Jason,' Doug Shatz said.

The man who had once raped a young woman named Maria and who had been convicted after Jason had convinced the Spanish girl to report him, had changed considerably. He was no longer a rangy adolescent; he had sprouted muscles and looked like a bodybuilder.

'Let go of me,' Jason yelled.

Doug gave him a venomous stare just as a tree trunk seemed to crash down on to the back of Jason's neck, forcing him to his knees. Dizzy and stunned he looked up at the hand Doug had hit him with. As white-hot pain spread from one shoulder to the other, Shatz crouched down beside him.

'You do not tell me what to do, you understand?'

He said it like a teacher reprimanding a headstrong child. Jason smelled booze and cigarette smoke on the man's breath. Suddenly Doug drew a knife and held it up close to Jason's eyes.

'What I want you to do is come with me, very quietly. You hear me?'

Jason nodded.

'One move and I'll do to you what I did to your wife.'

Doug yanked him up. Jason had no strength to resist. The man wrapped an arm around his midsection, as if supporting him. The tip of the knife cut into Jason's back.

He considered resisting, or fleeing. Later, it turned out that his best chance to flee was during those few minutes, while Doug was leading him through the hospital toward the parking lot, where a white Mercedes Benz was parked off in a back lot. But Jason didn't try anything. He was stunned, defeated, shattered.

Doug opened the doors, hit Jason in the back of the neck with a karate chop again, and tied him up with rope he had retrieved from the van. Jason felt dizzy. His world was spinning around him as first his hands were tied behind his back, and then his ankles were trussed. Doug shoved him into the back compartment of the van and closed the doors. As Doug slid behind the wheel and drove off, Jason noticed a heap of black clothes in a corner of the van.

THIRTY

Mitch

Jason had no idea how long he lay bound like a wild animal in the back of the van. He had lost all sense of time. The man who had murdered his wife was behind the wheel, and he felt utterly broken.

Finally, the van came to a stop. Doug disappeared from behind the glass partition between the back of the van and the front seat. Jason heard the clatter of a garage door going up. Then Doug reappeared and drove the van inside. After that, he opened the back door.

As he had expected, Jason found himself looking out into a garage. One he recognized.

Another door opened, and a man in a wheelchair appeared. Jason stared at him. His missing ears, nose, lips and eyelids were not as noticeable today as were the scars on his face. They seemed to be more prominent, as if betraying emotions that smoldered beneath the skin.

There were people, Jason knew, who thought Lou Briggs looked like Frankenstein's monster. And with good reason. Lou gave him an amused look, as if he were wondering what den of evil Jason Evans had landed in this time.

Jason continued to stare at Doug, who, like a bouncer, had taken up position before the open back door. He had his arms folded over his chest.

'Been to visit the hospital, Jason?' Lou asked.

Despite the murderous glance Jason threw at him, Lou remained unmoved.

'Doug had a minor slip-up. But he'll finish the job later.'

Jason shut his eyes and opened them again. 'My wife is dead. She died at twelve fifteen. I was there.'

The words that spilled from his mouth were hoarse, almost imperceptible.

Lou's eyes widened. 'Really? Well, what do you know? The problem solves itself.' He made a harsh, metallic sound that could have passed for a cruel laugh.

Jason bit his lip. Impotence, anger and grief were merging and rising up uncontrollably. *'You filthy bastards!'* he screamed.

Lou made a gesture as if he had felt a mosquito bite. Annoying, nothing more.

'You and I have a lot to discuss, Jason,' he said impassively. 'I know this is all a terrible shock for you. Believe me, I know. But will you behave, or won't you? If you refuse, I'm afraid I will have to make this quite unpleasant for you.'

'I don't give a damn!' Jason cried out. 'Just kill me too, you son of a bitch, and get it over with!'

Lou sadly shook his head. 'How disappointing. Don't you want to know why Kayla had to die? Or your Uncle Chris, for that matter?'

Jason's jaw fell.

'But before I tell you, I need an update from you,' Lou said. 'So I'll know where to start. What have you found out for yourself? You told your wife, God rest her soul, that you discovered something in San Francisco. What was it?'

Despite his horrifying mix of emotions, Jason's gaze turned inquisitive.

'Ah yes, you don't know this,' Lou said. 'Just before Doug delivered the first photograph to your office, he broke into your house.

It wasn't hard. You always forget to lock the porch doors. He planted a few bugs inside your house. In the phone, behind the cupboard. They kept us pretty well informed about everything that went on between you and Kayla. Including the last conversation you had with her, when you said you were returning to Los Angeles.'

Jason shook his head in disbelief.

'Those photographs came from me, you know,' Lou continued. 'Doug was only the delivery boy. And you won't be surprised to learn that he was driving this very same van when he pushed you off the road, that night after your dad's party.'

Jason bit his lip.

'I asked you what you discovered in San Francisco. I'll be honest, that phone call was my cue to act. I thought you were on your way over to my place, and I wanted to beat you to it. I wanted to get revenge on Kayla first, and then on you.'

Still lying in the back of the white Mercedes Benz van with his arms and legs tied, Jason was unable to move, convinced he was about to be murdered. He felt a powerful urge to give his anger and sorrow free reign. After all, what difference would it make? He was in Lou and Doug's power, and they could finish him off whenever they wanted. And they would. Lou had told him so himself.

Something else inside him awoke. A different kind of anger. These men had taken Kayla away from him. He was still alive. And as long as he lived, he could fight. He *wanted* to fight. He wanted his own revenge – although it would be hard to come by under these circumstances. But as long as he was alive he could at least hold on to the possibility. He had to use his head. He had to stay calm and collected. Lou wanted to talk, and as long as he kept the man talking, he was still alive, still able to act.

'Yes, I *was* on my way to your place,' he said. 'I found out that you had been inside Chris's house. I found your ring. It had rolled beneath a cupboard. That's why you were rubbing your right hand the last time I came over to see you. You were missing your ring.'

Lou grinned. 'So *that's* where it went. Do you have it on you?'

Jason bit his lip again.

'Search him,' Lou said to Doug.

The wide-shouldered man, still dressed as a male nurse, crawled into the back of the van and started searching through Jason's clothing.

'Doug never forgot that stunt you pulled on him, you know?'

Lou said. 'Thanks to you, we became partners. Without you I would
never have heard of him. Still, Doug mostly has a business view of
things. I'm his best paying customer. For me, there are other priori-
ties. But I'll tell you about them later.'

Jason processed that remark. Lou was not done with him yet.
That meant they weren't going to kill him right away. He didn't
know how much time he had left, but he *had* some time, it appeared.

Doug found the ring in Jason's pocket and handed it to Lou, who
rubbed the piece of jewelry on his pants and slid it on his finger.

'Now I feel better,' he said, holding up his hand and smiling
at it.

He trained his eyes on Jason. Gazing at him intensely, he rolled
his chair closer to the back doors of the van.

'Go on, what else do you know? This is most intriguing.'

It was almost impossible for Jason to control himself. Lou, the
man he had trusted, was a murderer. He worked with a hit man, a
thug who deserved to spend the rest of his life in prison. Kayla was
their victim. Jason had never thought that he would be capable of
murder, but at this moment he knew he was. But what could he do?
More to the point, why had he let Doug take him by surprise at the
hospital? Why hadn't he tried to escape or cry for help? The answer
to those questions was obvious. He had been too shattered, too
stunned by Doug's unexpected appearance.

Try and stall for time, his survival instinct shouted at him.

The fact that the Polaroid photographs had come from Lou, and
that Doug had been the attacker, did not deter him. If anything, that
knowledge gave him strength. Everything he did in the next few
minutes or hours – or however long he had left – he would do for
Kayla. But for now he had to keep Lou engaged in conversation
for as long as he could.

'Chris was at the funeral for the Chawkins family,' he said. 'I
know I must have some connection to Mikey, who died in the car.
A few weeks later, I was born. My pyrophobia may have something
to do with what happened to Mikey.'

Lou kept gazing at him with great interest.

'And so?' he prompted.

'I think that, somehow, Mikey is inside of me. It occurred to me
that maybe I'm his incarnation.'

Lou tapped a finger on his chin.

'Go on.'

'That's about it,' Jason said. 'The photographs were about Mike Chawkins. Chris went to his family's funeral. You and Doug killed him. But I don't know why. And I don't know why you felt that Kayla had to die. Or what you have against me.'

Lou shook his head. 'I thought you would have come up with more than that by now,' he said dejectedly. 'But I'm starting to believe that you really *don't* know.'

He sighed, as if Jason had professed ignorance about water being wet.

He looked at Doug. 'We're doing this.'

Doug picked a metal plate from the garage floor and wedged it between the floor and the back of the van. Then he pushed Lou, still in his wheelchair, inside and parked him next to Jason.

Doug grabbed his black clothes and slammed the van's back doors. A moment later, Jason heard the rattle of garage doors sliding up again. He struggled to sit up across from Lou by leaning his back against the spare tire fastened to the side of the van. His wrists burned from the chafing rope.

Soon after, the van's engine fired up and the van rolled backward out of the garage. Doug shifted gears and the car started moving forward. Above Doug's head, visible through the glass partition window, smoke spiraled up. Doug was dressed entirely in black – his executioner's uniform – and he had lit a cigarette.

Jason looked around. He was thirsty and his throat hurt. But he was still alive. It seemed they were not going to kill him inside Lou's house.

Against the partition were a number of brown burlap bags. From one of them protruded several long sticks. Jason also saw a bale of hay, wrapped in foil.

He looked back into Lou Briggs's eyes. The man sat straight-backed in his wheelchair, watching him.

'Since we have some time, I'll tell you my story, Jason' he said casually. 'I'll tell you all about it.'

As the van continued on down the road, Lou made a sound as if he was having an epileptic fit. But it was only his garbled laughter.

'It's like a stage play,' he continued quietly, barely audible above the hum of the engine. 'Imagine a theater. The scenery is all set, the light in the room is dimmed, the spotlights go on. The first actor on stage is Pete McGray. You, the audience, know Pete. He's a lazy drunk who talks with his fists. A second actor who will soon come on stage is Donna Campbell. For all the wrong reasons, Donna feels attracted to Pete. A romance develops between the twenty-four-year-old woman and thirty-year-old McGray. You might say Donna should have known better, but unfortunately she didn't. Not at the time, when she let herself be won over by Pete. Oh, her brother Chris had warned her often enough, but in those days she was stubborn and didn't listen to him. Her brother always thought it was because she had been forced to skip childhood and grow up too fast. Donna lost her mother at the tender age of fourteen, and her father had left her long before that. She hadn't heard from him since. She never found out what happened to him, how long he lived after that, or where he died. The only person she had left in the world was her brother, two years older than she and something of an oddball.'

To Jason, despite his misery, it was like having a cold hand around his throat as this mutilated madman told him things that, as far as he knew, were known only to him and a handful of other people. What Lou was saying was true. All of it.

'Donna's past was no picnic,' Lou went on. 'A children's home here, a guardian there, never a place to really call home. She doesn't want to live with her brother in San Francisco, even though he invites her to do that more than once. But she is restless, insecure; she feels hunted. Donna Campbell is different from Donna Evans. As Donna Evans she will eventually be transformed, but in this act of the play she is not there yet. She moves from one city to the next, sleeping with one guy after another. She never has any serious problems, however, until in Salt Lake City she runs into Pete McGray. Pete seems to be the one. He is big and strong. She is madly in love with him and for a few months she is happy, the longest Donna has been happy in her life to date.

'But then she gets pregnant. And with that comes the end of the fairy tale. Pete wants her to have an abortion. She refuses; she's determined to have her baby. A change comes over Pete. Suddenly he is not such a nice man any more. He starts boozing, and when he's drunk, he hits the mother of his unborn child.

'One day, inevitably, things blow up. This is a few weeks after Donna finds out she is pregnant. It's July thirteenth, to be exact . . .'

Lou paused, allowing Jason time to recall that he had received the first photograph on July thirteenth. Then he continued. 'In a fit of rage Pete beats her up, even drawing blood. When he comes to his senses, he's shocked by what he has done and flees from the house. He leaves her there, injured. She calls an ambulance and is admitted to the hospital, where she recovers. She then calls her brother, who takes her under his wing.

'Donna survives, but her unborn child does not. And as if that weren't bad enough, the doctors tell her she will never be able to conceive again. Pete has destroyed her present and her future.'

Jason moved his backside a little to straighten up against the spare tire. It dawned on him that Lou had just said something that was new information for him. It seemed unimportant, since everything was unimportant compared to what Doug had done to Kayla, and his own impending death; but maybe it *did* matter. Lou was trying to explain *why* he had done what he did. Could Jason use that against him somehow?

'Pete is my biological father,' Jason said. 'My mother told me that. Why would you think that . . .?'

Suddenly it felt like something was clogging his throat. The answer revealed itself.

Chris.

Only Uncle Chris could have told Lou all of this.

At the same time he thought of Pete McGray, a man he knew only from the rare times his mother had talked about him. Once she had shown Jason a picture of him. A slovenly man with long hair and unshaved cheeks had stared back at him. Jason had not understood how his mother could have fallen in love with a loser like that, and neither did she, in hindsight.

Pete had sired him, she had told Jason. Then she had ended the relationship and found happiness with Edward Evans. Donna did not want to be reminded of Pete. Could Jason accept that and leave it at that? Jason had been young when he had this conversation with his mother. He had willingly agreed, and after that he had mostly forgotten about Pete.

But had his mother lied? And if Pete wasn't his father after all, who was?

How had Lou figured it out? Why would he care?

Perception dawned suddenly, as if a door into wisdom had opened.

'As you know, Pete doesn't get a happy end either,' Lou continued.

'He gets stabbed during a bar brawl. Apparently he was in the wrong place at the wrong time. His death, however, was no great loss to the world.'

As Lou paused, Jason's thoughts churned. A sense of *knowing* had formed inside his mind. It made him nauseous.

At the same time, he thought of his mother. He had known about her tumultuous past, but in all these years he had never doubted her sincerity and that she had become a better person by what she had been forced to endure. But nothing added up. The image he had always had of her was now transformed into something black and unrecognizable.

'Let's get on with the play,' Lou said, shifting around a little in his wheelchair. He was visibly enjoying the opportunity to tell his story.

'It's all coming together now. After losing her baby, Donna is depressed. Of course, she is also furious with Pete. But she knows she needs to get on with her life. Then it happens. On August eighteenth, 1977, she is driving along Highway 98 near Sacramento Wash. She has said goodbye to Salt Lake City and plans to make a new life for herself in California. A little over five weeks have passed since she last saw Pete McGray, when he left her bleeding on the floor, moaning and writhing in pain. As Donna is driving along, she sees black smoke rising up ahead of her. When she draws close, she sees a car on fire. Donna pulls over and runs toward it to see if she can help. She witnesses a terrible thing. The car has flipped over on its roof, and there are two screaming people in the front seat. They're stuck and can't get out. And then she sees something else. Crying, wailing babies in the back seat. Two of them . . .'

Lou fashioned a v with two fingers.

'The flames haven't yet reached the newborns, monozygotic twins called Mike and Mitch, not yet three weeks old, but it won't be long before they do. She has to act. She has to make a choice. Who should she try to save first? There's no time to think. Donna squirms into the burning car, through the hot, stinking fumes, struggles toward the babies, and grabs the first one she comes to. She retreats from the car with the child – just in time. There's an explosion and new flames shoot up from the cracked windscreen. Nailed to the ground in shock, she stands there for a moment, convinced that everyone inside the car must now be dead. But she's wrong. Black smoke is wafting out. She's afraid to approach it now; she's panicked and scared to death. Imagine that.'

Jason tried to. In his mind's eye, as if he were watching a movie, Highway 98 appeared. Broken asphalt under the searing sunlight on a sweltering hot August day. The air shimmering from the vicious flames consuming the Chawkins' car.

There is Donna, a young woman, mother of an unborn, murdered child. Three people have just died, right in front of her eyes. She's shaking, she's trembling, maybe even crying. There are three dead bodies in the car, that's what she is thinking. But she doesn't know that there is one other survivor. Someone she has not saved.

'Do you get it now, Mike?' the mutilated man in the wheelchair asked.

Jason nodded in resignation.

Yes, I get it now, Mitch.

THIRTY-ONE
Secrets

He who had murdered Kayla and Chris showed his macabre grin as he continued his story again.

'Another car is approaching in the distance. The next few seconds are crucial in everything else that is going to happen. Donna thinks that the three people inside the burning car are dead. Then she makes *the* decision.'

Jason did not need to guess what decision Mitch was talking about.

'She puts the baby inside her own car and drives off. In the other car, closing quickly, is a man named Johnny Halper. He was a gas station attendant and a chronic alcoholic. He had been drinking heavily the night before. In the morning of August eighteenth he had not skipped his usual breakfast, a generous shot of Jack Daniels, as the police will ascertain later. Despite that, he acts bravely and decisively when he arrives at the burning car. He in fact performs a heroic deed. He too squirms inside, sustaining serious burns in the process, but manages to pull the other baby from the flaming inferno. The adults are burned beyond salvation, but the baby in his arms is still alive, although it has suffered many serious burns. By the way, Johnny is unaware that there was a woman who saved one of the babies. Donna drove off too quickly. And besides, the only thing he was paying attention to was the car on fire. And if he hadn't acted the way he did, I would not be here to tell you all this.'

From somewhere came a rattling sound followed by a metallic *clonk*. Jason had no idea what that was. A new cloud of smoke rose up above Doug's head; he had lit another cigarette as he drove on.

'The baby Johnny pulls from the car survives. But he is fated to go through life with severe disfigurements. Despite a series of surgical procedures over the years, that is one thing that can't be remedied. And the child, later the man, is confined to a wheelchair most of the time because of irreparable contractions of his muscles.'

Mitch Chawkins paused for a moment. Maybe he thought that Jason should feel sorry for him. Had he forgotten what Doug, in his name, had done to Jason's wife? He remembered Joe Bresnahan's words. *There's one missing – now where did that one go?* He had thought that Joe was talking about a picture that he had misplaced; now he could imagine that the old man had been talking about the other baby. Had Jason asked him about it at the time, he would have found out more about the mystery nightmare he was living in. But he had neglected to do so and what was done was done, for better or for worse.

Jason, formerly known as Mike Chawkins, clenched his teeth and struggled to pry his wrists and ankles apart. But it was to no avail. Doug had done too good a job tying him up.

'Let's go back to Donna,' Mitch said. 'Like I said, she assumes the people in the car have perished. So she takes off with the baby she rescued from the flames.'

Jason briefly remembered the visions he had had while lying on Mark's couch. It was becoming clear to him who the figure wreathed in flames – the fire spirit – had been. Donna Campbell, the woman he had always known as his mother.

Mawkee, he thought. *She called me Mikey, before I became Jason.*

'With me,' he said hoarsely.

Mitch grinned horribly. 'Yes, with you, though at first that was unclear. You and I were only a few weeks old at the time, identical twins. So who could say which one is Mitch and which one is Mikey? Fortunately, one might say, our parents found out soon after we were born that we aren't totally identical after all: our organs are mirrored inside our bodies. It happens sometimes with identical twins. The phenomenon is called *situs inversus*. Apparently it's also the reason I suffer from colds more often.'

Mitch paused for a moment, pensively tapping his finger against his chin.

'Without the fire, or had Donna made a different choice, I would have looked like you,' he whispered. 'But I got burned, and you . . . well, we can see how *you* turned out.'

Mitch swallowed, shook his head, and said, 'OK, enough of that. Now on with the show. So Donna drives off with you. In the beginning, in those first minutes and hours, her feelings revolve mostly around shock and panic. After all, she has seen three people die in agony, right before her eyes.

'And then, of course, she realizes she has committed a crime – she has stolen you. In utter confusion she drives away as fast and as far as she can. By nightfall, after she has calmed down somewhat, she calls the only person she trusts implicitly: her brother Chris. He listens to her story and urges her to join him in his house in San Francisco.

'She can stay with him while they figure out what to do. Donna agrees, and drives there. In the next few days she nearly drowns in panic; without her brother's constant support her mind would surely have come undone.

'Her brother makes some phone calls and does research about what happened on Highway ninety-eight near Sacramento Wash, and who the victims were, according to official reports. Then he decides to go to Mount Peytha City to attend the Chawkins funeral. Even though it's risky, he wants to express his sympathy in some way. And he wants to find out what people are saying about the missing baby. It turns out that nobody so much as mentions the baby.

'Donna is plagued by regret and remorse. There are times when it gets so bad that she wants to report the missing child to the authorities. But then she realizes that she cannot do that. She can't go back now. Chris doesn't report the theft of the baby either. What he wants most is to maintain his relationship with Donna. He fears he will lose her if he turns his sister and the baby over to the police. So he says nothing about it all those years.

'Chris advises her to talk to Pete. If she wants to keep the baby, she will have to convince the world that this is her and Pete's child, and Pete will have to corroborate her story if anyone should ask. Because Donna wants nothing to do with McGray, her brother pays him a visit. It isn't a long or difficult talk. All Pete wants is to be rid of Donna, and he doesn't care about anything else – he will do whatever it takes.

'Then Chris comes up with a scheme to conceal the truth. They need a birth certificate saying that she and Pete are the baby's parents. They can't register him in Utah. Too many people there know she wasn't pregnant any more in August of 1977. San Francisco, the city where she was born, is a more logical choice. It's where Donna grew up, and where her brother still lives. They concoct a credible story about her visiting him and how the baby was born much sooner than expected. Her brother talks Pete into coming to San Francisco as well, to help manufacture the paper trail. They take photographs of Pete and Donna with the baby. Then Chris takes them both to the registry office to co-sign the birth certificate. Her brother even manages to find someone who is willing to testify that he has delivered the child. This man owes her brother something – what he owes is irrelevant – and he pays off his debt with his signature on the fake birth certificate.

'And so, on September second, Jason is born. Jason was the name she would have given her unborn child – the one Pete had murdered – if it had been a boy. Mikey dies, and *her* child is born. Oh, there are a few raised eyebrows about the size of her newborn, but no one is suspicious enough to delve deeper. After that, Pete leaves and Donna never sees him again. Her brother advises her to leave San Francisco behind and make a new life elsewhere. She picks Los Angeles. There she meets Edward Evans and falls in love, for real this time. She marries him two years later. For the rest of her life, Donna sticks to her story that Pete is Jason's father and that she broke off her relationship with him after her son was born. The secret she takes to her grave is McGray's abuse of her and her subsequent miscarriage.'

Mitch paused yet again. Jason was thirsty as hell. His throat felt scorched. He kept trying to move his wrists and ankles away from each other, surreptitiously, without drawing Mitch's attention. It was still hopeless. He coughed and said, 'But surely that's impossible? Everyone must have seen that the other baby was missing. There must have been an inquiry.'

Mitch leaned back. He raised a skinny hand and his forefinger pointed at the roof of the van. 'Of course there was an inquiry. Donna got away with it because no one saw her leave the scene of the crime. They put Halper on the rack. They suspected that *he* was the one responsible for your disappearance. But he insisted that he knew nothing about a second baby, and finally the chief of the Mount Peytha City Police Department – Joel Kaplan was his name, he died about a decade ago – had to accept his story. Halper's head was Swiss cheese. He was an alcoholic and God knows what else, but he was also an honest man, and he had been a hero that day in saving my life. After that, Kaplan turned up all kinds of theories. Maybe you hadn't been in the back seat. Maybe our mother had held you, and the fire had consumed all of you.'

Mitch gazed ahead, looking oddly vulnerable.

'I don't know,' Jason started hesitantly. 'Did he really think that? I would imagine there are always traces left after a thing like that. I mean, I can't imagine a human body going entirely to ashes in a blazing fire, not even that of a baby.'

'You're right,' Mitch agreed. 'The human body doesn't burn easily. Well, what would you expect? We're made up of seventy-five percent water, aren't we? Even crematoriums have to pulverize the bones of the deceased after the cremation.'

Mitch's hazy expression did not change. 'Another theory was that you weren't in the car at all. Maybe a relative or friend was minding you that day. But you were never found, no matter who they asked.'

Agony pierced Jason's heart. Until now he hadn't considered that if Donna was not really his mother, his family was not really his family either. He must have real blood relatives out there somewhere. Who were they – besides his psychotic brother Mitch?

'Kaplan didn't know what to do any more,' Mitch continued in the straightforward tone of a news reporter. 'Everything and anything was possible. Of course, he also put forth that you might have been kidnapped, that someone could have plucked you from the burning Chevy. That's why, besides Halper, they also questioned Silverstein. But that line of investigation proved just as pointless and fruitless as the others. To make a long story short: your disappearance has remained a mystery to this day. According to Kaplan you were the unlucky one, and I was the lucky one.'

Mitch grinned bitterly. 'The chief, I have to add, was a man who was averse to working up a sweat. He liked practical solutions. He was the kind of person who sweeps the house and hides the dust beneath the carpet because he doesn't know what else to do with it. In this case he could think of nothing better to do than push people into putting your name on the headstone. You were gone, most likely dead, maybe burned beyond recognition, and in the end that became the official account. You disappeared beneath the carpet, so to speak. Nor did the press become involved in the case. In those days it was much easier to keep bothersome things like a missing baby from the papers. The world believed that you were inside the coffin. And the grieving Chawkins family did not raise any commotion either. Your grave was covered up with sand and oblivion.'

Jason said nothing. There was nothing *to* say.

Mitch continued. 'This happened in 1977. I survived and grew up. As a *freak*, cast out by everyone. I was in constant emotional and physical pain. No burn specialist could remedy that. That was the price I had to pay for my "good luck". Until I was ten years old, I lived with my Uncle Sam and Aunt Dina; after that I lived with Uncle Kent and Aunt Kate. That didn't turn out so well, and at the age of fourteen I was put in my first shelter. It was hell. If you look like me, you have no friends, no hope, no life. Trust me on that.'

The expression on Mitch's face reflected all kinds of memories resurfacing. Dismal, painful shadows from a dark past.

'You know what I mean. Despite that, people always kept telling me how glad I should be that at least I had survived. I grew sick of hearing such rubbish. The only thing I retained was a sharp mind. And the Internet has been a blessing to me. Without anyone needing to see me, I could make a decent living. And I also changed my name as soon as I was legally allowed to do so. I no longer wanted to live with that cursed name.'

Jason licked his parched lips. The pain of the rope around his wrists, tied to his back, was becoming unbearable. Meanwhile, the van kept on heading toward an unknown destination. What was Mitch planning to do? The question was on Jason's lips, but he dared not ask. He let Mitch talk and forced himself to keep alert.

'As I grew older I went in search of the man who had condemned me to my "good luck". Steve Silverstein had been sentenced to thirty years in prison. He made parole in 1999. Not long after his release, he suffered a fatal accident.'

Mitch's lips expanded into a wicked grin.

'The brakes on his Toyota failed. That's what the police report claims, at least. It happened when he was driving down a slope, along a deep precipice. Steve didn't stand a chance. He lost control of the car and plummeted to his death.'

Mitch related this story as if he were reading a newspaper article.

He had also murdered the driver of the truck that had rammed his parent's car.

Jason was not shocked. Mitch was spiteful, gone mad from the many years of suffering inflicted on him. Certainly he was capable of this degree of violence.

What interested him more was how Mitch could have sabotaged Steve's car. Had he had help from Doug even then? No, probably not. He had gone in search of Doug after Jason had told Mitch about him during previous visits. That meant that he had to have worked with another hit man back in those days.

'After Steve's death, the riddle of your disappearance remained,' Mitch went on. 'Let me tell you, I didn't believe for one minute that you had burned to a crisp. That theory made no sense. I had been pulled from that car alive, our parents' remains were still recognizable, and of you there was no trace? Impossible.'

Mitch leaned forward.

'I will be even more precise,' he said sotto voce. 'I *knew* you were still alive.'

Jason tried to crawl backward to avoid Mitch's penetrating stare, but he was propped against the spare tire as far as he could go.

'I *felt* it. We're identical twins, for fuck's sake,' Mitch grated.

Jason opened his mouth to speak, but no words came out.

'I'll go you one better,' Mitch went on. 'I always *knew* that I wasn't alone. Call it faith or whatever else you want. And I also had dreams, or visions, in which I kept seeing a hazy figure that seemed to belong with me.'

Shadows inside the van made Mitch appear taller and more threatening.

'I spent years searching for you.'

Mitch drew his ravaged face closer to Jason, intent on his loathsome mission.

'Finally I had something to go on. Thanks to an idea I had a couple of years earlier, to have a sketch of myself made without . . .' Mitch hesitated. 'Without the burns. What would I have looked like if Steve Silverstein hadn't been alive, or if he had been sober, at least on *that* day? With the sketch, I kept Googling PYROPHOBIA, and for birth dates close to my own. Nothing. Then came the day I thought I had found you. A man from Oakland seemed to resemble my sketch. I checked his data at the registry office and studied his family background – you don't want to know what's possible on the Internet if you're at all proficient at hacking. But it couldn't be the man from Oakland. Then I found your profile and photo on *ipyrophobia.com*. Right away, I felt sure that this time I was on to something.'

For an instant, a glint of yellow fire glowed in Mitch's eyes.

'You were the spitting image of my sketch. And you were almost the same age as I was. That was reason enough to take a closer look at you.'

Mitch leaned back, satisfied.

'I wasn't convinced right away. I just couldn't believe I had actually found you. Even when I saw this one facial characteristic in you, the doubts remained.'

Jason's eyebrows rose.

Mitch paused again. Not for long.

'Oh, come on! Be honest. You really don't see it? It was getting ever more apparent to me, especially when you came over to my place the last time, with my own photographs, and I had to pretend I was crazy, incapable of finding a tomb in a cemetery.'

Mitch spread out his arms, inviting Jason to take a good look at him.

Jason squinted his eyes and studied his twin brother as he never had before. He saw the scars, the skin that resembled a freakish red mask. In his mind's eye, Jason looked at Mitch's skin smoothing out. Then he added eyelids. Lips. A nose. Ears. And, what made the most difference, he gave the bald man in the wheelchair what he lacked most – thick black hair just like his own.

Then he got it.

In his mind's eye, he could see in Mitch the mirror image of himself.

Mitch's admission that he had murdered Steve Silverstein had not unnerved Jason. But this was a shock. His mind's eye closed and the moment of recognition fled, like the image of a dream upon waking.

He opened his eyes and gazed out at Mitch. The similarities were gone.

But not completely. He could still see similarities. The shape of Mitch's face was no different than his own. His chin protruded in the same way with the same diagonal cleft. Only now did he see it.

Mitch followed Jason's gaze. Quietly he said, 'Have you never felt that you were incomplete?'

Jason shook his head.

Mitch shrugged. 'Oh well, I've always been looking for you. Not the other way around. But it doesn't matter. My doubts remained. I'll tell you what finally did convince me you are Mike. No, I didn't go looking for other similarities, although I'm sure there are a couple more, such as our penchant for Polaroid photography. I took a different approach . . .'

Mitch thought for a moment. Suddenly he uttered a cackling laugh.

'But why should I tell you? You already know.'

'You interrogated Chris,' Jason said, his throat as dry and raspy as sandpaper.

Mitch clenched his fists. 'Precisely! Doug and I could have gone over to Edward's, or we could have questioned you some more about your past. But when you mentioned Chris, your mother's only brother, her last surviving relative, I decided to go see him. After all, Chris had been the person closest to Donna, certainly around 1977. It turned out to be a very enlightening visit. I had a suspicion beforehand that you were Mike, because of the physical similarities and the incidences of pyrophobia. If you *were* Mike, then maybe Chris would know something about it. The question was: how much did he know? Well, he knew *all* about it. More than I had expected! Everything I told you, I got from him. And it wasn't even that hard to get him to spill his guts out. I don't think he ever told anyone else his big secret. Imagine that, keeping it to himself for more than thirty years! But I am quick to add that Doug is an expert in getting people to talk.'

So apparently Chris had not kept it all to himself. He had once said something about it to Jason, although he had forgotten what it was. But it seemed it had inspired him to make his children's drawing of burning graves, with 'Mapeetaa,' an adulteration of Mount Peytha City, written on one of the headstones.

'And then you killed him.'

He heard his own words, and they hurt.

Mitch turned his head a little.

'Yes, of course. I couldn't let him go after that, could I? Besides, *I* didn't do it. Doug helped him out of his misery. I couldn't do it alone, and besides, I keep Doug handy for just that type of need. But I was the one who found the medical data about Chris's illness. He hadn't put the files away carefully enough. He admitted, after some prodding from Doug, that he didn't have long to live. After we had strung him up in the attic, we left a goodbye note and did our best to make everything else look like it was a suicide case. I believe we managed pretty well.'

Jason bit his lower lip. Fresh, hot anger boiled up like magma.

'That's how I found out that you were my brother Mikey who had been presumed dead,' Mitch ranted on, unperturbed. 'I understood that I hadn't been the lucky one at all. On the contrary! *You* are Sunday's child. You're not mutilated, you look good, you have a beautiful wife, and you have everything in life you could possibly want. Because *you* were the first to be saved. I could have been you. *I* could have had your life. But it's too late for that now. I knew I would never get justice. But I *would* have revenge and satisfaction. You would suffer like I suffered. I resolved to make it happen.'

'Why in such a roundabout way?' Jason asked furiously. 'You killed Steve Silverstein, Chris and Kayla. Why not stick a knife between my ribs, if you can't cope with the fact that I have a better life than you?'

Mitch nodded slowly, as if that option had not occurred to him before.

'I could have. But why? I thought it would be much more interesting to let you find out for yourself who you really are. I gave it quite some thought. Hence my lie about getting disfigured as a teenager, in a house fire. And the photographs, for instance. Years ago, I knew a boy named Michael Glass who tried to cheer me up. He had a Polaroid camera, took my picture and said, 'I don't think you're ugly. Ugliness is not about how you look on the outside, but about what you are on the inside.' We've all heard that sort of drivel before. Still, I took heart from what he said. He gave me his camera, and I have kept it ever since. Michael wanted me to use it to see who I really am. I decided to use it to make you see who *you* are: Mikey Chawkins, dead and buried according to official documents, died August eighteenth, 1977.'

Mitch chuckled. 'I was honored that my pictures affected you so much, you even came to me for advice. But it was more than a psychological game for me. I wanted to make you feel what it is like to be alone, when the things you hold most dear are taken away from you. When you called from San Francisco, saying you'd found something, I made my next move. Before I was going to get satisfaction from you, I wanted you to feel Kayla's death.'

Jason closed his eyes, his strength and resolve ebbing rapidly. A wave of sorrow welled up from his core being.

'I'm finished with my story,' Mitch said. 'When we heard she was still alive, I sent Doug over to the hospital. He brought you over to my place, before you could come to me.'

He shrugged. 'And that's about it. That's all I have to say.'

In his mind's eye, Jason saw Kayla. She was dressed in white, standing in a green pasture on a sunny day, somewhere near Ralph. And Donna and Chris. But Kayla's face was not sunny. Her eyes were dark. The same gaze as the last time he had seen her. They had parted with an argument, the distance between them much greater than he could have imagined even in his worst nightmare. That argument had been their goodbye.

The wave crashed over him.

THIRTY-TWO
Final Resting Place

iery tongues rolling in from pitch-black darkness. The inferno is quickly spreading. The fire is undulating around him, clenching white-hot fists. He is unable to move. Scorching flames are beside him, beneath him, above him. Then they assume a shape,

turn into a figure. The burning creature has a face. It is Donna
Evans, née Campbell. She is the fire, and her torch-like arms reach
out for him. No, not for him, past him. He stares at her fiery hands,
and only then realizes who is sitting beside him. It's Mitch, and he
is no longer mutilated. He is instead the spitting image of Jason.

This time she'll save me, *he hears him cry over the furious raging*
of the fire. This time *you'll* stay behind, Mawkee.

Then Mitch is gone, just like the burning Donna figure.

But why is the fire still burning?

This time there is no escape. He is the flames' prey, and the fiery
fists pound straight into his face, like a sparking hammer. The pain
is terrible. His hair is on fire. His nose, burning like a torch, drops
from his face. He claps his hands against his head, and then sees
that he is holding a blackened ear.

His screams get louder—

And then he awakened to find Mitch, the Frankenstein monster,
glaring at him. Jason was still in the back of the Mercedes van,
with his wrists and ankles tied. Apparently he had dozed off. How
was that possible?

He remembered his last thought being of Kayla, and that had
been too much for him. He must have blacked out.

Mitch shook his head and averted his gaze. Jason used the
opportunity to try once again to lever his wrists and ankles apart.
But the pain flared up, and he was barely able to suppress a cry
of agony. He snorted frantically through his nose. He broke out in
a cold sweat and gagged, dizzy, as if he was aboard a ship in a
storm after being struck on the head by a falling mast.

But still he did not give up – he could not give up.

He kept struggling to get himself loose, not wanting to think
about how bloody and raw his wrists had to be by now.

It was dark outside, maybe night-time already.

And still Doug kept on driving.

Finally, the van stopped. Doug slid from the driver seat, and then
Jason heard the familiar fumbling at the back door. It slid open with
a clatter. Jason lay gazing up at the black night sky. What time was it?
He had no idea.

Doug reappeared behind the bright light of a flashlight he was
holding in his hand.

Jason coughed. His throat was parched. He yearned for water, anything liquid.

Doug pulled him out of the van by his legs. He slid from the edge and clenched his teeth, anticipating a painful slam on to the hard ground. Barely a second later, a torturous ache exploded in his pelvis. Although he had resolved not to give Mitch the satisfaction of watching him suffer, he couldn't help crying out and cursing.

Doug leaned over him, peeled off a strip of duct tape, and placed it firmly over his mouth.

Jason was on his back on the hard ground, stifling his pain in forced silence.

Doug took a brown burlap bag from the back of the van and placed it beside Jason. As he did that, Mitch hoisted himself up from his wheelchair and awkwardly shuffled over.

'Give us a hand here,' he said to Doug, who caught Mitch beneath the armpits and lifted him up as if he were as light as a feather and planted him on the ground behind the van.

'Do you need your wheelchair?'

'No,' Mitch said. 'I won't be able to move around with it in this terrain. You take care of *him*. I'll manage.'

Doug nodded. He wrapped his arms around Jason, underneath his armpits, and started dragging him away from the van. Mitch followed, shining the flashlight. Doug was manhandling him roughly, and Jason worried that his arms might become dislocated. He screamed, but there was no one to hear him. Even if it hadn't just been the three of them, no one could have heard his cries, smothered as they were by the duct tape.

Shatz pulled him along as if he were a corpse already. His heels made tracks in the sand. Then, despite the darkness, he recognized his surroundings. He could see the bars of a high, dark gate. Familiar oaks stood on either side of it like towering sentinels.

His heart skipped a beat.

This was North Gate, at St James Cemetery.

Why had they brought him here?

Mitch's lilting voice echoed through his mind.

I want satisfaction.

Mitch had the blood of Steve Silverstein, Chris Campbell and Kayla Evans on his hands. What was he planning for Jason? His options for escaping were rapidly expiring, if he had any to begin with. Again he tried to loosen his bonds, and again it felt like a sharp knife was cutting into his flesh. His wrists felt wet, which could only mean that blood was seeping from his raw wounds.

Doug dragged him past hundreds of graves wrapped in dark shadows. The moon emitted a silvery glow. Jason estimated it would have to be two or three o'clock in the morning. It was a fair guess, if they had left Los Angeles around five or six o'clock.

Doug set him down in front of a grave. Mitch shone a light on the headstone.

It was the Chawkins' grave. In the circle of snow-white light, the names of Robert, Amanda and Mike appeared.

'Keep an eye on him,' Doug said. 'I'll get the rest of the stuff.'

He walked off, leaving Jason alone with his brother.

'What do you think happens next?' Mitch asked.

Why don't you go ahead and tell me, Jason thought.

Mitch grinned. 'Start saying your goodbyes. This is where you are going to meet your end. Your name is already on the headstone. All that's missing is you.'

Jason's eyes widened.

Was he going to bury him? In . . . his own grave?

Mitch made the cackling noise again. It rose up into the night sky like the howls of a wolf. No, of a demon.

Doug returned with the burlap sack with its protruding sticks, and the bale of hay. The sticks turned out to be tools: a pickaxe and a spade. He spit on his hands, rubbed them together, and started yanking the sods from above the burial site.

Mitch also was busy. From the sack he took a shorter stick, planted it in the ground beside the grave, took a step back, and carefully touched it with a burning match. The head of the stick caught fire. It was a Tiki torch. In its glow, Jason could see Mitch's scars moving and twitching, as if worms were crawling beneath his skin. Mitch was just as afraid of fire as Jason was. But he at the moment was more worried about what Doug was doing.

He was opening the Chawkins' grave, and it was obvious who would be laid to rest there.

I'm dead.

No, not yet. But time was running out. Mitch and Doug would

want to be out of here before dawn. The grave needed to be closed by then, with him in it, and they would not want to leave traces.

Like a madman, he yanked at the ropes binding him. It did no good; the flaring pain just kept on getting worse. Mitch looked back and grinned at his useless struggles.

Jason pulled, tore, wrenched. Then it felt as if a real knife was cutting his flesh. He cried out in hopeless despair. A black mist rose up in front of his eyes. Tears rolled down his cheeks.

Doug picked up the spade and started deepening the hole. He worked quickly, ruthlessly. Heaps of sand appeared beside the hole, piling higher and higher. About five or six feet down he would strike the moldy coffins of his parents. Doug would probably not go that deep, but then he didn't have to. Four feet would be deep enough to ensure that Jason's body would never be found.

When Doug finished digging, he climbed up from the shallow pit. Then he tore open the bale of hay and spread it out on the sandy bottom of the pit. What for, Jason wondered.

Mitch gripped the Tiki torch. He gazed fearfully at the flames and then at Jason. But his voice was firm.

'Almost thirty-two years ago, they dug a grave for you that so far you've been able to cheat. But no longer.'

The torch lent his eyes a barbaric glow.

'It is written that you burned to death and were buried in this grave. That's how it is written, and that's how it shall be.'

Doug Shatz stood there with his sleeves rolled up. His face was black from sweat and sand. Mitch lifted the torch over his head and seemed to be murmuring a prayer.

It was clear to Jason what was going to happen. He pushed himself back on his heels, like a caged animal that flings itself at the bars of its prison in desperation when the butchers arrive. It was useless. He was going to die a horrible death, the same death as in his nightmares.

Mitch lowered the torch, having recited his prayer or whatever it had been, and pointed the burning end at him.

He was going to set Jason on fire.

A hellish scream, a primal roar, pushed forward. In his own ears, the duct tape did nothing to stifle the sound. Like a madman, with every last ounce of strength he could muster, he tried to wriggle free. His upper body and legs were bucking wildly; sweat oozed from every pore.

Mitch waved his rod of flaming death around like a burning flag. His cheeks were puffed up with excitement, but his eyes were empty, void of any trace of humanity. Jason could clearly see all this in the glow of the wafting fire that made Mitch's appearance seem even more devilish.

Jason roared, bucked, wriggled. Sweat stung in his eyes. Maybe he was breaking his own teeth, because he heard grating, bone-splintering noises in his ears.

'Put him in there,' Mitch said to Doug, indicating the grave.

Doug leaned over Jason and dragged him toward the hole. He was shoved into the freshly dug grave, on to the fresh hay. Doug climbed back out of the grave, leaving Jason a foot or so above the bones of his mother and father.

Jason stared at the night sky as tendrils of fog appeared in front of his eyes. He kept screaming, wrestling, fighting. Beneath him, skeletal hands burst from the ground; cold finger bones touched his bare skin.

Even now he was tearing at the ropes. He no longer felt pain. Memories flashed in front of his mind's eye. Kayla's smile. Her pearly teeth, sparkling eyes, sweet scent. She caressed him and said she loved him. Their first kiss, on Sunset Boulevard under the soft light of a harvest moon. The time she said he meant the world to her, in the fractured red glow of the morning sun over the foaming surf at Venice Beach. And further back. Edward playing with him, tossing him a ball, him jumping to catch it. Still further back and . . .

He is a baby again. Donna is standing in the desert, near a car with black clouds of smoke and flames leaping from broken windows. Her face is smudged with soot and tears, her hands are pressing against her mouth, her eyes are bulging; she is in shock. Then she turns around, toward him. He is close to her on the sand, and underneath her pain he also sees relief and happiness that he at least is still there; and he sees her love, the love that has blossomed already. He wants to crawl to her, touch her, but he can't. He is unable to, something is holding him back. But he wants to touch her so very much.

I helped you then, because I could, *she says.* Now I can't. You have to do this yourself. And you *can* do it.

No! *he yells,* I can't. I'm going to die!

Yes, *she says, forcefully.* You *can* do it. It'll hurt, it'll hurt a lot, but don't you think it hurt me when I rescued you from that car?

Of course. Rescuing him from the flames ravaging the car must have caused her unimaginable pain.

You were strong back then, you have to be strong now, *are the last words Donna whispers to him. She smiles through her tears, her lips move, and he understands that she loves him, that he will forever be her child.*

Then she fades away from his view. Along with the burning car, the desert. He realizes where he is . . .

The night returned.

Mitch stood over him, on the edge of the grave, holding the burning torch.

'Hurry up!' Doug yelled beside him. His voice sounded strangely hollow, far away. *'Set him on fire!'*

He still felt Donna, but fading, less *there.*

A flame broke from Mitch's torch. No, there were more, as if drops of fire sparks were raining down into the grave. Jason pushed himself away from them, but when the glowing droplets hit the hay beneath him, smoke spiraled up in a ghastly array of newly born flames.

Jason turned on his side, his back to the gently crackling fire. He moved his wrists toward the glowing heat. Then the heat hit the rope – and his flesh – and he bit his tongue to stifle a bellowing cry of anguish.

Fire licked his skin, seared it, cooked it. Jason clenched his teeth, shut his eyes. He yanked the rope with a furious rage he didn't think he had in him. The rope held, but it was getting hotter and hotter. How long could he stand the pain? How long before—

Jason gave one final God Almighty yank. And suddenly the burning rope *did* loosen.

Jason stripped it off his wrists with a few jerks of his fingers and thumbs. Maybe his very skin was burning, he didn't know. And he didn't care.

He threw himself on his back and rubbed his wrists in the sand beneath the hay. Then he pushed himself upright again and clawed like a madman at the rope around his ankles.

He felt no pain; he was beyond pain. He just did what he had to do.

When he had freed his legs, he tore the duct tape from his mouth.

Mitch was staring at him, as if not believing what he was seeing. Doug too. Even in Doug's eyes he now saw fear. Immobilized, Mitch glanced at the dancing flames in the grave, and then at Jason.

Doug grabbed for the torch in Mitch's hand. In the same instant Jason rolled over on his hands and feet, his shoulders hunched up like a wild animal in a tight spot. Shouting a raw cry of rage, he jumped up from the pit.

Doug lunged for the pickaxe, but Jason was quicker and seized the handle. Beset with insane rage, Jason looked into Doug's eyes a moment before swinging the pickaxe at him. The blade dove into Doug's stomach. He grabbed at the jagged wound, and stared in amazement at the blood spurting out of him. His knees buckled and he fell face down on the grass.

Sparks of fire narrowly missed Jason's face. Mitch had swung at him with the torch. Another primeval growl erupted from Jason's throat. He drew back his lips and exposed his teeth like a jungle animal smelling blood.

Mitch swung the torch at him yet again, but Jason easily sidestepped it. He then lunged at Mitch and lifted him off the ground.

In his arms, dangling above the ground, the torch in one hand and its flaming head down, Mitch snapped at him with his lipless teeth, as if trying to bite him.

'Mike . . .' The word came out low, guttural.

'Mitch,' Mike heard a throaty sound he didn't recognize, even though he had made it.

The brothers had been reunited by fire.

Mike lifted Mitch higher. Then he slammed him into the open grave on top of the guttering torch.

More smoke started spiraling up from the hay and bigger flames rose up, burrowing themselves free from beneath Mitch, whose body jerked and convulsed as though he were receiving electrical shocks.

He screamed. He screeched. The sound was deafening.

Mike fell down. Only now did he feel intense pain. A scream bubbled up from his throat. He held out his hands and looked at them. His scorched wrists were raw, bleeding badly. He could smell his own burned flesh. His fingertips felt as if there were needles in them. Most of his fingernails had been torn off. More blood was seeping from open wounds.

A bestial cry erupted from his mouth. He screamed until he had no voice left.

Mike crawled away from Doug Shatz, lying there with the sharp edge of the pickaxe sticking out of his abdomen. His eyes and mouth sagged open, as though in utter amazement of what had just happened. His chipped tooth was red, just like the rest of his teeth, lips and face. Blood clots matted even his hair.

Reeling, Mike stood up. He smelled burning meat and heard a crackling fire.

Inside the open grave was his now forever silent brother, face-down in the earth, within a fire that was devouring a leg, an arm and his bald head.

More orange-yellow flames erupted in a ghostly dance of death.

THIRTY-THREE
Return

Weeks had elapsed since the horror at St James Cemetery. Every day, Jason relived fond memories of Kayla. They offered an album full of unforgettable events, scenes and gestures. The day they met at The Duchess. Their dates afterward, their first kiss. Moving in together and decorating their house. Trips to Utah, Arizona and Nevada. Their wedding day. As they stood before the altar and Reverend Jeremy Hofmeister had asked him whether Jason would take Kayla to be his wedded wife, he had been the happiest man on the planet; *this* amazing woman was willing to be his wife.

At first, when he talked about anything, it was mostly about Kayla. Brian Anderson came to see him and turned out to possess unexpected paternal traits. His vacation came up and ended, and he went back to work. Barbara didn't nag him and Carol didn't trouble him with her problems. Even Tony was a bit more talkative than usual. Everyone in the office closed ranks around him, to protect him.

Gradually Jason noticed that everyone's interest in his plight was waning. Life was returning back to normal. People got on with their daily lives.

He couldn't blame them, of course; it was the way of the world, and he reminded himself that he ought to be moving on as well. And he would, although he knew his life would never be the same again.

There was, however, one change that had surprised him. A lot.

When he had finally come home after that night in St James Cemetery, he hadn't crawled into bed. Even though he felt as tired as a human could feel, he had taken a long shower despite his bandaged hands.

Then he had gone in search of a candle.

Jason knew there were candles in the attic. Kayla had never wanted to get rid of her collection because she hated wasting money, which throwing out perfectly good, expensive candles came down to. These were Kayla's prettiest ones, the ones she had bought to create a festive mood during the holiday season but had then stored away in the attic, wrapped in a piece of cloth.

They had been lying there for at least three years.

That night Jason had taken the candles downstairs.

And he had lit one.

As he stared at the flame, he remained perfectly calm, without a trace of distress in his mind or heart. He had kept looking at the flame, and it hadn't bothered him to do so.

Even his pyrophobia no longer seemed to matter. It was one more thing that belonged in the past. He had sat there, silently gazing into the flame.

Then he had closed his eyes and prayed.

September sixth. Another Sunday. He got out of bed at seven, showered, and rolled new medic bandages over his wrists and the burned areas on his skin that doctors had told him would never completely heal; scars would always be visible, but at least the pain was gone. Then he made himself some breakfast and went out for a short walk. By eight thirty he was inside his LaCrosse, fixed up and good as new, taking his usual route. On weekdays the drive took him an hour; on quiet Sunday mornings it was about forty-five minutes. And so it was only twenty past nine when he parked outside the Thurber Institute.

The building was large and dreary. A squat, tan-painted block of concrete. The only thing worth noticing was the garden. In it he had noticed apple, mango, guava, hydrangeas, rhododendrons and any number of other plants and trees.

Jason went inside and crossed the familiar hallways toward the familiar room. He opened the door and there she was, in her wheelchair by the window. She saw him, put down her paperback book – she had started Stephen King's *Duma Key* – and greeted him with a faint smile.

'Mornin',' he said as he kissed her.

'Morning.'

She still looked frail, and she was. Her physical injuries were healing slowly. In itself this was a miracle, given how serious they had been. In the first few hours after Doug had slashed her with his knife, the doctors had not given her much hope. When Jason was fighting for his own life several hours later, he was convinced that Kayla must have died in the meantime. He had told Mitch she was dead, because otherwise Mitch would have sent Doug after her again.

Physically, Kayla was still here. Mentally, however, she was not yet her old self.

When people asked him how she was faring, he always said she was improving, making progress. How she was *really* doing was something he talked about only with her parents and his father. About the change that had come over her. She was a shell of her former self; still Kayla, but without the sparkle or the soul that had defined who she was – or had been.

The Kayla in the rehabilitation clinic was reticent, distant, not interested in much of anything or anyone.

This Kayla Evans just didn't seem to care.

She had changed. Drastically.

'Sleep well?' he asked.

'I guess.'

Her attention was drifting already. She gazed out the window at the garden she had all day to stare at, then at the paperback in her lap, then at Jason. The emptiness in her eyes hurt him profoundly, in ways he found hard to articulate.

He told her what he had been up to since he had last seen her. That had been the night before, so there wasn't much to tell. He then asked her how she was doing.

'Fine,' she said with a shrug.

He pulled up a chair and sat down. 'When are we going to talk?'

She gazed at him as if she didn't understand what he had said.

'We can't go on like this, Kayla.'

She turned her head away. 'I don't feel like talking.'

He had been nothing but reasonable and understanding until today.

In the first days after the attack, when he was still being questioned by the Mount Peytha police, her survival had been foremost in his mind. She had hovered near death. The medical team at the Pacific Valley Hospital that had saved her life on the third of August had lost her for a brief interval. Jason had heard about this later from John Havemann, the surgeon who deserved an award for achieving what many had assumed was the impossible. For a minute, all brain activity had ceased and she had been clinically dead on the operating table.

At first the mere fact that she was still alive had been more than enough. In the days that followed, his fear of her relapsing turned out to be unfounded, and that too had been more than enough. Kayla had been in a hospital bed, wrapped in bandages, her eyes closed, her face swollen, but every time he saw her like that, he had also thought: *things are going to be all right, the doctors say she will recover and that most of her scars will disappear.*

The most serious problem had been with her legs. Her spinal cord had been injured by a deep thrust of Doug's knife, and her doctors were unable to tell him if she would ever be able to walk again. Everything depended on her therapy and how much effort she was willing to exert.

And that was still the problem five weeks after her night of horror. She didn't seem to want to work hard for it; anything but. Worse, she gave the impression she wasn't willing to apply herself to *anything* any more.

Jason had asked her therapists at the Thurber Institute how he should deal with this. He had had a long talk with Jacob Becerra and Jean Curtius, both of whom felt that it was about time for a less gentle approach. She was stable, there was no danger of relapse, but she wasn't making any real progress. Kayla was stuck. What exactly she was stuck in remained the question, but if she didn't achieve some kind of breakthrough soon, Jacob and Jean said it might be wise to contact a psychologist. The longer it took her to flip a mental switch, the greater the odds she would have to spend the rest of her life in a wheelchair.

Jacob and Jean had given him that message a few days ago. He had promised them that he would try to get through to her. If that didn't lead anywhere, he said, they could start psychotherapy the week after.

He had carefully tried to break the ice with her. But all of his efforts had been for naught. The best he had achieved was her promise that she understood and would start soon. Really she would. That had been Friday. He had felt better when he went back home that night. Yesterday he had concluded, however, that she hadn't meant a word she had said and had just been making false promises to get him off her back.

Today was a new day, and he decided on a less subtle attempt.

'Don't *feel* like it? Well, get over it.'

It sounded harsher than she had expected. Harsher than he had thought possible himself.

She turned her head toward him and raised her eyebrows.

'You start therapy tomorrow, Kayla.'

It's for your own good, he considered adding, but he swallowed the words. She simply *had* to do this. If he didn't stop treating her like a child, she would spend the rest of her life in that chair. This was her weakest moment, she wasn't doing anything herself, and so she needed this slap on the wrist. If he didn't do it, she would hold it against him forever. He was her husband, for better or for worse.

'Why can't you leave me alone, Jason?'

'I just can't.'

'I'm not ready yet.'

It sounded like a plea.

'So *get* ready. Is something bothering you? If so, let's talk about it. I'm ready to listen.'

There was a spark in her eye at last; a spark of angry fire. It wasn't pleasant, but at least it was a sign of life.

'How do you expect me to get ready? I'm a mess.'

'You can be your old self again once you start putting in some effort. Jacob and Jean think your chances are excellent . . . but you'll have to work for it.'

'No, I can't. Just forget about it, Jason.'

'If you're not willing to even try, you're right: you'd better just forget about it. But why are you giving up on yourself? It's not like you, and it's so unnecessary.'

She considered that. He could see her struggling with herself, and it was a long time before she answered.

'I don't know if I have the energy. My head feels stuffed with cotton. I don't care about anything, and I can't help it.'

There were dark half-circles beneath Kayla's eyes, as though she hadn't slept in a week.

'You could start with a tiny step. That would be something, at least. The rest will come, eventually.'

'Later, not now.'

This wasn't Kayla. This wasn't his wife. Her body may have returned from the dead, but it did so without its soul. It was almost as if she'd left it on the eternal meadows in the afterlife.

'Do you *want* to get well, Kayla?'

She stared at the floor. Then, weakly, she shrugged.

'*I* want you to, and so do Jacob and Jean. We're all encouraging you. But still you do nothing.'

Kayla kept her silence.

He decided on a different approach. If the gentle method didn't work, he'd have to go for something stronger. He hated to, and she would curse him for it, but he was running out of options.

He hoped he was doing the right thing.

'You love no one.'

'Huh? What?'

Now she looked at him, her eyes wide.

'We're all trying to get through to you, but you're deaf to us. How long do you think we'll keep on talking to a wall?'

'Why are you treating me this way?'

Her eyes welled with tears. He couldn't stop now. He had to use a crowbar to pry open her passivity, for her own good.

'If you won't fight to get well, Kayla, then you're not worth fighting *for*,' Jason said coldly.

She stared at him like an innocent child that doesn't understand why it has been smacked around the ear. Jason tried to remain steadfast, but he felt himself deflate like a balloon filling with a fresh infusion of guilt.

He had done this – *he* alone was responsible for his wife's undoing. In the end, her injuries were the result of a chain of events *he* had set in motion. And now he was yelling at her, hurting her to the core of her being. Would she forgive him for it, if she ever recovered?

Kayla remained silent. She just sat there, dejected.

He didn't know what else to say.

Early in the morning, the day after he had told Kayla so bluntly that she wasn't worth fighting for, Jason received a phone call from Jean. His wife's therapist – petite, skinny, but with enough Mexican temperament to make one want to avoid an altercation with her – told him Kayla had had a bad night.

Jason told Brian Anderson that he needed to leave the office and raced toward the Thurber Institute as fast as he could. Jean, it turned out, had given him an accurate accounting. Kayla had destroyed a painting and shattered a vase, and the mirror over her wash basin was in shards on the floor. Two burly men in the night shift had had quite a hard time restraining her. Jean related all this in a calm voice, not at all typical for her.

He wondered how a woman in a wheelchair could have wreaked so much havoc, but Jean felt that if Kayla was capable of doing all *this*, therapy should be a piece of cake. His wife was now, after her nocturnal rampage, slouching in her wheelchair, exhausted and free of restraints; but her eyes were roaming restlessly. She still hadn't fully calmed down. When he covered her hand with his, she started gushing words.

She had become furious last night. With Doug Shatz who had nearly killed her, and with the evil genius behind it: Mitch Chawkins. She had also been furious with Jason. Not only because of the emotional beating he had given her yesterday, but because of *everything* since the Polaroid photographs had turned their lives upside-down. And she had been mad at Ralph, because he had died and abandoned her.

The entire world had let her down, and that had made her act in an insane manner.

'I can see that,' he remarked, letting his gaze travel around the room.

After her fit of madness she announced that she was ready to start therapy. He was pleasantly surprised when, in the days that followed, she seemed to mean it this time. Free of the rage inside her, she was starting to apply herself to her exercises.

Apparently what she had needed was some kind of outlet for her trauma. Doug's attack, the stress of the last few weeks, the tension she had felt since the moment Ralph Grainger had died – for years she had kept it all pent up, and that night it had reached a tipping point.

During the days that followed he witnessed her regaining strength in her legs, little by little. The wheelchair was taken away after two weeks and replaced with crutches. After another seven days she was told she could go home soon. Jason was overcome with emotion. He was going to get his wife back.

On September twenty-seventh she was discharged from the clinic. He drove her back to Fernhill and opened the door for her at Canyon View. She stepped inside hesitantly, as if she were getting a tour of a house she might want to live in. He took her in his arms and said, 'Welcome home, my love.'

The wonder of being home quickly dissipated. People came by to congratulate her on her recovery. Family and friends stopped by to wish her their best.

All's well that ends well, so the great bard once wrote.

Kayla found peace within herself during those days after September twenty-seventh. A sense of quiet and calm she had never known settled over her.

She had been so close to death it had almost been as if she had been able to say goodbye to Ralph. Maybe it was just her imagination, but it had felt like he had whispered a message to her from the afterlife. For her, the message meant she needed to accept the past. Things were what they were. Sometimes they were painful, but apparently that was part of the deal, and it was pointless to dwell on what was now said and done.

It softened her remorse about not doing enough to prevent Ralph's cardiac arrest. And it was an answer to the question whether his untimely death had been more or less preordained.

Death was still a mystery, but she accepted it. She had looked death in the eyes and was less afraid of it now. An era had come to an end.

What remained, revolved around Jason.

She brought it up on the last night of September, outside on the porch. Although autumn had been announcing its presence for some days now, tonight there was a balmy Indian summer breeze. Beneath the stars, he held a bottle of beer, she a glass of wine.

'What's bothering you?' she asked.

Jason sipped his Corona and said nothing for a while.

'What do you mean?'

Her eyes sought his.

'We're not done yet,' she said. 'We're about to make a new start, Jason Evans, but first we need closure on our old life. You haven't received that closure yet.'

He shrugged. 'You know what I've been through. It's not so strange that it got to me.'

She had heard the entire story when she was still in intensive care, but only after the worst of it was behind her.

Jason had found out that he had a twin brother. This brother, Mitch, had wanted to kill her *and* him. He was working with a hit man, Doug Shatz. Together they had taken Jason back to St James Cemetery in Mount Peytha City, where Mitch had wanted to bury Jason in his own grave. But first the madman had set fire to her husband. Jason had managed to free himself in the last moment. He had killed Doug with a pickaxe and had struggled with Mitch, causing him to fall into the grave on top of his own torch. Mitch had died a horrible death in the fire.

The police had held Jason for several days. He had been subjected to lengthy interrogations. But soon after, they had found evidence against Mitch and Doug. Doug's knife was the first piece of evidence to turn up, with Kayla's blood on it. The police then discovered hidden bugs inside Canyon View, and in Mitch's house the police found several tapes with the voices of Kayla and Jason on them. Forensics had been able to prove beyond a doubt that the macabre photographs had been fashioned on Mitch's computer.

The police also discovered that Jason's story about his past was true. His mother was not his real mother, nor was Pete McGray his father. His real parents had died in a burning car wreck, together with him in the official records. He had a grave. He *was* Mikey Chawkins and his name was on a headstone. Mitch had wanted revenge for the life that had been stolen from him.

Jason was no longer suspected of murder or any other crime. In fighting for his freedom he had acted in self-defense. Not long after that horrifying incident in the cemetery, he had gotten a visit from an older man, who had introduced himself as Sam Chawkins. He was a brother of Robert, his father; Sam was therefore his uncle. Sam had been appointed by the family to contact their cousin who had been presumed dead. Jason had talked to him and said he was not ready yet for an introduction to a group of people who were strangers to him. Sam had been understanding. He had left it up to Jason to contact them at a later time, when he was ready.

Her husband's entire life had been turned upside-down. That was confusing of course, she understood that. But now she was referring to something else.

'What are you still fretting about?'

He gazed at the stars. 'I told the police that I freed myself from the ropes. First the one around my wrists, then the one around my ankles. That's why all my fingernails were torn. But I also had a vision, the strangest one yet . . .'

He told Kayla about the image of his mother, of Donna. That he had returned to 1977. And that, for a short while, he had really *been* Mikey.

Here was something else she could not comprehend. But it did not make her angry; not any more.

'Then it was love that saved you,' she said definitively. 'Donna's love. The love of your mother.'

He smiled. 'Yeah, let's keep it at that.'

'It's impossible to understand everything,' she said.

'That's true,' he admitted. 'Sometimes things happen, and you have to accept them for what they are. Sometimes you just need to move on.'

He leaned over and kissed her. 'I love you very much, Kayla.'

She smiled at him. 'What a happy coincidence. I happen to love you too, Jason.'

THIRTY-FOUR
Illusions

Fifteen months later, a bleak wind cut through his clothes as he got out of the car and helped Kayla lift Robert from the baby seat in the back seat of his LaCrosse. The infant, warmly dressed against the cold, wailed as if some terrible injustice was being done to him.

'Oh dear, is it that bad, sweetheart?' Kayla said, holding her little boy close. 'Let's go inside, then, to grandpa. It'll be a lot nicer inside than out here.'

As she walked up the path, Edward opened the door. His face lit up when he saw his grandson. Jason closed the car doors and followed his family.

'Merry Christmas, Dad,' Kayla said.

Edward gave his daughter-in-law a kiss. 'Merry Christmas, and to you too, Jason. And to you of course, Robert. Your very first Christmas!'

'Hi Dad, Merry Christmas,' Jason said, shaking Edward's hand.

'Come on in,' Edward beckoned with animated gestures.

Robert's grandfather had decorated the house, making it extra special this year; he had been looking forward to this Christmas, with the four of them, for weeks. The fireplace was lit, and the flames crackling agreeably around the logs.

Jason glanced at the many presents underneath the Christmas tree. Edward had certainly put a lot of effort into making this holiday special. On the mantle beside the tree, in its familiar place, was a framed picture of Donna. Eternally smiling, she gazed lovingly out at her family.

Jason stood up and looked around the room. The china cabinet beside the dining room table held more framed portraits. He saw a picture of Uncle Chris, smiling broadly. Jason peered intently at the photograph. For a second it seemed as if Chris was winking at him.

A smile crossed Jason's face.

'Merry Christmas to you as well,' he whispered. 'Wherever you are. I hope you've found her again. I'm sure you have. You're back together, aren't you? I'm thinking of you.'

'What are you doing, Jason?' Kayla asked.

'Nothing, just musing.'

'Well, come muse over here. Your son needs to be fed. I'll help your father set the table. Make yourself useful.'

'Your wish is my command.'

'Don't overdo it.'

He walked back and took Robert from her. 'So you want your bottle? Do you, little piggy?'

The baby smiled.

Grandfather Edward smiled with him.

Some things in Jason's life had turned out to be illusions. But sometimes illusions had to pass for the real thing. There was nothing else for it. After all, life went on.

Maybe, some day, he would reunite with his real family. With Sam Chawkins and his other relatives.

Maybe. Some day.

When the time was right.

In the meantime he had Kayla and Robert.

And Mikey, the shadow that was always with him.

This was his life, a *full* life, and it was enough.

More than enough to make him happy.

Lightning Source UK Ltd.
Milton Keynes UK
UKOW04f0621110116

266139UK00001B/18/P